AND THE SPARROW FELL

AND THE SPARROW FELL

A Novel

ROBERT J. MRAZEK

AN IMPRINT OF CORNELL UNIVERSITY PRESS
ITHACA AND LONDON

First published 2017 by Cornell University Press

Printed in the United States of America

Library of Congress Cataloging-in-Publication Data

Names: Mrazek, Robert J., author.
Title: And the sparrow fell : a novel / Robert J. Mrazek.
Description: Ithaca : Cornell University Press, 2017.
Identifiers: LCCN 2017007113 (print) | LCCN 2017008423 (ebook) | ISBN 9781501713934 (cloth : alk. paper) | ISBN 9781501712258 (epub/mobi) | ISBN 9781501709616 (pdf)
Subjects: LCSH: Vietnam War, 1961–1975—Fiction.
Classification: LCC PS3563.R39 A84 2017 (print) | LCC PS3563.R39 (ebook) | DDC 813/.54—dc23
LC record available at https://lccn.loc.gov/2017007113

Cornell University Press strives to use environmentally responsible suppliers and materials to the fullest extent possible in the publishing of its books. Such materials include vegetable-based, low-VOC inks and acid-free papers that are recycled, totally chlorine-free, or partly composed of nonwood fibers. For further information, visit our website at cornellpress.cornell.edu.

DEDICATED TO

ROBERT POREA, CORNELL '67

Who was a helicopter rescue pilot in Vietnam
And on a mission to save lives gave his own

AND TO

CATHERINE SUSAN MRAZEK

I shall tell you a great secret, my friend.
Do not wait for the last judgment. It takes place every day.

Albert Camus, *The Fall*

Are not two sparrows sold for a farthing?
And one of them shall not fall on the ground without your Father.

Matthew 10:29

MARCH 15, 1968

ITHACA, NEW YORK

ONE

I doubt too many people in this world can say they have known a goddam saint, but my younger brother Tommy comes as close as anybody I'll ever meet. No one would ever confuse me with a saint. I'm pretty sure murderers don't qualify.

I won't pretend to be Socrates. At twenty-two, I haven't figured very much out yet. Maybe I never will. I'll say one thing at the outset. This story isn't pretty, but I will tell it just the way it happened. If only Kate could know what I know now. She would understand. She might even forgive me and forgive herself enough to love me.

The sixties didn't start out like this. Back in 1961, I remember seeing a picture of JFK standing at a summit conference with the other leaders of the free world. Harold Macmillan, de Gaulle, Adenauer, all of them doddering old men refusing to leave the stage. But JFK took the stage away from them. Well, for a while at least. Boy, he and Jackie sure gave off the light.

I actually met him when I was fifteen. It was at our home in Cold Spring Harbor when he was running for president and my mother organized the event so that the Locust Valley lockjaw ladies along the Gold Coast could come by to make sure he wasn't really a stooge of the pope.

I was standing at the front door when he arrived and holding my dog-eared copy of *Profiles in Courage*. He grinned at me and said I was obviously a connoisseur of great literature. Then he pulled out a fountain pen and signed it. Up close I saw that the fingers on his right hand were all red and chapped.

I guess I'll begin with what happened a few months after he was elected. It was the Sunday in February 1961 when my brother Tommy claimed he found heaven at the bottom of St. John's Pond. I didn't take the idea seriously at the time. I didn't take anything seriously back then except girls. In every important way, I was my father's son.

For at least a week that winter, I was pursuing a girl named Denise McLaughlin. For me that was a long-term relationship. She was seventeen years old. I was a skinny fifteen but already over six feet tall.

Denise had silky black hair that flowed all the way down her lower back. She also had a sweet oval face and big brown eyes that always seemed like they were about to cry.

The best thing about Denise was her slim, willowy body. What she did with it mostly was ice-skate. Her mother started her off in figure skating when she was three. Mrs. McLaughlin's goal was for her to score the Olympic gold medal at Innsbruck in 1964. My goal was to score with Denise.

I was in my sophomore year at Friends Academy. Denise was a senior at Huntington High School. After her parents divorced, her mother became active in our church. Denise and I ended up together in the Methodist Youth Fellowship.

I was there only because my older brother Dave had told me that MYF would look good on my résumé when I applied to Cornell. She was already a member when I joined. At the first meeting, one of the choirboys took me aside and told me she was easy.

It didn't make sense to me, particularly when the girl was as gorgeous as she was. But I meant to find out. After telling her how much I enjoyed skating, I asked if she could teach me some moves that would help me make the hockey team at Friends Academy.

Denise told me that the last thing she wanted to do on a Sunday was go ice-skating. She had to get up at four o'clock every other morning of the week to be driven by her mother to Brooklyn so she could practice skating for two hours with her Hungarian coach.

After I gently reminded her of our new bonds of Christian fellowship, she reluctantly agreed. We made a date to meet at my house at two o'clock on Sunday afternoon and then walk over to St. John's Pond.

"That's the one with the lovely white church by the edge, isn't it?" she asked over the phone, and I said it was.

For a century, the first families on the North Shore had gotten married in that church or been buried out back. Henry Stimson is parked back there, but I didn't choose it for historical reasons.

At the far end of the pond was an abandoned boathouse with a small room above it. On its wide-planked floor was a decrepit double mattress, indelibly stained from past erotic encounters. That was where I was hoping to maneuver Denise.

I was watching from my bedroom window when her mother dropped her off at the stone entrance pillars flanking the gateway to our property. She stared up at the big house for a full minute before slowly walking up the gravel lane, her ice skates hanging from her right shoulder.

In those days, the place still looked imposing. A Wall Street securities trader named Ingersoll had paid a fortune to have it built as a summer home in 1924. He went bust in 1929. The twelve-bedroom mansion was a wedding present to my parents from my mother's father, Thomas Sprague, of the Rhode Island Spragues. My brother Tom was named after him.

Sprawled on a bluff overlooking Long Island Sound, it rises four and a half stories high, with a wraparound porch and a big pillared entrance portico. Thanks to my father, whose whole family came from Texas, the flag of the Lone Star State flew from a fifty-foot-high pole near the gatehouse. Gigantic oak trees shaded the three acres of lawn.

As I said, the house still looked imposing, at least after dark. Even in daylight it looked impressive if you were glancing at it from your yacht out on the sound. It was only when you got up close that you realized the place was starting to fall apart.

It wasn't that the lawns didn't get mowed, or the rhododendrons weren't trimmed, or that the tennis court didn't get rolled, but by 1961 the white clapboards were peeling, the black shutters were sagging, the windows needed caulking, and a legion of termites had gorged themselves on enough support beams so that you had to walk uphill from the center hall to the dining room.

If the house hadn't been crammed with books, oil paintings, telescopes, photographs, aquariums, and family memorabilia, you would also have noticed that the plaster walls were cracked and a lot of the furniture needed refinishing. The condition of the house was like the condition of our family.

From my bedroom window, I saw Denise reach the stables at the head of the drive. The stables once housed a herd of Ingersoll's polo ponies. By 1961, the last occupant was the old man's '41 Packard convertible, the car he had been driving when he met my mother at the naval air station in Pensacola before the war. It was crumbling just like their marriage.

By the time I reached the main staircase, Denise had found the doorbell and the old man had gone to answer it. Aside from Tommy and me, he was the only one home at the time. Looking down the banister, I saw the two of them standing together in the foyer, his six-foot-one frame towering over her.

"Good afternoon, Commander Ledbetter," she said, glancing up at him nervously, and then quickly averting her eyes.

He still enjoyed being addressed by the last rank he had held before being kicked out of the navy in 1952. That was ten years after he had won the Medal of Honor for sinking a Jap aircraft carrier in his Dauntless dive-bomber.

He was clutching four inches of martini in his pewter Annapolis goblet and gazing down at Denise with an air of appraisal and speculation. It probably stemmed from her decision to wear a red satin stretch-fitting body stocking, the kind that was popular back then with the speed skaters I'd seen training on television for Squaw Valley. Over her shoulders, she had loosely tied a white cable-knit Irish wool sweater. All in all, she looked pretty fabulous.

"Thanks, Travis, I've got it," I called down to him as the staircase creaked and groaned beneath me.

I began calling my father by his first name on the day I turned twelve. That's when something happened that forever changed our relationship. My birthday party was in full swing when my mother asked me to track him down for the cake-cutting ceremony. I found him up in our attic playroom with her best friend, Jane Carpenter. Mrs. Carpenter was the wife of our church pastor, Rod Carpenter.

They were sitting on the throne chair that my older brother Dave had built when we were playing King Arthur and the Knights of the Roundtable. Mrs. Carpenter was mounted on Travis's lap and facing him.

I may have been twelve, but I knew what they were doing. She had gone back downstairs and Travis was putting his pants on when he glanced over and saw me kneeling behind my sister Hope's huge dollhouse.

"Ricky," he said nonchalantly. "So how long have you been up here, buddy?"

That evening he sat me down to discuss the facts of life, Ledbetter style. Travis was no Dr. Spock when it came to parenting skills. He lived by his own set of rules. By the time I was fifteen, he had become my all-knowing mentor and role model.

As alike as we were in personality, I favored the Sprague line physically, being tall with blond hair, blue eyes, and regular features. Travis had black hair and brown eyes, a blunt, square-jawed face, and the slab-chested body of a bronc buster.

"Hi, Richard," said Denise with a thin smile, looking up at me on the staircase.

I remember the coal furnace in the basement had broken down again and I could see her breath condensing in the cold air of the foyer. I led her down the hall into the living room, where a log fire was keeping it warm until the plumber came. Travis followed us into the room.

"I'm going to get my skates," I said.

"I didn't know you skated, Ricky," said Travis, grinning.

"I'm going out for the hockey team," I came back.

When I returned a few minutes later, Travis was telling her about a friend he knew before the war who had skated in the 1936 Games at Garmisch, and was later killed at Guadalcanal. I said I was ready to go, and Denise excused herself to go to the bathroom.

"Ricky," he said after she was out the door. "That girl could go all the way at Innsbruck. She's got the most important asset an Olympic figure skater has to have."

"What's that?" I asked.

"A gold medal ass," he said, heading off to refill his goblet.

We were going out the front door when Tommy brushed past me with his own skates over his shoulder. He had on the little white French Foreign Legion kepi he had begun wearing after we had both read *Beau Geste*. Afterward, we had built a miniature version of Fort Zinderneuf in the sand dunes below the house. I was Beau and he was Digby.

"Where the hell are you going?" I demanded, worried that he would foul up my plans.

"Skating, Beau," he replied as he bounded off.

We were in the middle of a severe cold snap. It took a couple of weeks of freezing temperatures for St. John's Pond to ice over, and when we got there, it looked fairly thick and solid all the way across.

A harsh wind was blowing off Long Island Sound, and the sky descended until it seemed no more than a few hundred feet above us.

The clouds were a solid mass of gray, almost lead in color, which only added to the bleakness of the afternoon.

In the distance, a group of high school kids were playing hockey at the far end of the pond. Right across from the church at our end, I saw Tommy barreling along by himself with his head thrown back.

While putting my skates on, I realized they were an old pair of Dave's and one size too small for me. I figured that the sooner I got them on, the faster I could fake an injury near the boathouse and take them off again.

Denise took forever to get ready. It was clearly a precious ritual for her. First, she put on two sets of long white cotton socks, and slowly pulled each one tight. The skates were then laced up with careful precision. My toes were already starting to ache by the time she finally secured the laces around the back of her ankles with fancy loops. I looked across the pond to see Tommy lunging forward, his legs pumping furiously, as he careened into a wide turn near the tidal sluice gate.

When Denise was finally ready, she tiptoed over to the edge of the ice. With one almost imperceptible thrust of her left toes, she glided away. After a dozen yards, she dipped forward with swanlike elegance until her outstretched fingers almost touched the ice. Simultaneously, her left leg, now fully extended, rose gracefully into the air. I watched her coast into a series of perfect figure eights.

It was goddam dazzling. All I could think of was taking my ice-cold hands and warming them between her perfectly formed thighs. I wasn't sure what to do with my feet, which were really starting to hurt.

Meanwhile, I floundered along in her wake, ferociously scissoring my legs to maintain forward progress. A moment later, she was floating effortlessly back toward me, her black mane sailing behind her. She tweaked my left ear as she flashed past.

"You'll never make the hockey team," she called out. "You're hopeless."

Swerving into a stationary spin, she whirled faster and faster until her body became an astonishing blur. I watched as her hands moved upward in slow motion from her sides like flowers seeking the sun, rising higher until her arms formed a perfect canopy above her head. I gaped at her, spellbound, as she ended the spin in an explosion of ice chips.

"You're the most amazing girl I've ever known," I said, exaggerating only slightly.

She saw how much pleasure it had given me, and flashed me the barest hint of a smile. I was imagining her lying with me on the boathouse mattress when my reverie was interrupted by her sudden scream.

"*Your brother!*" she shouted, pointing toward the other side of the pond.

From that distance, the only thing I could see was a tiny arm waving up at the sky. It was no more than a foot above the ice, and looked like the antenna of a praying mantis. As we skated toward it, Denise grabbed my hand to drag me along faster. I saw his head above the ice as we came up to the tidal sluice gate, where the ice wasn't so thick. Tommy was still wearing the kepi. His expression looked surprisingly calm. He hadn't said a word, much less called out to us.

When we were about twenty feet away, he disappeared down the hole. The ice around Denise and me began to crack with a sound like pistol shots, and we stopped short. A few seconds later, his kepi floated to the surface.

Everybody comes back up at least twice, I remember thinking. That's a given. Denise started hyperventilating and began tearing furiously at her hair as she dropped to her knees.

"Oh, no!" she cried.

There were no bubbles in the water where he had gone down. I looked up at the sky. It was right on top of us like a lead coffin. Denise was kneeling beside me with mucus pouring out of her nose.

"Go get those hockey players," I said, staring down again at the black hole.

The water in the hole was flat and still. There was no time to take off the skates. I started lurching toward the jagged opening. When I was three feet away, the ice began to break up. Then I was in the water too.

Cold is a word that doesn't describe it. I didn't know what the term thermal shock meant at fifteen, but I was about to learn the definition. I was already cold when I went in the water. Now it felt like a thousand needles were jabbing at me all at once. Then the water was over my head.

The faint light above me disappeared. I reached out for Tommy in every direction. He wasn't there. I couldn't help swallowing water. My lungs seemed ready to burst. A voice began screaming in my ear.

He's gone!

I kicked for the surface, but the skates weighed me down. There was blackness everywhere. A feeble light appeared above me. I came out of the water and breathed in great gulps of air.

I could see the hockey players in the distance. They were surging down the ice from the other end of the pond in smooth, powerful strokes. Denise was leading them. Strangely, the water didn't seem so cold anymore.

For some reason I actually felt calm as I took a deep breath and dropped back into the darkness. Weighted down as I was by the wet winter clothes and skates, it was impossible to swim. By windmilling my arms and kicking my feet, I gained some momentum and searched through the void. I lost all sense of direction in the blackness.

My fingers encountered something slimy and horrible. It took me a second to realize it was just putrefying leaves at the bottom of the pond. As I recoiled backward, I felt my breath going again.

Tommy had been down there too long. He was dead. *Save yourself,* a voice whispered in my ear. I had no more air inside me. I swallowed more water. In a panic, I kicked for the surface until I saw the faint light above me again. Then my head hit the underside of the ice with a heavy thud. Inside my brain it sounded like a bowling ball being dropped on the floor. But I was below the floor.

In a spasm of demented fury, I flailed my arms and screamed the worst obscenities I knew. At least in my mind. Then I collided with something that felt like a sodden rag doll. It was Tommy, already drowned.

I thought I could hear the sound of more pistol shots as I pulled him close to me and the circuits began shutting down in my brain. They say your whole life passes before you in a moment, but I didn't see any of it. I had drowned too.

As if my mind was no longer part of my body, I felt myself being dragged out of the water and pulled into a boat. I opened my eyes to see Tommy already lying there on the duckboards between the two bench seats. His skates were stuck up in the air at a cockeyed angle. His head rolled toward me and I saw what could only be a death mask. His face was a hideous purple and blue.

To this day I'm not sure how we got to the surface. I was told that a few of the hockey players used a log to break up the ice while others dragged the wooden skiff over from the shore. Tommy had been locked in my arms when they found us together under the ice.

The Cold Spring Harbor Rescue Squad worked for a long time to save him. In bringing him back, they cracked two of his ribs. When I came around again, we were lying together on that old stained mattress in the boathouse, the one where I had been hoping to score with Denise.

They had covered us with coats and sweaters. All I could see of Tommy was his face. It was still grayish-purple, and his lips were swollen up like little inner tubes. As I watched, his body spasmed and a mouthful of bile ran out from between his lips. Then he began to shiver so hard I thought he was convulsing. When I hugged him, his eyes fluttered open before closing again. For a moment I thought he had died.

Then I heard his boy's voice in my ear.

"I was in heaven, Beau," he whispered.

I turned over to face him. His nose was only inches from mine. A grotesque attempt at a smile split the purple mask.

"I was in heaven," he repeated.

"You were in heaven at the bottom of the pond?"

He nodded.

"I was there. It was so beautiful."

"Yeah, sure," I said, convinced he must still be in shock.

When I looked up again, there was a crowd of strangers filling the room, all staring down at us. That's when I heard someone say, "What that kid did for his brother was really brave."

"He's a hero," added Denise with a smile.

Growing up, that's all I ever wanted to be. A hero. Just like Travis when he won the Medal of Honor for sinking that Jap carrier, and like JFK when he saved his shipmates in the Solomon Islands aboard *PT-109*.

TWO

I arrived at Cornell University in the fall of 1963 as a freshman in the School of Arts and Sciences. That was after graduating from Friends Academy near the bottom of my class. Unlike my older brother Dave, who graduated from Cornell cum laude, I was a family legacy. And I was a hell of a tennis player.

Our grandfather Thomas Sprague was in the Cornell class of 1917 and had gone over to France as a lieutenant in the American Expeditionary Force under General Black Jack Pershing in World War I. He came home a committed pacifist.

Later on, he helped to bankroll the campaign of Norman Thomas to be the first Socialist president of the United States. That's pretty funny because he inherited his own fortune from our great-grandfather Samuel Sprague, who had amassed his wealth by exploiting the workers in his New England shoe factories.

My mother, Edith Sprague Ledbetter, graduated from the Arts and Sciences school with a major in English literature in 1938. That was the same year she made her debut in New York society along with Brenda Frazier in the debutante cotillion at the Ritz-Carlton Hotel.

At the start of my freshman year, I remember my first faculty adviser telling me, "Mr. Ledbetter, I want you to look at Cornell as an incubator with so many programs to offer you that we pride ourselves on leaving it up to the maturity and self-discipline of each student to plan his or her own course of study."

What he failed to gauge, at least in my case, was that I had no maturity, much less self-discipline. Along with the required courses, I explored the boundaries of learning through classes like "Introductory Stagecraft," "The Taxonomy of Cultivated Plants" in the Ag School, "Oral Communication," and "The Digestive Physiology of the Dog." I learned all my mathematical theory in a high-low poker game run by best friend, Pete Demetropolis.

There were occasional bumps in the road. The first one came freshman year.

I needed eight credit hours in a foreign language and I decided on French. In the summer of 1962, I had spent two weeks with a French family in Grenoble as part of the student exchange program at Friends Academy. It was cut short when Reynaud *père* found me in bed with his oldest daughter, Gabrielle, but by then she had helped me acquire a pretty good French accent.

In addition to the grammar lessons in French from Professor Arbuckle, we had to participate in a French recitation class that met six mornings a week in the basement of Morrill Hall. I've never been an early riser, and mine was at eight in the morning. The night before each class you were supposed to memorize a stupid exercise like "Collette Goes to the Butcher" or "Françoise Buys Fruit."

One person would play Collette and the other the butcher. We had been organized into teams and I had been stuck with Mike Grubb, who was the leading scorer on the freshman lacrosse team but usually more hungover on a Saturday morning than I was. He would sit there slumped across the scarred conference table, blank-faced and unshaven. Your typical Sigma Nu scholar.

In some ways, it worked to my advantage. When Mike would say in French that his favorite fruit was a yellow shoe, I would give the graduate assistant a Gallic shrug as if it wasn't my fault.

I escaped with the lowest passing grade of 60.

The most devastating thing that happened freshman year, or the rest of my time at Cornell, occurred on a Friday afternoon in the fall semester. I was in the middle of tennis practice when Coach McKinlay asked us all to gather round him.

"President Kennedy has been shot in Dallas," he told us. "They don't know if he is going to live."

We all crowded into the coaches' lounge to watch the developments live on a small black-and-white television set. We were still there when Walter Cronkite announced the news that he was dead.

It was impossible for me to absorb. In my mind's eye, I could still see him standing at our front door in Cold Spring Harbor with that crooked grin on his face when I held up my dog-eared copy of *Profiles in Courage* to him.

The next three days and nights went by in a blur, most of them spent in the TV room on the first floor of Founders Hall, where I lived freshman year. It brought together all the guys in our dorm—the jocks and the wimps, the WASPs and the Jews, the wild partiers and the do-gooders. We all sat there in shock, watching as the president's body came home with Jackie in her blood-soaked dress and was unloaded off *Air Force One*.

With brief shower breaks and sandwiches from the Barf Bar, we found a small measure of release in watching it all unfold live. How did one make sense of the spectacle of seeing Jack Ruby murder Lee Harvey Oswald in front of our eyes, then endure the hours-long funeral procession along Pennsylvania Avenue, and finally the infinite sadness of JFK's burial at Arlington at the age of forty-six?

I think he was the hero of the world's hopes.

That Sunday morning before Oswald was shot, I took a break and attended a church service at Sage Chapel along with hundreds of other students and faculty members, most of us beyond tears by then, sharing the same thousand-yard stare at the enormity of it all. There was no comfort.

It might sound crazy, but I felt I enjoyed a personal kinship with JFK that set me apart from the rest. I could close my eyes and see him as a young officer again, not much older than me, with the sun in his hair on the bridge of *PT-109*, bare-chested and smiling.

I could will myself in my mind to be there with him at Rendova in the Solomon Islands, listening to "Chattanooga Choo Choo" on his Victrola, and waiting for the next mission against the Japanese destroyers coming down the slot from Rabaul. In those same islands where Travis was then flying off his carrier to help stop the Japanese advance.

His death left our lives at Cornell a lot emptier.

His loss didn't make me devote myself to being a more serious scholar. By then I knew he had been no student grind either. A navy pilot friend of Travis's had visited us in Cold Spring Harbor a year or so earlier. He had been a close friend of JFK at Choate and Harvard. One night I was listening when he said to the old man, "Jack Kennedy was a happy-go-lucky cocksman who cut a bigger swath through the ladies than even you. You can believe it. I was there." It gave me another sense of kinship with him.

. . .

Tommy came to Cornell when I was starting my junior year. With his perfect grades at Friends Academy and perfect College Board scores, he wasn't a legacy like me. He could have gone anywhere he applied. By then we were probably as different as two brothers could be. Whenever I went home, he was usually gone, and vice versa. If I was Travis's son, he was Thomas Sprague's grandson.

Together, grandfather and grandson pursued one seemingly lost cause after another. I remember once when Grandpa Sprague and a group of his friends rowed a longboat across Long Island Sound to protest the building of a nuclear submarine in Groton, Connecticut. Tommy manned one of the oars.

During the summer of 1964, while I was swimming, sailing, and waterskiing with my friends on the sound, he and Grandpa Sprague went down to Mississippi to become Freedom Riders and help make sure the Negroes had the right to vote. Tommy was in the same place where the three young Freedom Riders were tortured and murdered by the Ku Klux Klan.

By the time he got to Cornell, Tommy and I were traveling different paths. I was still into tennis and hadn't lost a match in two years. At my mother's urging, I tried to connect with him at different times, inviting him to double-date with me on a trip down to Manhattan for a society party, or to travel along to Princeton for one of my tennis matches. I always promised him a hot date.

In turn, he would invite me to an organ recital at Sage Chapel or to a seminar on the idea of women earning equal pay with men, or "meals of reconciliation" he and others at Cornell United Religious Work had arranged with Negro students who were angry at the lack of programs and courses geared to their interests.

I had no interest in religious work or religion. My mother forced us to go to Sunday school from the age of five. At twelve, we graduated to attending services with her. For me, it was like going to the dentist every week to get a cavity drilled without Novocain. My only genuine prayers were for the minister to announce during the service that there would be no sermon because he didn't have anything new to say about Jesus dying for our sins.

. . .

I had one last scare when it came to graduating with my original class.

It was the result of my stupid decision to take a course taught by one the stars of the history faculty, Professor Walter LaFrance. The course was titled "The New Empire: American Expansion (1860–1898)." Its principal attraction was the fact that it met only once a week.

The class size was large enough so that no one would notice my absences over the winter when I flew south to the Bahamas. The final grade was based on two term papers, and I had several to choose from, all written several years earlier by Dave. He had gotten an A in the course.

Disaster loomed when Professor LaFrance decided to replace the second term paper with a final examination. There was no point in trying to cram for it. I had missed most of the lectures on which it was based.

The exam took place in the amphitheater at Goldwin Smith Hall. The key to my survival was simple. There were exemplary scholars scattered all over the amphitheater. I had dated one of them and I didn't think she still hated me. I settled in between her and another student who looked like a young Audrey Hepburn. Just behind us, the big windows facing East Street gave me all the light I needed with my 20/10 vision to borrow some relevant ideas.

The grad assistants began circulating the exam. It consisted of one short paragraph that read, "What were the economic forces propelling America to world power in the nineteenth century? Be sure to address the thesis that American policymakers have depended for direction on the compass of utopian idealism."

What can I tell you?

As we waited for all the papers to be handed out, Professor LaFrance began casually walking up the center aisle of the amphitheater, scanning the faces of students on both sides of the aisle. He slowed down when he reached my row near the top. Looking over the heads of the students between us, he pointed directly at me.

"Excuse me," he said. "Are you a student in this class?"

I looked back at him as earnestly as I could and said, "Yes, sir. This is my favorite course."

Some asshole in one of the rows below me started laughing.

Professor LaFrance cracked a little smile. He had a very distinguished head with a full crown of grayish-brown hair. I grinned back at him as if it was a private joke between the two of us. He crooked his finger at me to join him in the center aisle. I didn't have many options at that point. With everyone watching us, he motioned for me to follow him back down the steps of the amphitheater. When we reached his desk at the bottom, he pulled his own chair out and invited me to sit down by myself.

The paper I ended up writing focused on the impact of Stonewall Jackson's death at the Battle of Chancellorsville and how it affected the fortunes of the Confederacy during the remaining years of the war. I tied it into the fact that the South had no armament factories and its economic power hinged entirely on cotton. It actually wasn't bad.

A week later, I overcame my sense of dread and went over to Goldwin Smith Hall, where all the grades were posted alphabetically in a big glass-fronted case near the main entrance. My eyes were immediately drawn to a grade that was circled in red. There was an asterisk next to it. I saw that it was next to my name. I had received an F as my final grade.

I followed the asterisk down to the bottom of the grade sheet. There were the handwritten words *If it had been possible to issue a lower grade than an F this student would have received it.*

THREE

For me, the vanguard of the campus revolution arrived at Cornell on a raw morning in March 1967. At least, that was the first time I encountered it. The SDS, or Students for a Democratic Society, had probably been drafting their manifestos for months, but I hadn't heard about it.

It was snowing again, another blast of arctic wind that filled the air with ice particles. Your typical Ithaca spring. It was around seven in the morning. In those long upstate winters it was still pitch-black then, but you could feel the place begin to come alive in the dark like a slumbering giant.

Most of the students seemed to be wired into the same natural energy source. As if in harmony, lights would begin winking on in the Baker Dorms and University Halls. In concert, an army of undergraduates would begin shambling into steaming shower rooms before putting on a double layer of winter clothing. With the first sickly rays of dawn peeking over East Hill, they began converging on the campus from every direction. Filled with determination, they fanned out to conquer their twenty-four-credit-hour course loads or to discover a new galaxy in the universe.

After almost four years, my academic career was finally coming to a close. That morning, my athletic career was ending too. I was already late for a meeting with Fred McKinlay, the coach of the varsity tennis team.

The windswept snow peppered my face like birdshot as I headed toward the suspension footbridge that crosses over one of the two-hundred-foot-deep gorges cutting through the Cornell campus. Unlike the students walking along beside me, I had just left the smoky warmth of a marathon poker game at the Seal and Serpent house. We had been playing for thirty hours and I was practically out on my feet, but eight hundred dollars richer.

Halfway across the bridge, I glanced down into the cataract of black water raging through the gorge and remembered the day when Tommy and I had almost drowned. That started me thinking about him, and whether he was still enjoying his sophomore year. Although I hadn't seen him in months, my mother wrote that he had decided to major in religious studies and was planning to attend divinity school.

Coach McKinlay was already in his office at the tennis complex when I arrived. The green-painted concrete block walls were covered with photographs of the players he had coached over his long career, mostly guys with hair the length of toothbrush bristles wearing madras sport coats and white bucks. There were also pictures of Fred competing against the best players of his era like Pancho Gonzalez and Ken Rosewall. Now he prided himself on turning out players with his own brand of hustling play.

That morning he looked like he was nursing a bad stomachache. I interpreted it to mean he had finally decided to kick me off the team. What he didn't know was that I was looking forward to it. After playing tennis competitively since I was five years old, I had as much interest in it as I did in reading Nancy Drew.

"That's some tan for Ithaca" were his first words as I sat down in the molded plastic chair across from his desk. I had recently returned from a quick trip to Nassau but knew better than to respond.

"You think I'm a stupid jerk, don't you?' Fred demanded.

"No, Coach," I said.

"Don't patronize me," he came back. "I've known you for four years."

He ran his fingers through his thinning gray hair and gazed up at the sainted players' pictures on the wall. That seemed to give him the courage to continue.

"You're hurting the team, and I can't allow that. I've given you every chance to redeem yourself, and you've squandered them all."

"I know," I said. "I'm sorry, Coach."

Down the hallway, I could hear the team starting to hit on the practice courts.

"You're not a natural like Dave but you know how to win, how to compete. You could be the best player in the Ivies and well beyond that if you really applied yourself."

Dave had played first singles at Cornell for three years. At one point, he was ranked as one of the twenty best college players in the country.

"I'm also fully aware of what your mother's family has done for this university—and for the tennis program," he said finally.

My mother's name was engraved over the entrance to the new university courts. That was the only reason I was still on the team.

"So," he began, and stopped again.

I started to worry he was about to give me another shot.

"I haven't had a chance to practice as much as I would have liked, Coach," I said. "I'm putting a lot of effort into my course work right now. I need to graduate to qualify for Naval Officer Candidate School."

His hooded eyes got even narrower.

"What a load of crap," he said. "Like the time you came in here sophomore year to tell me you had broken your arm over Christmas vacation so you couldn't practice. You remember that? Except that one of your teammates saw a vet student over at the Veterinary School putting on your cast. As of today, you are no longer a member of this team."

I smiled to show him there were no hard feelings.

"You're happy about this, aren't you?" he said.

"No, Coach," I said.

"Get the hell out of my office."

It was still snowing hard as I made my way across the arts quad toward Willard Straight Hall. Earlier that month I had rented one of the alumni guest rooms on the top floor to take much-needed naps after poker games. Having my monthly allotment of Grandpa Sprague's trust made things a lot easier.

"The Straight," as the Cornell student union is called, is a stone building slightly larger than Grand Central Station and built like a Crusader fortress. It holds two cafeterias, including the Ivy Room, where students gather to hang out, along with a warren of club and study rooms, innumerable fireplaces, a movie theater, gaming rooms, and the campus radio station, WVBR.

I was crossing the promenade leading to the big double entrance doors when I encountered the forward elements of the campus revolution. About a dozen people were clustered around the doors. They were all wearing red armbands. A girl in an army helmet had started to loop a long length of chain through one of the door handles. As I attempted to open the other door, a guy with shoulder-length hair and a scraggly beard stepped around me. He passed the chain through the second handle and padlocked it.

"This building was just liberated in the name of Students for a Democratic Society," he declared after turning to face me.

He was wearing what looked like a red granny dress trimmed at the ankles over dirty chinos and desert boots, and he reeked of body odor. *Be tactful,* I remember thinking. This guy's got the keys to the padlock. He can't help being a complete asshole.

Before I could tell him how much I respected his Stalinist idealism, he looked up at the small crowd behind me and announced, "Today, we are demanding that the university give all course and curriculum control to the SDS Student Coordinating Committee. Until they meet this demand, the Straight is shut down. Totally."

My reply just slipped out.

"Look, shithead, I have an important appointment with my faculty adviser in there."

"You'll have to conduct university business somewhere else," he said, sneering.

Two other guys dressed like him began rolling empty oil drums across the promenade toward the entrance. Behind them came two more carrying thick planks of pine lumber.

"Who phoned the Syracuse TV stations?" I heard the first one call out.

A timid-looking girl wearing combat fatigues checked a batch of notes attached to her clipboard.

"I asked Arnie to do it, but he told me that Jody told him that the People's Action Council was in charge of all media contacts and so Jody said she would do it."

"Jody? Jody's a freak!" he shouted angrily.

That was my introduction to SDS, but I was too tired to give it further thought at the time. Walking around the building to the back entrance, I discovered that it wasn't padlocked yet. I made it up to my alumni room and sacked out for the rest of the day.

. . .

There were several inches of snow on the windowsill when I came alive again late that afternoon. After shaving and taking a shower, I headed downstairs. By then, the iron chains on the front doors had disappeared along with the revolutionaries.

Inside the main hall of the Straight, it was typical evening pandemonium. In the glow of the fireplaces, students were milling about, checking the ride boards, waiting in line for concert tickets, or warming themselves after coming in from the snowstorm.

I checked the news headlines pinned to the bulletin board near the ticket counter.

ALICE B. TOKLAS DIES

NAVY SKYHAWKS BOMB HANOI

Picking up my mail, I found the letter I had been waiting for from the Navy Department. I ripped it open. Travis had made it happen. It was the assignment that I had asked for. I headed back upstairs to share the good news with Pete Demetropolis.

Inside the game room, a dozen pub tables were packed with students playing chess, backgammon, bridge, and gin rummy. Near the casement windows on the far side of the room were four pool tables. Pete was slouched in one of the step-up chairs that lined the wall behind them.

An open leather briefcase was resting on his lap. I knew it was filled with an array of prophylactics in colorful plastic packets. His shrewd black eyes were focused on a kid wearing a three-piece suit who was staring wide-eyed into the briefcase. I flopped down in the chair next to Pete and watched the driving wet snow splatter against the windows.

"I'll be honest," said Pete to the kid. "A handsome guy like you raises expectations in women. In addition to protecting yourself from a nasty infection, you have to think about your reputation on campus for the next four years. This baby is made from the stomach lining of a cheetah. It will drive a girl bat shit."

"How much is it?" asked the kid nervously.

"Twenty-five dollars," responded Pete. "But I like you and you're a new customer. I'll give you three for twenty bucks."

The kid brought out a leather wallet, counted out the money, and headed off.

"Another satisfied customer," I said. "So where is the action tonight?"

"No action. The snow has killed off everything except Las Vegas Night at the Moravia Grange Hall."

"That's too long a drive in this weather."

"Yeah, I know," he said. "But they're the biggest fish within forty miles. You want to try it?"

I shook my head and pulled out the envelope I had received from the Navy Department.

"What's this?" he said suspiciously after seeing the official military insignia.

"My navy assignment. The old man wangled it for me."

"Really," he said without enthusiasm. "When do you go in?"

"Right after graduation."

"I can't interpret all this legalese shit. What did you get?"

"I'm going straight into the navy's swift boat program as soon as I finish Officer Candidate School at Newport. It's for guys who grew up on the water and know all about small boats. They start you out in Vietnam as a second in command, and three months later you skipper your own boat. I'll be a captain."

"I'm sure they're quaking in their sandals in Hanoi. What's a swift boat?"

"They're high-speed gunboats that patrol the rivers in the Mekong Delta. In and out fast . . . a lot of action."

Pete pivoted around so suddenly our noses almost touched.

"Are you nuts?" he said heatedly. "You're still fixated."

"What are you talking about?" I said.

"You remember the night in the Bahamas when you came up with your plan to organize an expedition to search for the hulk of *PT-109*? This idea speaks to the same mentality."

In truth I knew there wouldn't be much left of *PT-109* after twenty years since the hull was made of plywood, but the thought of locating it was like finding the Holy Grail.

"So what are you going to do after graduation?" I asked.

"There's one exemption I like for anyone under orthodontic care. You pay the dentist to fill your mouth with braces just before you go for your physical. The whole package costs around a grand. Guaranteed. I'm also thinking about entering a yeshiva."

"You're not Jewish."

"I could be," he came back.

"You've got to be kidding," I said.

"No, I'm not. Why the hell would I want to go to goddam Vietnam and get my ass shot off by some little bastard in black pajamas? Christ, they're killing two or three hundred guys a week over there!"

"So you're going to be a goddam draft dodger," I said.

His cheeks flushed molten red.

"Ricky, in some ways you're a real moron, you know that?" he said as if I was retarded. After several seconds, his eyes softened a little. "Listen . . . let's go over to The Palms and get a couple of beers."

"Make it the Chapter House," I said.

Pete was my closest friend, although as I think about it now, I really didn't have any others. I first encountered him at the beginning of freshman year, when he came through the Baker Dorms selling the same line of prophylactics. Pete's father had died when he was seven and he had to pay all his own college expenses. When the war in Vietnam began heating up, he made good money selling bus tickets to protest rallies in New York City on a nonexistent bus line. By his junior year, he was running a high-low college poker game. Later on he put together a townie game that included cab drivers, dish washers, and short-order cooks. They loved their poker straight . . . no high-low, nothing wild. In that first year, I cleared over three grand from both games.

When we came out of the Straight, kids were lined up along the top of Libe Slope with plastic serving trays from the Ivy Room. It's an incredibly steep hill, which makes for great sleigh riding. It can also be dangerous, and in winter the school ground crews place baled straw around the trees that dot the slope.

Looking up at the leaded windows of Uris Library, I could see the figure of a girl, her hands and face pressed against the glass as she looked out into the storm. In the Straight parking lot, we dusted the snow off my Austin-Healey and headed over to the Chapter House.

There is something about a storm that creates a party atmosphere, and the Chappie was in a holiday mood. Its wood-paneled rooms were packed with students beneath the faded photographs of bygone athletic warriors. The crush along the mahogany bar reminded me of a rush hour subway train in Manhattan. There was going to be live music that night from the Oz and Ends, and I could hear Ozzie and his bandmates warming up in the dance area with "Hold On, I'm Comin'."

We had almost reached the end of the bar when I felt something hit me in the back. When I turned around, a hand came up and slapped my face. I looked down to see Tracy Logan. She was a cute blonde from Philadelphia with a stunning body, all in miniature. She was barely five feet tall. Her face usually had a sweet Shelley Fabares quality to it. Now it was full of anger.

"You promised," she said, her voice dripping with emotion. "You promised! I waited all night for you."

The absurdity of the whole thing struck me as funny. I couldn't help smiling, which only seemed to enrage her further.

"You rotten bastard," she cried, silencing the crowd milling around us. "Everyone told me about you, but I didn't believe them."

"Go ahead, Tracy . . . hit him again!" shouted a girl behind her, egging her on.

"I hate you!" she screamed, trying to punch me in the face. At six foot three I was a tall target, and her fist struck my chest instead. The crowd along the bar was gazing at us as if we were circus freaks at a small-town carnival. Standing behind Tracy, Pete Demetropolis was shaking his head in disbelief.

"So why didn't you call me?" Tracy shouted, hitting me in the stomach.

The punches were starting to hurt.

"I just lost track of time," I said.

I made the mistake of smiling again. A moment later her fists were flailing up at my face. I had to raise my arms to block them.

"Kick that fucking creep in the balls!" someone yelled.

I looked back down the line at the bar. The girl was standing on one of the barstools, her face contorted with rage. I vaguely remembered taking her out one night freshman year.

Tracy burst into tears. Pivoting away, she rushed headlong into the arms of the girl standing behind her. Together they disappeared into the crush. As we continued to the end of the bar, the girl standing on the stool kept screaming "Asshole!" and pumping her middle finger at me.

"Rick, you've created a new world-class benchmark for serious relationships," said Pete. "It's called the one-hour stand."

. . .

Within a few minutes, everything had returned to normal. After a couple of beers, we ordered cheeseburgers and fries. By the time our plates were cleared, the crowd had largely turned over, and Pete began to survey the action again.

On the television set suspended above our heads, Walter Cronkite was introducing a news segment. I saw it was a Vietnam story. A reporter stood in a jungle clearing speaking directly into the camera. I could hear the sound of small arms fire in the background and then a squad of American soldiers was running past the camera. The sound of gunfire grew louder.

What must have been an artillery round landed near the position, because the camera jerked for several seconds before it came to rest on one of the soldiers, a kid who looked like he was barely out of junior high school. There was fear in his eyes. Then I heard the chatter of automatic weapons, and a deep voice was yelling "Go! Go! Go! Go!" The camera stayed on the kid's face, still fixed with fear, but determination too. Then he was moving forward out of camera range. The reporter came back, and the segment gave way to a deodorant commercial featuring Sonny and Cher. I looked over at Pete, who was stuffing his face with Vienna sausage.

"Did you see that?" I said, poking him. "They're making history right now in Vietnam."

His mouth was still full, but he was staring at me again like I was from Mars.

"If you want to know what I think," he said after swallowing the sausage, "I think we've got an arrogant bunch of idiots in Washington who are taking advantage of hopeless morons like you. I also think you've been brain-damaged by all those war movies you grew up on."

He was right about the movies. Just about all my favorites were about World War II. They ran a lot of them on television when I was growing up. After watching *Twelve O'Clock High* or *Run Silent, Run Deep* or *Thirty Seconds Over Tokyo* on *The Late Show* on WCBS, I would go up to my bedroom. Lying in bed, I would close my eyes and pray that when I opened them again, I'd have come of age in the nineteen thirties in time to witness Hitler's rise to power, the fall of France, Pearl Harbor, and all the dramatic events that engulfed the world. What I would have given to have had the chance to fight alongside my father and Jack Kennedy in the Pacific.

Pete knocked back a pickled egg and said, "Don't you understand? They zap you for good over there. It's for real, you jerk."

That was the moment I first saw Kate. She appeared as a reflection in the mirror behind the bar. As I watched her come through the door, she shook snow out of her shoulder-length dark hair, pulled off a fleece-lined duffel coat, and hung it on one of the pegs near the door. My first impressions were of a girl with a pale face, chin held high, tall and walking very erect.

Farther down the bar, a blonde stood up and called out to her. The dark-haired girl moved toward her through the crowd. For the life of me, I don't know why she captured my interest. For one thing, she was wearing glasses and carrying a book.

The blonde was more my type, with the vacant looks of a centerfold. As the dark-haired girl reached the bar, she removed her glasses. Her eyes swept the room in both directions. They didn't stop on me. The guy on the stool next to her immediately surrendered his seat. She gave the bartender a smile along with her drink order.

This girl was obviously not into the college bar scene. I spent a fair amount of time in just about all of them around campus and had never seen her before. The bartender came back and placed a mug of coffee in front of her. She was different. Maybe it was the eyes. They were eyes that seemed to say, *I'm going to make a difference in this world.* Why this attribute would have suddenly appealed to me, I have no idea.

"She's not your type," said Pete, following my gaze.

"What type?" I said.

"Wholesome . . . mature . . . intelligent," he came back.

With a girl like this I had to come up with something fresh, something original. As I waited for her to look in my direction, I decided to arch my right eyebrow. The puzzle wrapped in an enigma. James Dean.

When she looked my way, I wasn't prepared for her reaction. She stared straight back at me. It lasted for at least five seconds before she dropped her eyes and turned back to her friend. Having often had that impact on girls since I was fifteen, I felt comfortable enough to work my way through the crowd until I was standing right behind her. Up close, her hair was the color of a new polished chestnut just peeled from the shell. For a tall girl she was almost boyishly slim. Again, not my type.

She was wearing a navy crew-neck sweater that showed a hint of white shirt collar at the neck. A gray flannel pleated skirt ended at the top of high black boots. Her right toe was tapping along to the Beach Boys' "Don't Worry Baby" on the jukebox.

The book she had been carrying was lying faceup on the bar. The title of it was *The Divine Milieu.* From the cover art, I could tell it had some kind of religious connotation, and suddenly remembered a line that had worked on a girl at a Methodist Youth Fellowship retreat one summer on Shelter Island.

"Tell me," I said, leaning in close to her right ear so I could be heard over the Beach Boys. "Do you believe in predestination?"

She swung around on her stool to face me. Her swept-back hair revealed high cheekbones and deep-set brown eyes.

"As perceived by John Calvin or Saint Augustine?" she asked in a low-pitched voice.

Obviously, she was smarter than hell. I had no idea who she was talking about. She waited expectantly.

"Actually, that's irrelevant," I finally came back. "What is important is that you recognize that one fleeting moment in your entire life when destiny brings you together with the one human being ideally suited for you."

Her eyes showed no reaction, although her blond friend started looking at me with interest.

"What kind of man would that be?" she asked, smiling for the first time. I noticed she had a slight bump at the bridge of her narrow nose. I wondered how it got there. Aside from lipstick, she wasn't wearing any makeup. Or rings or jewelry for that matter.

"The man who can make your life a never-ending odyssey of romance and adventure," I said.

The animation in her smile began to drain away. In a bolt of self-awareness, I realized how trite the words were. At the same time, I wondered why I was so desperate to impress her.

"Wouldn't it be fair to assume that sparks would be flying in both directions when that moment arrives?" she asked neutrally.

"Ahhh . . . generally speaking, yes," I replied.

She turned her back to me and resumed talking to her girlfriend. As my mind turned to suet, the blond girl continued to gaze at me over her shoulder.

"Of course, sometimes a person's antennae can become rusty through previous false alarms," I said to her back.

She continued to ignore me.

"That's a pretty cavalier attitude to take in the face of destiny," I said. "You could even be facing some fairly tragic consequences."

"You look like Robert Redford," said the blonde, who hadn't turned away.

I had heard it often enough in recent years to give her the familiar grin and say, "No . . . he looks like me."

I still had no idea what I was actually feeling. I only knew I hadn't felt anything like it before. And for some reason I didn't want it to end. The dark-haired girl checked her watch.

"With all this snow, we should probably leave now," she said, picking up her book from the bar. "The movie starts in fifteen minutes."

"Are you sure you still want to go, Kate?" responded the blonde.

A name—I was finally getting somewhere.

Kate got up from her stool. She was really tall for a girl. I'm six foot three, and the crown of her hair came to just below my chin.

"Yes, I'm sure," she said firmly.

"What are you going to see?" I asked.

She turned back to me.

"*Casablanca*," said the blonde. "It's classic night at the State Theatre."

All the hundreds of hours I had spent watching old movies were about to pay off. As the girl began working her way through the crowd toward the coat pegs against the wall, I followed in her wake.

"Great movie," I began. "You kind of remind me of Lauren Bacall. Listen, you can't be late. The first ten minutes sets the entire mood. Conrad Veidt is one of my favorite character actors. What a Nazi! Better than Helmut Dantine in *Northern Pursuit*. Of course, he's in it too. He plays the young Bulgarian at the roulette table. Bogie tells his wife to go back to Bulgaria."

Kate had put her duffel coat on and was now staring at me oddly. And why not? I sounded like a raving lunatic, totally out of my element. Desperately, I shifted gears.

"I'd be happy to drive you down. I'm parked right outside."

She just stood there looking up at me.

"I'm kind of an expert on *Casablanca*," I said.

I saw the first hint of a smile.

"Yes, I can see that," she said.

I felt a tap on my right shoulder and turned to see another girl standing there. She was someone I had picked up one night and screwed down in the Cascadilla Gorge near the Chapter House.

"Rick Ledbetter, I presume," she said in a tone that indicated she was prepared to join me again. She gently squeezed my crotch and slowly drifted down the bar.

"Small world," I said, shaking my head. "I met her at the Louvre last summer."

"Your name is Rick Ledbetter?" Kate asked, taking a step backward.

"Yeah," I said. "Let me just grab my coat."

Zigzagging through the crowd, I stopped to tell Pete I was leaving.

"You don't have to say anything. I can see the imbecilic rapture on your face. The blonde is gorgeous."

"Not the blonde, the dark-haired one."

I grabbed my coat and headed back to the door, shoving it open and stepping outside. The snow pricked my eyes as I looked up and down the sidewalk. Both girls had disappeared. I walked south to Buffalo Street, which led downtown and to the movie theater. In the streetlights, I could see that the sidewalk was empty for several blocks. I walked back to the Chappie with the snow flying in my face.

While Pete vainly tried to pick up one of the waitresses, I sat at the bar attempting to analyze these new feelings. I knew it couldn't be love at first sight. As Travis had always assured me, love was something you made. It was all about desire and consummation. Considering the number of girls I had scored with since I was thirteen years old, the whole idea was ridiculous.

FOUR

The SDS revolution stirred into action again one afternoon when I happened to be playing pool in the game room at the Straight. I had just lined up a shot when a monstrous shriek caused me to scratch with the cue ball. It was my introduction to the electronically amplified bullhorn. At the noise, everyone at the chessboards and pool tables headed over to the casement windows facing down onto the broad promenade in front of the main entrance.

"What's going on?" I asked Lou Jamieson, who was already at a window.

Lou had been my roommate freshman year and was a recruited Big 33 high school football player from Pennsylvania. He had the beatific smile of an altar boy and the personality of a Nazi storm trooper. Coeds adored him until they discovered his mean streak, which normally took about fifteen minutes. He was one of the biggest losers in our poker game and owed me four hundred dollars.

"It's just the pukes mouthing off," he said, staring out of the window with obvious contempt.

"The pukes?" I asked.

"You know . . . the antiwar faggots," he said.

I joined Pete at one of the windows and gazed down at a crowd that stretched out from the entrance of the Straight for almost thirty yards. More students were arriving every minute.

Three campus police cars were parked on the fringe of the crowd, their gumball lights swirling. Television crews were jockeying for position near a speakers' platform that had been crudely constructed by laying boards on top of fifty-five-gallon metal drums.

Since the snowstorm, the temperature had climbed back into the fifties, and the afternoon was golden bright. I wasn't sure how many people were there to participate in the demonstration and how many were just happy to be outside without freezing to death. A handful of people were waving large hand-lettered signs on poster-sized sections of white oak-tag. One of them read NO MORE WARGASMS. A coed was holding up a huge black-and-white photograph of an Asian girl with her legs missing.

The first speaker to climb onto the platform was Curt Sombrotto. He had lived down the corridor from me in Founders Hall freshman year. Later on he dropped out of school and I had lost track of him.

"The United States is waging an immoral war against the people of Vietnam," he said, holding the bullhorn in front of his face. "Dean Rusk says that we have to stop communism in Vietnam or all the other nations in Southeast Asia will fall like dominoes. Dean Rusk is a stooge of American imperialism."

His words were greeted with scattered applause from the cluster of students closest to the speakers' platform. They were all wearing red SDS armbands. The rest of the crowd seemed indifferent. Sombrotto went on for several minutes calling President Johnson a war criminal and McNamara a lackey of the military-industrial complex. He was followed by a guy who began shrieking that the university was a tool of the capitalist pigs on Wall Street who were financing the war for their own greed. I was about to turn away from the window and resume my nap in the alumni suite when Pete leaned over to me and whispered, "Isn't that your brother Tom?"

He was pointing down at the group directly under our window. I recognized him right away as he worked his way toward the platform. With the easy grace of the athlete he had been at Friends Academy, Tom vaulted onto the speakers' stand. His brown hair was cropped short, and he was wearing the kind of Ben Franklin spectacles that Trotsky favored before they put the ice pick in his head. Someone tried to hand him the bullhorn, but he waved it off. As I watched, he jammed both of his hands into the back pockets of his corduroys and faced the crowd.

"It seems to me that if there is such a thing as a just war," he began in a low voice that carried up to my window, "and I would submit that World War Two was a just war, there is also such a thing as an unjust war, and to fight in one should be a matter of individual conscience."

Unlike with the previous speakers, there was nothing strident about his language or his speaking style. He spoke to the crowd in a measured way, almost as if he were standing in our living room in Cold Spring Harbor instead of on that big open promenade.

"At the end of World War Two we learned at the Nuremberg trials that following orders is no defense if you know in your conscience that what you're doing is wrong. Now, almost every nation that fought alongside us in the Second World War believes that what we are doing in Vietnam is wrong."

Some of the students at the far edge of the crowd seemed to be leaning forward to hear him.

"Even if Secretary McNamara is right when he says that cluster bombing and search and destroy missions are winning the war, he is wrong if he believes these things represent what our nation should stand for in this world. And what if history someday records that thousands of young Americans fought and died in a war that never should have been fought? This war. The war in Vietnam."

Someone hocked a glob of spit out the window. It splattered on the head of one of the people standing on the speakers' platform. I turned to look at who had done it. Lou Jamieson grinned back at me.

"That's my brother down there," I said.

"I was aiming at the other puke," said Lou.

"Most of the Vietnamese are poor," said Tom as I turned back. "They are not Marxist ideologues. They don't know the difference between Karl Marx and Groucho Marx. In most ways these people are just like us. Parents of the children in Vietnam have the same hopes and dreams that their children will someday have a better life, just as our parents do for us."

I still wasn't sure why they all seemed to find him so compelling. It definitely wasn't the kind of bombastic speech that the other protesters had used to try to arouse the crowd.

"What a bunch of pussies!" declared Lou loudly. "You know why they're so idealistic all of a sudden? It's because General Hershey wants to get rid of the grad school deferment. Now that they may have to go to Vietnam themselves, they've suddenly decided the war is wrong. Six months ago you couldn't pay those assholes to demonstrate against the war. As long as it was someone else dying over there, they couldn't be bothered."

Pete stepped back from the window.

"If you're so anxious to fight, Lou," said Pete, "why don't you quit school and join up?"

Lou came over and poked his finger hard into Pete's chest.

"I'm all set to go into the National Guard right after graduation, Demetropolis."

Pete seemed momentarily taken aback. "Oh, wow! Hey, I'm sorry man. I didn't realize. I mean we all know the Guard gets right into the thick of the battle action. Wow. You'll be right here in the North American Theater of War. Write to me from Louisiana. I'll send you a care package."

"Fuck you," said Lou.

When I looked out the window again, Tom had finished his speech and a small wave of applause was sweeping across the promenade. With a shy smile, he jumped down from the platform and someone else was hoisted up to replace him. It was a girl wearing combat boots and an empty ammunition belt strapped around her waist. She had an Afro hairstyle that exploded out of her head for two feet in every direction.

"That's the chick that poured mustard on Averell Harriman's head when he came up here to speak," said Pete.

It was Phyllis Lobianco. The last time I had seen her was three and a half years earlier, during freshman orientation week. Back then, she was quite traditional and sported a cute Prince Valiant haircut. She had also seemed very mild-mannered. Someone handed her the bullhorn, and she raised it to her mouth.

"I'M AN SDS WOMAN FIGHTER!" she shouted. "WE'RE DEMANDING AMNESTY FOR EVERYONE ARRESTED AT YESTERDAY'S DEMONSTRATION."

Pete chuckled and said, "Can you imagine Marx and Lenin demanding amnesty from the Cossacks of old Czar Nicholas?"

My eyes were following Tommy as he navigated through the crush around the speakers' stand. People were stopping to congratulate him as he passed by. One guy was gazing up at him as if he had just scored the winning touchdown against Princeton.

Phyllis began reading from a letter she claimed she had received from a Vietnamese woman who said that the American soldiers were raping and torturing women with broken Coke bottles. As she went on, my mind wandered back to the first time I met Phyllis at a freshman mixer during orientation week. Back then she had proudly proclaimed herself to be a student in the College of Home Economics, where they had classes on how to raise a baby, dental hygiene, tap dancing, needle craft, and how to convert a garage or basement into a family room. I ended up taking a couple of them.

That night, she told me she was searching for the man she could devote her life to as kind of a perfectly trained housewife. Of course, I had some affectations of my own in those days. My clothing repertoire included a burgundy silk ascot that puffed out of my shirt collar like an inflamed thyroid. I also posed a good deal with one of Grandpa Sprague's meerschaum pipes.

After smoking several pouches of Cherry Blend tobacco, I felt like my tongue was on fire. I was forced to concentrate on keeping it suspended between the roof and floor of my mouth, which prevented me from talking and led to my early reputation as a serious student as well as a good listener. I was interrupted from my daydream by an elbow from Pete.

"Look over there," he said.

From the direction of Sage Chapel, another group of students was heading en masse toward the crowd. I recognized several members of the varsity football team. Someone in their group took up the cry "PEACE THROUGH NAPALM!" Two others held up a banner that read HELP STAMP OUT FLAMING ASSHOLES.

From inside their group, what looked like golf balls began to sail through the air toward the speakers' platform. As they smashed against the wall behind the platform, I saw they were eggs. Beyond the promenade, a black Lincoln Continental came slowly up University Avenue. It stopped at the edge of the crowd, and several men in dark suits got out. One of them was holding a 35 millimeter camera with a two-foot-long telephoto lens.

"The FBI, I presume," said Pete.

I watched Lou Jamieson walk over to one of the pool tables and pick up a white cue ball. As he walked back toward the window, I sidled over to him.

"What's that for? I asked.

"They're throwing eggs," he said. "It's just a jumbo egg."

I grinned at him.

"Look, Lou, just so you understand," I said. "If you fracture someone's skull with that cue ball and the campus police come up here to find out who did it, I'll be the first one to tell them it was you."

He gave me a malevolent smile.

"Why the fuck would you care?" he demanded.

"I don't," I said. "But I'm not going to risk having the navy take away my commission because the police end up accusing me of being an accomplice to an asshole like you."

Lou outweighed me by twenty pounds, but I had taken his measure long ago. He was a coward and would always back down from an actual fight.

"You won't get another fucking dime of what I owe you," he said, dropping the cue ball back on the table with a loud thud.

"Fine, Lou," I said. "And when I tell everyone you welched, try to find another game."

Phyllis Lobianco was still going strong when I returned to the window.

"We are going to shut the war machine down. ROTC will be stopped, and the war recruiters will be stopped!" she shouted.

That was when two more students wearing red armbands hoisted a galvanized trash can onto the speakers' platform. One of them proceeded to start a fire with several rolled-up newspapers.

"Ahh, the burning garbage pail ritual," Pete murmured. "More young men of principle burning their draft cards."

Five of them were already in line near the garbage pail. The first one looked close to tears as he loudly stated that he was burning his draft card in opposition to the war before dropping it into the pail. From the fringe of the crowd, I saw the agent with the camera take his picture. Pete pointed to the last person in the lengthening line.

"Looks like your brother is about to join the barbecue," he whispered.

Tommy was slowly making his way toward the front again. I remember thinking that there was still time to stop him. I ran out through the door of the game room and down the stairs. Coming out of the Straight, I headed toward the place where I had last seen him. As I worked my way through the mob, someone shoved past me. It was Grant Devlin, the provost of the university. Grim-faced, he was also trying to force his way to the speakers' platform.

"Hi, Beau," came a voice close to my ear.

Tommy emerged from the mass of bodies with his familiar grin. Up close, I could see that he had lost weight since I had last seen him. Behind the rimless glasses, his blue eyes were very bright in the gaunt face. Always slender, he now looked thin and a little unhealthy, as if all the family holiday feasts had melted off him, leaving his body lean and hard.

"Are you okay?" I asked, genuinely concerned.

"I'm fine," he said as a coed handed him a pen and a piece of paper.

"I think you're going to be president someday," she said.

I watched the color rise from the neckline of his shirt. It was obvious he thought the notion was as ridiculous as I did. Nevertheless, he took the paper from her outstretched hands and signed it.

Something suddenly lumbered between my legs and almost lifted me off my feet. I looked down to see a gigantic Saint Bernard. Dogs are allowed to roam free at Cornell, and this one had been spray-painted orange, probably some fraternity guy's idea of hilarious fun.

"Tom, you were magnificent," said a voice behind me.

I looked over. She looked back. It was Kate, the girl from the Chapter House. She seemed just as startled as I was. Caught in her gaze, I stood there with an idiotic smile on my face.

Kate, this is my brother, Rick," he said. "Rick, Kate."

"We've met," she said.

"Hey," I said, remembering why I had rushed down there. "I hope you're not planning to put anything in the garbage pail with those other morons."

Tommy shook his head. Over his shoulder, I watched another student drop his draft card onto the flaming pile. A ragged cheer went up from part of the crowd.

"I already returned my card to the Selective Service Administration," Tommy said, the haunted look momentarily returning to his eyes.

"You did what?"

"I returned my card to . . ."

"Goddam it. What's Travis going to say?"

Kate turned to face me, her arm around his waist.

"Tom is just following his conscience," she said.

"Well, that's original," I said. "I suppose you helped him reach that decision."

"As a matter of fact I did," she said, glowering at me.

Behind her, Provost Devlin had mounted the speakers' platform and was trying to gain the attention of the crowd. He looked very out of place in his double-breasted suit and Phi Beta Kappa key. In his early forties, he had an air of arrogance about him.

"This demonstration is an illegal use of university property," he announced in a loud, pompous tone. "On my responsibility, I will now ask the campus police to disperse the crowd."

Phyllis Lobianco, who was still on the platform with him, raised her bullhorn toward the crowd.

"THIS MAN IS A WAR CRIMINAL!" she yelled.

Ignoring her, Devlin waved to the campus police lieutenant standing at the edge of the crowd. As he turned to leave the platform, Phyllis held the bullhorn next to his left ear and screamed "WAR CRIMINAL! WAR CRIMINAL!"

Devlin never even blinked.

"Fuck off, Miss Lobianco," he said.

Phyllis smiled triumphantly and aimed her bullhorn at the crowd.

"PROVOST DEVLIN HAS JUST TOLD ME TO FUCK OFF!"

Around half the crowd started applauding.

"When did you do it?" I asked Tommy.

"What?"

"Send in your draft card."

He looked at Kate before responding.

"Last week," he said.

"Why didn't you talk to me first?"

Kate was still glaring at me. Just like Travis, I wasn't exactly a rock of support when it came to family crises, but Tommy and I shared a bond that I didn't have with anyone else in the world.

"Okay . . . there's still time to set this straight," I said. "You don't want to do something you'll always regret. Breakfast tomorrow. Obie's Diner. Eleven o'clock."

"Eleven o'clock?" he repeated.

"Why not? You have other plans?"

He just grinned and said, "Okay."

"Good . . . see you then."

Several questions were running through my mind as I walked away. The first was how Kate knew Tommy. And what was their relationship? To my knowledge, he had never even had a girlfriend in high school. As far as I knew, the kid was sexually retarded.

FIVE

After freshman year, I never took classes that were scheduled in the early morning. I usually slept in from evening activities, and that day was no different. By the time I had shaved and showered, I was late for breakfast with Tommy. I found him sitting in the first booth at Obie's Diner, hunched over a coffee mug and smoking a cigarette. An open pack of Camels lay on the table in front of him.

"When did you start smoking?" I asked.

He had been a champion cross-country runner at Friends Academy and had always embraced a strict health regimen.

"A few months ago," he said, shaking his head. "Bad habit . . . I'm trying to quit."

"Sorry. I overslept," I said truthfully.

"It's okay," he replied, sounding like he meant it.

"Have anything you want . . . my treat."

"Thanks, but I ate earlier," he said.

"Well, I'm ravenous."

I ordered a Boburger, waffles, home fries, and a large glass of freshly squeezed orange juice.

"Where did you learn to speak like that in front of a crowd?" I asked as the waitress brought my juice.

He looked at me and said, "From you."

"I've never done anything like that."

"Yeah, but you're the greatest bullshit artist the world has ever known," he said, cracking a smile.

I had no idea if he was joking. This Tommy was a lot different from the kid I remembered from only a year ago. As he took a deep drag on his cigarette, I wondered when all the most recent changes had taken place.

"I guess it's easier if you believe in what you're saying," he said. "What it really comes down to is a matter of conscience."

"Conscience," I repeated, as if it was the first time I had heard the word.

"Yes," he said.

Over Tommy's shoulder, I watched Obie drop a thick slice of American cheese on the hot hamburger meat frying on the grill. When it began to melt, he piled on a handful of chopped fried onions and a slice of tomato, and topped the whole thing off with a fried egg.

Before my breakfast arrived, I decided to come right to the point. Using all the tact and sensitivity I displayed in any Ledbetter family crisis, I plunged into solving his problem.

"So what's all this shit about your turning in your draft card?" I asked him. "I know you're not an asshole like those other clowns."

He laughed out loud.

"This is serious, goddam it. It's like telling the Feds, 'Please indict me.'"

"You really want to talk about this?"

"I've got all the time in the world," I assured him.

Tommy removed his glasses and carefully polished the lenses with a napkin, all the while staring at me with a searching look on his face. It was hard to keep returning his gaze.

Maybe that was what Kate found attractive, I thought. It definitely wasn't his dress code. As usual, he was wearing shapeless corduroys and a light-blue denim work shirt, open at the collar. He reminded me of a young Henry Fonda as Tom Joad in *The Grapes of Wrath*. The big shock of unruly hair over those sad eyes.

"Dad's probably going to disown me for this," he said next.

"That's a fair assumption," I agreed, but after thinking about it for a few moments, I wasn't really sure. For the rest of us, Dave, my sister Hope, and me, Travis had been like the trainer of circus seals with a fish bucket, tossing rewards to us as we competed for his attention.

But after what happened at St. John's Pond, Tom went his own way, and the old man never said a word. I remembered Travis once referring to him as "our immaculate conception."

"The whole thing is so overwhelming," he said.

"What thing?"

"The war in Vietnam . . . how it affects each of us, you, me, all of us."

"What's so overwhelming about it? It's pretty simple, I think," I said.

"Why are we there, Rick?" he asked.

"To stop communism," I said.

I waited for him to respond, but he didn't have an easy comeback this time.

When he didn't reply, I said, "Can you tell me why you decided to do this?"

"I doubt I can answer that to your satisfaction," he said.

"Why not just try?"

"It's very hard to put these things into words without sounding . . . I don't know, self-righteous I guess."

"Try."

"Well . . . I believe this war is wrong. To accept that it's wrong without acting on it is to help perpetuate it. That may sound simplistic but that's how I feel."

"You're damn right it's simplistic. Where would we be if everybody just made up their own laws?"

"I wasn't finished," he said as the waitress appeared with my breakfast. When I bit into the Boburger, the soft egg yolk began slowly dripping down between my fingers.

"Tommy," I began after wiping my mouth. "Vietnam is just like a big poker game. We started out over there playing nickel-dime and now we're up to pot limit. They keep raising the ante to see if we've got the guts to play. And they've got to learn we can't be bluffed out."

Another example of my intellectual depth at that moment. In any event, my thoughts were all coming together, pouring out like the senior thesis I'd never written. Or ever would.

"It all comes down to whether these little countries know they can depend on us to protect them from communist subversion. You remember in *Key Largo* when Lionel Barrymore asks Johnny Rocco what he wants . . . and finally Bogie answers for him and says, 'MORE'?"

This was really good, I remember thinking.

"And then Edward G. Robinson thinks about it and smiles and says, 'Yeah, that's it! MORE!' Well, that's the communists. They'll just keep taking more until we stop them. And if we don't stop them over there, they'll end up right here."

There was a pained expression in Tom's eyes, as if he was feeling a headache coming on. Looking back, I realize he might as well have been trying to pour out his heart to the waffle on my other plate. At least the waffle would have helped him regain the weight he had lost.

"Look at this," I said, pulling out my wallet. Removing the faded photograph I always carried, I placed it on the table in front of him. In the picture, Travis and four other navy pilots in his squadron were standing in front of a line of dive-bombers on the deck of the *Yorktown*. As they grinned into the camera, they seemed almost nonchalant. They were in summer tans with leather flying jackets. Travis had on his Mae West and was holding flying goggles in his right hand. They were bareheaded.

"That photograph was taken just a week before the Battle of Midway," I said. "When it was over, Travis was the only one of those guys left."

Tommy gazed down at it for several seconds and then looked up at me again.

"The golden gods of war," he said.

"What I would give to have been alive back then," I said, staring at the photograph. "All those events that engulfed the world . . . to have put my life on the line at the most critical juncture in human history."

"But that was World War Two," said Tommy. "This is Vietnam. I'm not trying to sound superior about this, but there is no moral clarity to this war, and I can't support it. I'm also willing to pay the penalty for opposing it."

"You're ready to go to prison?" I said.

"I am. It's almost inevitable. I go before the draft board for a final hearing over break. By the way, could Kate and I drive home with you?"

"Kate? The girl at the rally?"

He nodded yes.

"How did you meet her?" I asked.

"She's a religious studies major too. We met at CURW."

"CURW?" I asked, forgetting what the letters stood for.

"Cornell United Religious Work. Our adviser is a Jesuit priest named Dan Berrigan . . . a remarkable man and a mentor to me. I hope you can meet him."

"Sure," I said. "Where is she from?"

"San Francisco."

"Are you making it with her?"

There it was, out on the table.

Tommy stared at me, looking astonished. Then he laughed out loud. For the first time since I'd sat down, he seemed to relax. Pulling out another Camel, he lit it and took another deep drag.

"What does that mean?" I demanded.

"It means it isn't something I want to talk about," he said. "I'll say this . . . we've become really close friends."

"What's her last name?"

"Kurshan," he said.

"That sounds Jewish," I said.

He nodded and smiled.

"You're seeing a Jewish girl?"

He nodded again.

I had never dated a Jewish girl. We were Gold Coast WASPs, and most WASPs didn't mix with Jews unless they needed a lawyer or a dentist. For another thing, none of the Jewish girls seemed easy. I decided not to push it any further. They were just close friends. That's what I took from it.

"Rick, I'd like you to hear me out on something. Then I'd appreciate it if you would tell me what you think."

"Okay. Sure. Fire away."

When he began again it was in a much more passionate tone. The first thing he brought up was the just war argument, the same one he had advanced at the demonstration, culminating in what we had learned at the Nuremberg trials.

"How can you equate the goddam murderers in Nazi Germany with what our government leaders are doing to stop the communist subversion of South Vietnam?" I came right back. "We're talking about men like McGeorge Bundy and Robert McNamara and Dean Rusk—all of them chosen by JFK. Now, if they have all decided there is a good reason for us to be fighting the goddam communists in Vietnam, then who is my little brother to decide in his own infinite wisdom that they're wrong?"

"Please hear me out, will you?" he repeated with a rare note of exasperation. He was smoking his cigarette in quick, nervous tokes. I nodded at him to continue.

He started going on about American soldiers dying bravely in a war without any moral foundation. Then he was off onto something about the *Summa Theologica* and Thomas Aquinas.

A Kodachrome image suddenly carried me far away from the diner and the sound of Tommy's voice. Kate and I were standing together on the beach at Paradise Island in the Bahamas. The sun was broiling hot and she was wearing a simple linen shift like Carroll Baker in *Baby Doll*. Tom's face momentarily swam back into focus.

"I'm not advocating violence, but I do believe in the tactic of civil disobedience. It's part of the long American democratic tradition that started with the Boston Tea Party, and then the Underground Railroad and right through to Dr. King and the civil rights movement. If I have to go to jail for my actions and I'm willing to accept this punishment, then in a sense I'm upholding the legal order, right?"

I nodded at him as earnestly as I could. I already knew where a lot of it had come from. Grandpa Sprague. And now Tommy was also following this Catholic priest Daniel Berrigan.

Another vision of Kate presented itself. It was right out of *Tom Jones*. The two of us were still on the beach in the Bahamas. We were only inches apart. A bead of sweat was trickling down her throat until it disappeared beneath the collar of her linen gown. I imagined it rolling along toward the hollow between her breasts.

Tommy's voice began to rise in intensity.

"Rick, it's very hard to deal with the thought that you could die fighting over there," he said. "At this point, those of us against this war have to come out from behind our exemptions and put our bodies on the line. And I'm willing to do that."

I nodded and told him I was late for a class. He apologized for dragging it all out. Of course I didn't have a class.

"Maybe we can talk again on the ride home," he concluded. "I'm late for a class too."

He picked up his cigarettes from the table and headed out the door of the diner. Although it was nearly freezing again that morning, he had forgotten to wear a coat.

SIX

What I did next was as raw as anything I had done in my life to that point, which is saying something. But as I said at the beginning, this story isn't pretty. My next move was straight out of Travis's playbook. I remember justifying it to myself on the basis that Tommy had described Kate as just a close friend.

I guess part of it was a selfish desire to have something I couldn't. Up till then, girls were always falling into my lap. I didn't have to pursue them. They pursued me. Why should she be different? I know that another part of it was the intense attraction I felt for her. It was something I had never experienced before, still couldn't figure out, and was impatient to explore.

Anyway, I used a guy from the poker game who worked in the registrar's office to find out more about her. She was a year older than Tom and had transferred to Cornell after spending her freshman year at Stanford. She was majoring in religious studies and carrying a 4.0 average. She lived at an off-campus boardinghouse. Her address cost me ten dollars. The boardinghouse was on Roberts Place near the suspension footbridge over the Fall Creek Gorge. I started staking the place out later that same afternoon. There were only two ways for her to leave, and I had both of them covered in the rearview mirrors of the Austin-Healey.

An hour passed. I read *The Sporting News*. The sky began to get dark. I turned on the radio and listened to Bob Considine delivering the evening news. The Third Marines were taking heavy casualties at a place called Con Thien after being attacked by an entire division of North Vietnamese regular troops. Go, marines. No one went in or came out of the house. I wondered if I had bought the right address. At around nine o'clock, four girls went in together. She wasn't one of them. On the radio, Murray the K was coming in loud and clear on WOR. Question Mark and the Mysterians sang "96 Tears." I imagined dancing to it with Kate.

Two more coeds came in at around eleven. Another went out. A little after midnight, I walked over to Louie's Barfmobile on Thurston Avenue. Back in the car, I ate a meatball hero with a pint of milk. Murray the K signed off. The last light in the boardinghouse went out. That started me wondering where she was spending the night. At around two o'clock, I decided she wasn't worthy of my devotion. I went home and went to bed.

At six in the morning, I woke myself up with the realization that she could have been inside the house the entire time. By six thirty I was back on duty with a thermos full of coffee and a sack of Devil Dogs on the passenger seat. At seven fifteen, it got light enough to read the gauges on my instrument panel. Looking for something to keep me occupied, I found several library books stuffed behind the jump seat. One of them looked remotely interesting. It was by Carlyle and was about the French Revolution. After being soaked by snow and rain a few times from my leaving the top down, the book was warped into the shape of a flattened pumpkin. Most of it was stuck together and you could read only certain pages.

I found something useful almost immediately. Back before the revolutionary court sent Georges Danton to the guillotine, he had come up with the following advice for his followers: "*Il nous faut de l'audace, et encore de l'audace, et toujours de l'audace.*" My rough translation was something to the effect that we needed audacity, more audacity, always audacity.

At seven thirty the front door opened, and Kate Kurshan came down the front steps. She took a brief look at the brightening sky and then strode purposefully across the lawn in my direction. I hunched down in the seat, just as I had seen Bogie do when he was staking out Geiger's house in *The Big Sleep*.

In a moment she was past the car, walking fast toward the suspension footbridge that led over to the arts quad. She wore a tweed overcoat with a white scarf, baggy slacks, and lace-up brown boots. A book bag was slung over her shoulder and she was wearing red woolen mittens. She was already approaching the footbridge before I closed the gap. When I was about ten feet behind her, I called out "Hello." She turned and saw me, and then immediately speeded up. I trotted after her as nonchalantly as I could.

"Hey!" I was right behind her. "Isn't this a coincidence? I was just heading over to the arts quad myself."

She turned to look at me as I came up to her. I could tell she wasn't enthralled. She stopped short.

"Leave me alone, please," she said before taking off again.

"Hold on a second," I said, keeping up.

She whirled around to face me.

"Did you know that Tom talks about you constantly?" she declared, glaring at me.

I shook my head.

"Really, he idolizes you, although I can't imagine why."

I continued shaking my head.

"You should hear him tell the saga about how you saved his life."

"He exaggerates," I said, trying to sound modest.

"You don't have to convince me," she said with a derisive laugh. "I have no doubt you caused it all to begin with. But, somehow, it made quite an impression on him. You're his big hero."

"So, how do you feel about him?" I asked.

"I'm in love with him," she said almost defiantly.

"I heard you were only close friends," I said. "So how do you feel about me?"

"I don't feel anything toward you," she said. "That's not true. I think I am coming to dislike you very much."

"I don't believe that."

She pivoted away from me and began walking again. I followed along behind her. As she walked, the waves of her hair bounced softly off her shoulders in an exquisite rhythm.

"Why?" I said.

"Because you're shallow and arrogant."

"No, I mean why are you in love with him? He's just a kid."

She stopped again and laughed harshly in my face. Most people, no matter how attractive they are, can become pretty ugly when they get really angry. Here she was, looking at me with undisguised loathing, and yet she was beautiful.

"You're the child," she said. "The big hero. Tom is far braver than you will ever be. He has moral courage. Frankly, it's difficult for me to believe you two are actually brothers. Tom is sensitive, wise, caring, and idealistic. His whole life has purpose. He cares about people."

"Honestly, I care about those things too," I said.

"You have all the honesty of Uriah Heep," she told me. "It's funny. You have the same eyes he does. Tom's reflect a passion for truth and kindness. Yours are empty. All you have is good looks."

Three coeds approached us from the other end of the bridge, slowing down to stare.

"Tom makes me think about everything important in life," she said next. "And by his own example he challenges me to lead a better life."

"I don't want to make you do anything," I protested.

"No . . . you just want to make me," she declared.

She was walking again.

"I saw the way you looked at me at the Chapter House."

"How did I look at you?" she said.

"Your eyes . . . they're very expressive. You give off these little messages, and then the next minute . . ."

"I'm your brother's girl," she interrupted. "Doesn't that mean anything to you?"

"Yeah, I suppose."

"I bet."

"You weren't acting like his girl the night I met you."

She shook her head back and forth.

"You know what I thought when I first met you? I thought . . . look at him, he's in love with himself. Just another Ivy League face man who wants to use you for a mattress. And then I thought . . . who knows what I thought."

"That's not very Christian," I said.

"I'm not a Christian," she said hotly. "But I do know basic decency."

"It sounds like you've thought a lot about me. I'm flattered."

"You're flattered? I'll let you in on something else. I've already had my Rick Ledbetter, or more precisely he had me. I'm cured. He's the reason I'm here instead of Stanford. He happened to be Jewish, but he was a role player just like you, a real *yentzer*, an erotoman. I was his *nafka*."

I had no idea what she was talking about. The words were foreign to me.

"Since people like you and the *yentzer* never feel anything close to genuine human emotion, you figure everybody else is faking it too. You're takers. You give nothing. You're a walking cliché. You're not real, Rick. It's even worse in your case. You don't even know it."

She moved off again with those long, purposeful strides. I watched her cross over the bridge and disappear into the mist around the evergreens that fringed the gorge.

"I'm real!" I shouted after her.

Leaning over the guardrail, I looked down at the torrent of snow-swollen water rushing violently down the base of the gorge. I remembered reading Danton's last words as he lay on the guillotine, looking up at the blade. They were spoken to his executioner.

"Show my head to the people," he said. "It is worth seeing!"

I was walking back across the bridge when I saw something red lying on the pathway. She had dropped one of her mittens. It was red wool with white lambs embroidered on it. I studied it carefully, as if it might hold magical properties. When I got back to my apartment, I enshrined it over the fireplace.

Of course she was right about my lack of decency. I just didn't know what it was.

SEVEN

That Easter weekend of 1967 turned out to be the final wreck our family had been heading for since my parents first met at the officers' club in Pensacola before the Japanese attacked Pearl Harbor. When the weekend was over, we weren't a family anymore.

My parents had legally separated over the past winter. Travis had moved all his personal stuff to a friend's sailboat moored at their club in Cold Spring Harbor.

The March morning sky was dark with rain clouds when I arrived at Kate's rooming house. She and Tom were waiting outside on the front porch. There were little pouches under his eyes, and he looked exhausted. While he stowed their bags in the trunk, Kate made a point of avoiding me. She was wearing the same shapeless corduroys he was, along with a white oxford shirt and a blue windbreaker. Her hair was plaited in a French braid.

"I'm afraid it's going to be a tight fit," I said. "This car was designed for two."

When I patted the pillow on the transmission hump between the two bucket seats, she gave me a peevish frown. Climbing in, she managed to keep her body from touching mine, which wasn't easy. Her hair was still fragrant with the smell of honeysuckle shampoo. A few minutes later, we were racing out of Ithaca along Route 79.

The rain came hard a few minutes later. Flipping on the windshield wipers, I felt a jolt of sheer contentment, almost like a positive electrical charge. The drumbeat of the rain, the steady *thwick-thwack* of the wipers, the husky growl of the engine, and the smell of leather and honeysuckle created an almost hypnotic effect on me.

I turned on the radio. For the first time I listened to "I Had Too Much to Dream Last Night" by the Electric Prunes. It was unlike any rock song I had ever heard, weird but compelling with a driving beat, like the band was on drugs. Kate fell asleep with her head lolling on Tom's shoulder. There was very little traffic on the country highway, and

I had the Healey in overdrive most of the way down through Chenango Forks to Route 17.

We passed one dairy farm after another. Cows in the field, cows in the barn, cows standing forlorn next to the road, brown cows, white cows, black cows, and various combinations. Kate woke up when I got stopped for speeding at a well-disguised radar trap in Windsor. When the police officer informed me that I could avoid going to trial by immediately paying a fine of one hundred and fifty dollars to the local justice of the peace, she showed the first sign of genuine pleasure. I thanked the officer for his advice and drove to the judge's hardware store to pay the fine.

We stopped for lunch at the Antrim Lodge, the great old inn near Roscoe. Sitting near the fire, I asked Tom and Kate to share a bottle of the house red wine with me. They ordered tea. Their conversation immediately turned to Father Daniel Berrigan, the Catholic priest who was mentoring Tom and Kate at Cornell United Religious Work. They both seemed to idolize him.

Kate spent a good part of the meal describing how charismatic he was, how modest and self-effacing, and the risks he was willing to take with his life to help end the war. In a tone of obvious reverence, she pulled a piece of paper from her handbag and read aloud to me something he had said at a recent gathering.

"We have chosen to say, with the gift of our liberty, and if necessary our lives, the violence stops here, the death stops here, the suppression of the truth stops here, this war stops here."

Her eyes went liquid. Knowing I was supposed to be impressed, I solemnly nodded back at her. Then she told me how sexy he was.

"Sexy?" I blurted. "He's a Catholic priest."

She and Tom laughed.

"Yes," she said. "He is."

I couldn't finish my cherry cobbler. I asked for the check and we went back outside into the rain. When we were under way again, Tom fell asleep almost immediately. Kate stroked his hair for a few minutes before she went off too. This time, however, her body settled closer to mine. I glanced down at the black-and-white photograph of a young Jack Kennedy that was taped to the console below the dashboard. He gazed back up at me with a knowing grin.

. . .

A couple of hours later, Kate began to wake up as we slowed down for heavy traffic approaching the Throgs Neck Bridge. At that point, her head was resting snugly on my shoulder, her hair tickling my cheek. We were swinging onto the entrance ramp when she vaulted up in the air, landing on Tom, who came awake with a start. Her body didn't touch mine the rest of the way.

We were all wide awake when I finally headed up our gravel driveway past the stables in Cold Spring Harbor. When I cut the engine, Tom climbed out of the passenger seat and Kate scrambled out after him. I followed them down the path to the mudroom. Dropping our bags inside the door, we went through the butler's pantry into the kitchen.

My mother was standing at the big Garland commercial stove, her slim figure dwarfed by the gigantic copper exhaust hood. She was wearing a white apron and stirring something in a saucepan. As always, a Salem cigarette was jutting out of the ivory cigarette holder planted between her lips.

She employed a professional chef when we were growing up, and that was a good thing. My mother hated to cook. I think it was mostly because she thought she could will something to be finished before it was ready. For her, cooking wasn't a relaxing or creative thing but a kind of martyr's sacrifice. When Tom called out a cheery hello, she swung around to face us.

"I was getting worried about you," she said, giving him a welcoming smile.

"We decided to eat on the road," I said.

"Did it ever occur to you that I would be preparing something?" she came back.

I was about to say that was why I stopped when Tom said, "Kate and I were hungry too."

"Well, that's different," she said, pausing to take in Kate with a critical eye.

I could tell she liked what she saw. My mother was always quick to make judgments about people. Kate had already passed a significant test without even knowing it.

The swinging door to the dining room opened, and Flash nosed his way into the room. Flash was the old man's giant mastiff, around fourteen years old, and in steep decline. He trudged over to me, wagging his tail in slow motion. His eczema was worse than ever. Dave came in behind him, followed by his wife, Laura, and their two kids, Miles and Kristen. The next one through the door was my sister Hope, followed by a guy with shoulder-length blond hair who I assumed was her new boyfriend. Bringing up the rear was Grandpa Sprague. He tottered straight over to Tom and embraced him for several seconds in a bear hug. He didn't bother extending a greeting to me.

Everyone began talking at once, declaring how wonderful it was to be together again as a family at Easter. No one mentioned the absence of Travis. Grandpa Sprague finally came over to me. His skin was chalky white, and his hand felt like a small batch of twigs when he shook mine. There was no hug.

"I gather you have enlisted in the navy," he said in a tone that suggested I might have joined the Nazi Brownshirts.

"Like father, like son," I said.

He slowly shook his craggy head before moving on to Kate.

Miles and Kristen began screaming for attention and I retreated into the butler's pantry, combing through the well-stocked liquor supply. I had recently begun exploring the hard stuff, and my eye fell on a bottle of Calvados. Pouring myself a healthy measure of apple brandy, I took a swig and headed back into the kitchen.

Miles walked slowly and shyly up to Kate.

"You want me to give you a pinky?" he asked.

"What's a pinky?" she responded, kneeling to join him at his own height.

"You go like this," he squealed, tugging the right sleeve of her shirt straight back above the elbow. He quickly found the big vein in her elbow joint, licked his index finger a couple of times, and after going into an exaggerated pitcher's windup, began slapping his finger against the joint.

"About fifteen times like this does it," he said, giggling like an idiot.

She seemed to be transported with delight as he continued slapping at her, counting as he went.

"You oughta see a purple murple," he said next. "You take your fist and rub your knuckle into a guy's chest until it gets all red."

Leaning down to Kate, I whispered, "You can give me a purple murple anytime." Dave sidled over.

"How's the tennis game?" he asked.

"I haven't played lately," I said truthfully.

"When we got in today, I went out and rolled the court," he said with a wolfish smile. "Unlike the rest of this place, it's still in pretty good shape."

"Really," I said.

"How about eight o'clock?" he said. "It will be pretty cold, but we'll warm up fast."

I began rubbing my right arm and winced.

"I don't know, Dave. This tendinitis just won't go away."

"Yeah, right," he said in a disbelieving tone. "I'll wake you up for the match."

The constant chirping of the kids was already getting on my nerves, so I went back to the butler's pantry and poured myself another tot of Calvados, taking the glass with me up the back stairs to my room. Stripping off my clothes, I took a long shower, put Nina Simone on the hi-fi, and stretched out naked in bed. As she growled "I Put a Spell on You," the tension I was feeling began to dissipate in the comfortable darkness of the lair where I had spent the first seventeen years of my life. I drowsed off to the music, only waking to the sound of the hallway floorboards cracking and groaning as the others came upstairs.

"I think you'll be comfortable here," I heard my mother say from down the hall. "You have your own bath through that door, and there are extra towels in the closet."

There was a pause and then I heard Kate say, "May I tell you something, Mrs. Ledbetter?"

"Of course you can, child," she said.

"I just want you to know that Tom has changed my life. He's taught me so many things. I'm a better person just for having known him. And not just me. So many others, too. You should be very proud of him."

It was those sad Henry Fonda eyes of his, I remember thinking. What I wouldn't have given then for sad eyes.

"I am proud of him," my mother replied. "And after reading his letters over these past few months, I'm very much aware of the impact you've come to have on his life, too. He draws so much strength from your love."

"Oh, I hope so. I truly hope so," said Kate.

When my mother left, I slowly finished the Calvados, waiting for everything to quiet down. A half hour later, the house was finally still. I was feeling the alcoholic glow and toying with the idea of knocking on Kate's door to ask if I could bring her some warm milk when I heard her moving in the hallway from her room.

That's the good thing about termites. With every step she took, I charted her movement down the hall until she stopped outside Tommy's room. His door opened and closed. She never bothered to knock. Ten minutes passed. Maybe they were saying their prayers together, I thought. I waited expectantly, but there was no other noise. As silently as I could, I went to my door and cracked it open. No one was in the dark hallway. The only sound came from the aerator in the fish tanks at the end of the corridor.

I stood there trying to figure it all out. Perhaps she had some fresh insight on the principles of a just war that couldn't wait till morning, or a new tidbit to share about Father Flanagan, or whatever his name was. It came to me that my brother might not be sexually retarded after all. Putting on a pair of boxer shorts, I went down the hall, staying close to the wall, where the support joists hadn't been eaten.

No light was coming from underneath Tommy's door. I found myself getting angry and went back downstairs to the butler's pantry in the dark. I poured the last of the Calvados into the old man's Annapolis goblet and took a deep swallow. The heat that flowed down my throat did nothing to blunt the vision of Kate lying in Tommy's arms. I refused to believe he was screwing her. Maybe I had a lot to learn about women, but I did know him. Or at least I used to.

. . .

I headed back upstairs. As I passed my father's darkened study on the second floor, I noticed the flickering light from his portable television. Curiously, I heard no sound. In my groggy state, I made the mistake of being conscientious and went in to shut it off. Too late, I spied the back of my mother's head over the top of his leather armchair and gingerly began to retrace my steps.

"Please close the door and sit down, Richard," she commanded, her voice seeming to bubble up from a great depth.

The booze and cigarettes dropped her voice down an extra octave. She hadn't always been a serious drinker. When we were growing up, she might have enjoyed a glass of wine or two at dinner. Vodka had now become my mother's drink of choice, and I doubt a day went by when she wasn't polishing off the better part of a fifth. She never got drunk in the sense of losing control or getting sloppy like I did. She had the kind of iron will that could tame ninety proof Smirnoff.

It didn't seem to affect her health either. She was rarely sick, and her figure hadn't changed from when I was first old enough to notice. She had a taut swimmer's body with a wasp waist and long, tapered legs. The only concession to the aging process resulted from a lifelong devotion to the sun and salt water. The skin on her face had begun to develop the faintly cracked texture of an old catcher's mitt. It didn't mar the patrician bone structure that characterized ten generations of the Sprague side of our family.

I closed the study door and sat down on the sofa facing her. She picked up her empty glass from the stand next to Travis's chair and walked over to the liquor cabinet. Even on this routine pilgrimage to the Smirnoff bottle, she carried herself with casual elegance. Whether she was entering our family box at the Metropolitan Opera or spreading a blanket on the beach, she did everything with poise. Using silver tongs, she selected four ice cubes from the ice bucket and dropped them into the tumbler before pouring in two inches of vodka. Picking up a bottle of vermouth, she splashed a couple of drops into the glass while pausing to examine a photograph on the wall behind the bar.

The spirit of Travis pervaded the room. He had decorated the study to his own taste right after Grandpa Sprague gave them the house. The walls were dark walnut. There were no curtains. Interior shutters could keep it dark on the brightest day. Bookcases lined one of the walls, mostly filled with his family's personal historical accounts of the Civil War.

There were two paintings of clipper ships on the walls, along with groupings of framed personal photographs. One section consisted of shots of the small West Texas town where he had grown up. In one, he was standing with his football team in their hand-me-down uniforms and battered leather helmets. Another group was from World War II and included one of him receiving the Medal of Honor from President

Roosevelt. None of the pictures on the walls was less than twenty-five years old.

"So how is the last term going?" my mother said, returning to her leather chair.

"Uhh . . . you know, Mom. Same old stuff."

"How would I know?" she said caustically. "Your last postcard came from the Bahamas."

On one of my last trips south during the winter, I had made the mistake of sending a card to Hope, who must have passed it along to her. With practiced efficiency, she removed the butt end of a Salem out of her ivory holder and inserted a fresh one, lighting it with her Ronson. On the television, Marshall Thompson was silently attempting to save a wounded rhinoceros from white poachers on a *Daktari* rerun.

"Things are going great," I said.

"You're not playing tennis, I gather."

"No. This term I'm concentrating on getting my grade point average up," I said.

"I see," she said. "You should know that Coach McKinlay felt it was necessary to write me an anguished explanation of why he couldn't roll the stone of Sisyphus up the hill for you any longer."

"I'm sorry?"

"Why he had to boot you off the team."

"That's not entirely accurate."

"What isn't accurate?"

"That I, uh . . . had to quit."

"Frankly, I don't much care at this point, Richard."

"Really . . ." I began and then trailed off. She had a way of reading my thoughts sometimes.

Her eyes were drilling into mine. Without question, they were her best weapon. The irises were two different shades of green, pale in the center surrounded by a belt of emerald. They were a chameleon's eyes, capable of conveying sympathy one second and fury the next.

"I'd like you to do something for me," she said finally.

"Sure. You know that," I said.

"It concerns Tom."

"What now?" I came back.

"If you're going to take that tone, forget it!"

"What tone?" I asked.

"Wipe that damn smirk off your face!"

I retreated into the lock-jawed expression that the old man usually employed in these situations. She took advantage of the lull to take another swallow of her martini.

"I know what you're thinking," she said, her head slowly bobbing up and down.

I bit my tongue to avoid smirking again, concentrating instead on the old walking stick that was mounted on the wall behind her head. According to the old man, Geronimo had carved it during his captivity.

"You're thinking that your mother's into the sauce," she said, which was exactly what I was thinking.

"What are you saying?" I protested.

"Well, you're right. I am into the sauce. Hopefully, you'll learn to cope better than I have when you reach the dizzying heights of marital bliss," she concluded, her chin jutting out under the cigarette holder.

Like Travis, she was self-possessed to the point of arrogance. Part of her conceit stemmed from being brought up by Grandpa Sprague to believe that girls, at least his girls, had as much right to take on all of life's challenges as a man. I think her frustration lay in the fact that she hadn't.

Then it hit me. The answer to why she was in there surrounded by his old photographs and collections. In spite of everything he had done, she still couldn't get him out of her system. I suddenly felt a jolt of compassion for her.

"You know, it isn't healthy for you to spend so much time up here dwelling on the past," I said. "You need to start planning a new life for yourself."

"That's quite profound, Richard," she responded, her voice dripping acid. "The last thing I need in confronting my problems are some homilies you gleaned from the *Playboy* Advisor."

"Okay. Forget it," I came back. "I try to be helpful because I know you're hurting and you throw it right back in my face!"

I took another hit of Calvados out of the Annapolis goblet and started to get up.

"Sit down!" she demanded. "We both know how sensitive you are to other people's feelings."

I dropped back onto the sofa.

"In the last few months, I've had a great deal of time to think about all my failings as a parent—the paramount one being my inability to talk to my children with any sense of purpose."

"I've always thought . . ."

"Just shut up and listen," she said. "How well do you know your brother?"

"All my life," I said with boozy clarity.

She shook her head sadly.

"As you know, Tom has just made a very difficult decision, one that will have a profound impact on his life. There's little doubt in my mind he will go to prison for it. He has told me that when he appears before the draft board on Monday, he will refuse to accept status as a conscientious objector. Although he meets all the legal criteria that I'm aware of on the subject, he refuses to use them as a defense."

"So?" I said.

"He is trying to live up to a standard that is totally unrealistic in today's world."

"So where did he get that from?" I asked.

"Not from your father or me, certainly," she said. "Maybe my father . . . but however he came to it, the foundation of his faith is strong and unwavering."

"Well, it's his call," I said.

"Earlier tonight, Tom went to see Travis to tell him why he's doing this. When he boarded the boat, he apparently interrupted your father's seduction of that little slut of a lifeguard from the club."

"Which one?" I asked without thinking. I had shagged several of them myself over the years.

"I don't know her name," she said, ignoring me. "Your father started yelling something from his cabin about wet paint in the hatchway. He told Tom he would see him here at Easter Sunday dinner."

"He might have been painting the deck work," I offered, but she was already on to her next point.

"I'm confident that Travis will have no understanding or sympathy for what Tom is doing. These days Travis sees all of his carefully held values disintegrating around him."

She stopped long enough to replenish her glass at the liquor cabinet. This time she didn't even wave the vermouth over the vodka. I took another swig of Calvados. It was no longer burning on the way down.

"Richard, as even you should know by now, problems of this sort—Tom's decision, your sister's problems—these things are not your father's forte," she said, sitting down next to me on the couch. "They scare him so mightily that I'm confident he would prefer bodily torture over facing up to his responsibilities as a parent. I won't bore you with his performance as a husband."

The whole diatribe seemed so unfair that I was about to unload on her when she suddenly began chuckling to herself.

"Remind me sometime to tell you what happened when he was driving your sister to school one morning and had to contend with her shock at discovering she was having her first period."

I didn't see what was so funny about it. She stopped chuckling and seemed to lose her train of thought. I was ready to weigh in.

"Have you considered the possibility that Travis's values of duty and patriotism are a lot more needed when we're at war than Tommy's questioning of everything?" I asked.

She gave me the kind of indulgent smile a mother might use if her idiot son had just said something stupid to the dinner guests.

"It's obvious you don't know your brother very well, which isn't surprising to me. I'm not sure I do either. He has always been a little intimidating. In the last few years, I think he was helping me to grow up rather than the other way around. I never realized how much I depended on him until he left for Cornell."

Something went off inside me. I was so fed up with hearing about his divine attributes.

"You treat him like he is some ancient wise man," I said angrily. "If Tommy is right, then I suppose you believe that what I did by enlisting to fight in Vietnam is wrong."

"I didn't say that," she said. "There are times when each one of us has to make hard choices. Although you've made a practice of avoiding those most of your life, I'm genuinely impressed that you have committed yourself to something. However, I sincerely doubt that you considered your decision as carefully as Tom has his."

"If you want to know what I think, I think you're down on Travis and everything he stands for because he walked out on you."

She shook her head again.

"Richard, I'm going to let you in on a secret. You can write it off as one of the brilliant insights that accompanied my rediscovery of martinis. But I believe it with all my heart."

Reaching over, she took my hand in hers. The whole thing was starting to make me feel pretty uncomfortable.

"This requires me to be critical of your father . . . which as you know has become quite easy for me lately," she said, taking another sip of her drink.

"When I first met Travis," she said, grinning at the recollection, "he was so unlike anyone I had ever met before . . . the way he looked at me. God, he was so bold . . . no time for preliminaries, there's a war coming and this Texas stud is headed for the Pacific. But behind that façade he was smart and funny and luminous . . . a really wonderful man."

Luminous? What the hell did that mean?

"I was already engaged to a proper Bostonian at the time," she said, and then stopped, lost in her memories.

"So what happened to the Boston guy?" I asked, finally.

"Reg was first and foremost a gentleman. That was his occupation. He never held a job after graduating from Harvard. His family did his thinking for him. They thought it was a good match too."

She closed her eyes and sat there motionless. The silence lasted almost a minute.

"I thought I could tame him, you see," she said, and I knew she wasn't talking about the guy from Boston.

Opening her eyes, she focused them on me again.

"Richard, people stop growing at different times in their lives. I've known women who stopped growing in high school. Being captain of the varsity cheerleading team was the high point of their existence.

"Your father stopped growing in nineteen forty-five. Of course, his charm carried him a long way after the war. Before he left for the Pacific, he was a beautiful man, a courageous, caring, and decent man, but he left something behind out there when he came home. That war became the defining experience in his life. That was when he stopped growing."

She was practically right on top of me, those two-tone green eyes boring in the whole time. It hit me that I was sitting there in just my boxer shorts.

"There's a lot of him in you, Richard, his physical strength, his looks, his charm. You have a good mind. But you also have his immaturity, his selfishness, and his laziness, too. In spite of that, I have hopes you'll outgrow him."

Her face was only a couple of feet away from mine.

"I don't say these things to hurt you, but I want you to do a lot of growing in your life. I don't want you to be a middle-aged child like your father. I don't want you to reach thirty and suddenly act as if everything important in your life is finished. I want all of my children to stop and think once in a while about where they've been, and where they're going . . . and whether they think it's the right direction."

It was all I could do not to pull my hand away.

"You're shivering like a wet dog. How can you walk around this drafty house with no clothes on?" she asked.

Putting down my empty goblet, I tried to stand up. The force of gravity was suddenly incredible. I began lurching toward the door.

"Richard?" she called after me.

I stopped at the closed door, slowly turning around to look back. Her face was swimming in and out of focus.

"Darling, I want you to go with Tom to his draft board hearing on Monday. I've already done what I can behind the scenes. Will you do that for me?"

"Yeah . . . okay," I said.

"One more thing," she said as I fought to keep my balance at the door. "I want you to promise me that you will continue to grow."

I managed to get the door open.

"I'm not a goddam garden," I said before reeling off.

After making it up to the third floor, I rested on the landing for a while. Sometime later, I found myself crawling on my hands and knees down the hall to my room. The corridor was dark, which is why I noticed the light leaking around the door of Kate's room. It was slightly ajar.

I crawled over and pushed it open with my head. After focusing my eyes, I saw that her bed was turned down, but she wasn't in it. Her corduroy pants and shirt were crumpled in a tiny heap on the floor

It came to me again that I was really shellacked. I crawled back to my room and dragged myself up on the bed.

EIGHT

Dave started knocking on my door at eight the next morning.

"Shake the cobwebs off, buddy," he called out. "We have a match to play."

The excitement in his voice was intense. Laura had already told me he was playing his best tennis. I was curious to see how far he had actually come.

Considering all the apple brandy I had drunk the previous night, my hangover was endurable. Getting into my tennis whites and a windbreaker, I headed downstairs. A pot of coffee was perking on the kitchen stove. I swallowed four aspirin along with my first mug. Pouring another one, I carried it out to the gazebo on the bluff overlooking the bay. It was in the low forties, with scattered clouds and a harsh wind. Down in the eelgrass, a white egret stood motionless on one matchstick leg, staring toward Connecticut.

I could hear Dave warming up on the court. He was practicing his serve, and each booming *thwunk* was punctuated by his inevitable grunt. We both inherited our passion for tennis from Travis. As kids, we desperately craved his attention, and playing tennis was one sure way to get a piece of his time. He needed opponents, and even as kids, we were better than nothing.

My parents joined the Cold Spring Harbor Beach and Tennis Club right after he came back from World War II. Aside from good mooring facilities and a fine sandy beach, it had a huge indoor pool for year-round swimming. The club also maintained ten tennis courts, half of them clay, half grass. Although Travis didn't start playing tennis until he was in his late twenties, he quickly made himself one of the best amateur players on the North Shore. In the 1950s, he won every open tournament from Mamaroneck to the St. James Racquet Club. Tennis became his religion.

The only singles match I ever saw him lose in those days was to Don Budge when he came to Cold Spring Harbor for an exhibition.

Dave and I saw tennis as a way to make him proud of us, and the first thing my father taught us was that losing was unacceptable. You played to win. That was the solitary goal. If you lost to someone, you practiced even harder until you could beat him.

Growing up, we played all summer, every day, weather permitting. When I was seven years old, I began daily lessons with Udo Zangelein, the Swedish tennis professional at the club. I wasn't allowed to play doubles. That was for ladies and old men.

Back then, we started at eight o'clock in the morning with a break for ice-cold Cokes after every other set. We had an hour for lunch and then played most of the afternoon. On Sundays, we got to take on Travis at home. Dave and I were each allowed to play one set. They didn't last very long. He gave no quarter and played flat out. I didn't take a game off him for four years.

In those early days, he was almost Olympian in his physical impact on me. Every kid I knew wished Travis was his father. He was a superb all-around athlete and had split-second reflexes, but those weren't the only reasons for his success.

Travis had a tremendous ability to intimidate opponents. Part of it was his physique. At six foot one and one hundred and ninety pounds, he wasn't a muscleman, but there was a sense of indestructibility about him. He was slab-chested and had long, ropy arms and powerful legs that enabled him to scorch his ground strokes from baseline to baseline. His serve was a howitzer. He wasn't exceptionally fast, but he possessed something equally valuable—that instinctual sixth sense that great shortstops have—the ability to somehow divine where the ball is going to be hit. He always seemed to be leaning the right way.

The old man was constantly on the attack. I can see him now, charging at me bare-chested from the far end of the court, bellowing the rebel yell and daring me to put one past him at the net. In those early days, I rarely could. That's another thing. Unless he was playing a serious match, he never wore a tennis shirt. In fact, he rarely wore a shirt at all during the summer. His habitual attire consisted of pleated white cotton shorts that he bought at Shepherd's out in Southampton and then wore till they got ratty.

Dave was a natural at tennis. Udo Zangelein was the first to say he could compete at any level if he developed the mental toughness to go along with his talent. He won the New York State high school singles title at fifteen and then played first singles at Cornell. After graduation, he joined the junior circuit, aiming for the pros. At one point he was ranked in the top twenty amateurs nationally.

When I was thirteen and in love with a cheerleader named Mary Anne Mollico, I decided to give up tennis for good. There simply wasn't time for both pursuits, and I knew even then that I had to set priorities in life. When he heard the news, Udo sat me down in the little pro shop where he strung our racquets and fucked the members' wives on his workbench.

"Rick, if you work hard, you can be better than Dave someday," he said in his thick Swedish accent. "I ain't kidding you."

At the time, it was enough to keep me committed to tennis. Even without Dave's natural ability, I was good enough to go all the way to the semifinals of the state high school championship in my senior year at Friends Academy. Certainly it was tennis that got me into Cornell—that and the Sprague legacy. In my first two years there, I lost only one match. And then, just like Denise McLaughlin, who gave up figure skating at eighteen, I burned out. I just didn't care anymore.

Dave's eventual problem turned out to be his temperament, or as Udo called it, "tuvvness." At the Davis Cup qualifying matches, he lost to a guy he had beaten three times. Then he started getting psyched out in the first round of major tournaments. He began seeing a shrink. He kept losing. He saw a hypnotist. She didn't help either. He'd rant and rave over bad line calls. Toward the end of his competitive career he was almost suicidal. As usual, Travis was a rock of support when it came to Dave's personal crisis. After my brother broke down in tears one night, the old man told him to quit playing since he obviously didn't have what it took to make it. Dave ended up going to Yale Law School and was slated to join one of Long Island's most prestigious law firms.

That ended the Ledbetter tennis dynasty.

After finishing my coffee, I strolled over to the tennis court in time to watch Dave pound another booming practice serve across the net.

"Hey . . . I think you're ready to go back on the circuit," I said.

"No way," he responded with a grin. "I'm running for the state assembly."

"Really? I hadn't heard."

"It's going to be announced next week," he said. "I'm running as a Nixon Republican supporting our troops."

I had always hated Nixon after he ran against JFK. He had thankfully disappeared after losing the race for governor of California in 1962. I imagined him hanging upside down in a closet somewhere like a bat, waiting for his chance to return.

Since I didn't have my own tennis racquets, I picked out one of Dave's. It was a Lew Hoad model, just like mine. The grip was a little wide for me, but I could still get good topspin on my forehand. We hit for a while and, when we were both warmed up, volleyed for serve. He won.

The adrenaline was already flowing in me like a river. I felt the familiar tension that accompanied the start of every match since I was seven years old. Even though I hadn't played competitively for months, I felt complete confidence. The first game was enough to destroy it. Dave's first serve of the match was an ace. So was the second one. It flashed past me like a rifled slug. I didn't score a point in the first game.

"This could be the best you've ever served," I said truthfully as we changed sides.

I double-faulted to begin the second game. He hammered my next delivery back for a cross-court winner. The game went to deuce a few times before he finally broke me. In the third game, he held serve again. As I prepared to serve the next one, Laura came through the box hedges that ringed the court with Miles and Kristen in tow. They settled into canvas deck chairs at mid-court. Kristen clapped in delight as Dave and I blistered volleys back and forth across the net in a long rally. We went to deuce again before he broke me a second time.

"That makes it four–love," he proclaimed loudly for Laura's benefit, his face reflecting grim determination.

He served another monster to start off the fifth game of the first set. I managed to return the next one with all the force of a dying quail, and he put it away with a forehand smash.

"Thirty–love," he crowed, striding confidently back to the baseline.

The way he was playing, Ken Rosewall would have started to palpitate. It was time for action. Dave went into his windup and unleashed another magnificent serve. It was in by six inches.

"*Long*," I called out.

He stopped in his tracks.

"What do you mean, 'long'?" he called back. "That wasn't even close!"

"I was right on top of it, Dave," I replied evenly. "Believe me, it was just out."

"You've got to be kidding," he shouted.

I walked down to the service line and plunked my racquet head down a few inches beyond the tape.

"Really. It hit right here."

"That ball was in by a foot," he said, almost whining.

I smiled at him cheerfully. "All right, why don't we do it over?"

"Hell no!" he said emphatically. "The ball was in, and it's my point."

"I don't think that's fair," I said firmly. "I was right over it, and it should be my call."

"Don't hand me that crap, you lying bastard!" he yelled. "Laura . . . tell him it was in."

We both turned to see Laura retreating toward the house, dragging the children along in her wake. She had seen it all happen so many times before.

"Okay," I said. "You think it was in and I know it was out. Let's play it over."

"I can't believe you're doing this to me, Rick. We're not going to play it over. That serve was in. It's my point!"

He paced back to the baseline and again prepared to serve.

"It's forty–love!" he roared.

I began to walk off the court.

"WHERE THE HELL ARE YOU GOING?" he yelled.

I stopped and looked back at him. "Really, Dave, it isn't worth it. Look at you. You're getting all upset. Hell, it's just a game. We're brothers, for God's sake. Let's forget about it and go have breakfast."

He began snorting like a bull elephant. "Hey . . . Hey . . . Don't hand me that shit! That ball was in and it's my point. I'm leading forty–love. Let's play."

It was all I could do to avoid laughing in his face. I turned away to compose myself, knowing that it was almost time to finish it.

"It's Easter weekend, Dave," I said earnestly. It's really not worth arguing about."

"Don't do this. Don't do this to me, you bastard," he said.

I knew I was being a bastard, but the whole thing was ingrained in me.

"I can see you're working yourself up, Dave. It'll only turn into another grudge match. Really, let's forget it and go inside."

"You prick!" he howled. "You just can't stand to lose, can you? You're unbelievable."

When he finally started to stalk off the court, I raised my hands in mock surrender.

"All right, Dave. If that's the way you want to play it, fine. It's your point. Forget it. Here's what we'll do. Why don't we just say you won this game, and you won the first set? Does that make you happy?"

"It's not my game, and it's not my set!" he raved. "It's forty–love."

"Okay, it's forty–love, and you lead four–zip in games. Let's just play."

I went back to receive his next serve.

"What a crybaby," I muttered loud enough for him to hear.

His next serve was long by about three feet.

"SHIT!" he screamed.

"You want me to call that in too?" I asked with the politeness of an Eagle Scout. "Take another one."

He proceeded to double-fault two more times. It was all downhill from there. I took the next four games. We quit a few minutes later. As he came stomping back into the kitchen, everyone tried to ignore us.

"He's the worst cheater I've ever seen," Dave railed.

My mother cut him short.

"I'm going to have that tennis court bulldozed once and for all."

NINE

It was nearly eleven o'clock that same Saturday morning when I pulled into the club parking lot, inserting the Austin-Healey between a Rolls-Royce and a brand-new Bentley. I walked the familiar path along the edge of the tennis courts that led to the clubhouse.

Udo Zangelein was giving a cold weather lesson to a kid who must have been around the age I was when Udo started teaching me. Two limp backhands were enough to convince me that the kid wasn't going to be any prodigy. Udo saw me going past and stopped his forehand in mid-motion.

"Rick. You lookin' good. Let's get to work again."

Pointing at my wristwatch, I sped up. Udo had wasted an enormous amount of his personal time on me over the years, and I hated to tell him the dream was over. Farther along the path, I started hearing the muffled shrieks from the horde of kids in the indoor swimming pool.

On Saturdays it was organized mayhem in there. The club's main bar adjoined the swimming pool. Once an exclusively male domain, it had been integrated with women in the late nineteen fifties, as long as they weren't black or Jewish. The bar was originally modeled after the tap room at the Yale Club, but the women had completely renovated it, adding a soundproofed wall of plate-glass windows that enabled them to drink all afternoon while keeping an eye on their kids in the pool.

I could see my father's massive head across the room at the far end of the bar. His chin was raised as he drained the last of his highball. I threaded my way through the club tables, most of them occupied by women wearing ankle-length dresses and rubber-soled boat shoes.

"Commander Ledbetter, I presume," I said, coming up behind him.

He turned to envelop me in a bear hug. As he pulled away, his cheek grazed mine. It felt like being scraped by a starfish. His beard was so heavy that I often wondered how a woman could survive a night in his arms, much less be transported by it.

He looked damn good. There were new crow's feet etched around his brown eyes. His hair had more salt and less pepper. There were a few new veins visible in his blunt, crooked nose. The burn scar that ran from his left temple down to his jaw looked a little less livid. Otherwise he was the same indestructible force I had known all my life.

Waving his hand, he summoned over the bartender.

"Craig . . . my son Rick," he declared. "Obviously not as handsome as his old man, but he can't help that."

"What can I get you?" he asked.

"I don't know. I'm feeling pretty wasted," I said.

"Did you have any breakfast?" asked Travis.

"No."

"Then I would recommend one of Craig's Bloody Mary's . . . very healthy . . . definitely restorative. Could use one myself," he said.

"Fine," I agreed.

While Craig went off to prepare my breakfast, Travis swung around to stare through the picture window behind the bar at the silent bedlam taking place in the swimming pool.

"You're wearing your borrowing uniform," I said.

That was what Travis had always called it. His old navy Brooks Brothers blazer, a white button-down dress shirt, gray flannel slacks, and cordovan loafers, no socks. It was what he wore to weddings, funerals, and to borrow money from the bank.

"Yeah," he replied. "I was asking somebody for dough this morning."

Craig came back bearing the two Bloody Marys in frosted goblets, each crowned with a stalk of fresh celery. After the first two sips, the dull ache behind my eyes began to recede. There were chunks of horseradish in it. I could even smell the foliage on my celery stalk.

"I got my OCS assignment this week," I said.

He looked at me and nodded sympathetically.

"I only did what you asked," he said.

"Well, I got swift boats," I said with a smug smile. "Thanks."

"Beware of what you wish for," he said. "The few friends I have left in the Pentagon are damn worried about what's happening over there."

"What are they worried about?"

"They're worried that armchair warriors like McNamara aren't going to let them win it. And if they're right, there's going to be a lot of corpse-making for nothing. I'd hate for one of them to be you."

"I'll be all right," I said.

Without looking at me, he said, "Well, I'm proud of you."

That was all I needed to hear.

"So you're living on a boat?" I asked.

"A sixty-two-foot Pearson. I plan to sail her across the Pacific," he said.

"A world cruise?" I asked. It was something he had always talked about.

"Cruising is for the wealthy North Shore assholes I've been selling boats to for the last twenty years—men who play at sailing," he said. "No, I'm planning a voyage. Voyages are built by wanderers on a foundation of financial insolvency, for which I qualify in all respects. Anyway, I can get her for a song, which is something I need to talk to your mother about. How is she feeling?"

What he really wanted to know was how she was feeling about him.

"She's okay, I guess."

"What does that mean?" he demanded.

"She seems to spend a lot of her time in your study," I said.

The old man was grinning at me.

"So what are my latest shortcomings?"

I told him as much as I could remember, considering my condition at the time. He took it all very calmly, including the parts about his having never grown up, and being a middle-aged boy who couldn't stop reliving World War II.

"She's right, of course."

"I don't think she has any right to say those things," I said.

He grinned again, his whole face lighting up.

"When we met in Pensacola, your mother was the most dazzling woman I'd ever met. God. So classy. It didn't matter that she was rich. I couldn't have cared less. I wanted her and she wanted me. And she wanted to get married. So we got married. That was the mistake. We didn't really know anything about one another. Hell, we didn't have any time to find out anything."

When I looked past him, it seemed that half the people in the bar were furtively glancing over at him, which never surprised me. Whenever he came into a restaurant or a theater lobby, people's heads just naturally turned in his direction, as if he had a way of sucking up all the energy in the room.

Maybe it was his battle scars, or the sense of danger about him. Whatever it was, he seemed oblivious to it. I'm not saying he wasn't aware of his impact on other people, but he just seemed to accept it as a phenomenon he had no control over. There was nothing narcissistic about him. I rarely saw him look in a mirror.

"Yeah . . . we never should have gotten married," he said next. "Like most men, I pretended marriage was fine. I made all the right husband noises for the first few years. Then I stopped pretending. It just got too rugged."

My eyes were drawn to one of the women at the table closest to us. Her stare wasn't one of curiosity. She was glowering at him. I whispered to Travis, and he glanced over.

"Marie Haggerty. A friend of your mother's."

The woman continued to glare at him.

"When I came back, it became obvious we didn't have a lot in common. She hated my family. Texas peasants. The physical side was fine, which was a better start than a lot of couples. But she had big ambitions for me. The first one was politics . . . Medal of Honor winner runs for Congress . . . In Washington, the congressman and his lady wow Arthur Krock and Joe Alsop. Soon he becomes Senator Ledbetter and rides into the White House on the Sprague family fortune. The first lady does good deeds. Negro babies go to bed on a full stomach. Papa Sprague sleeps in the Lincoln bed."

I laughed out loud.

"That's a life?" he asked.

"I might have liked to sleep in the Lincoln bed," I mused.

"Anyway, I'm a Republican. At least, I probably would be if I voted."

The next round of Bloodies arrived on the house.

From where we were standing, I had a terrific view of the swimming pool. As I watched, one of the female lifeguards descended from her elevated stand and walked over to the bank of lockers along the far wall. She pulled out a hairbrush and began to stroke her hair vigorously before pinning it back in a no-nonsense bun.

"I assume as a soon-to-be college graduate you're familiar with Thoreau's thesis that most men lead lives of quiet desperation," said Travis. "Well, I've spent a good part of my life trying to prove him wrong."

Like many of the lifeguards hired by the club manager, the girl was stunning. Even the standard-issue black tank-top racing suit couldn't suppress a chest so bountiful that it made me doubt her ability to float. I watched in silent admiration as she slipped on an oversized Jets football jersey with NAMATH printed on the back and disappeared through the door to the locker room.

"I've pretty much had the life I wanted," Travis was saying. "I'm out on the water almost every day. I wake up happy every morning, something which always drove your mother crazy. And I've made enough to pay the family bills. Beyond that I don't care about money."

He was definitely right about that. Money stuck to his hands like liquid mercury. He was a boat broker, which meant he represented both sellers and purchasers of large yachts. His commissions could be pretty substantial, but the money that really supported our family came out of two trusts controlled by my mother.

"I sometimes think your mother knows me better than I know myself," he went on. "A day doesn't go by that the memory of some guy I knew out in the Pacific doesn't come floating into my head. When you live on the edge—just trying to survive—you spend something. Some men got it back when they came home. The lucky ones did. But she's right about that too—I used something up out there. I even know what it was. Loss. Loss, my son, is relative. What is the loss of a marriage or a job compared to the loss we got used to every day out there? Divorce is an inconvenience. Watching your best friend incinerated in a burning plane—that's loss."

He was in a different place for several seconds.

"Hell, I did love your mother," he suddenly said in a plaintive tone. "I came back, didn't I?"

Not all the Ledbetters did. His brothers all served in World War II. My uncle Marty flew both of the Schweinfurt raids as a B-17 pilot before he was shot down over Germany. Uncle Jack was a marine lieutenant when he was wounded on Bloody Ridge at Guadalcanal. Private Jim Ledbetter, the youngest in the family, went missing at San Pietro during the Monte Cassino battles. His body was never recovered.

I had often asked Travis what combat was like, but he would never talk about what he had done. The only time he came close was when a buddy of his from the *Yorktown* was visiting us and they got drunk together one rainy afternoon on the covered porch. I waited until Travis was well oiled and then asked him how he had won the Medal of Honor.

"It was nothing that any other guy with a genius for flying and undaunted courage couldn't have done," he said with a boozy grin.

"Come on, Travis," I said. "Really?"

"Really? Well, the truth is they gave one to every guy in the air that day," he said with sarcasm.

"Hell's bells," said his buddy, shaking his head. "Your father's plane was on fire from ack-ack and he still managed to finesse a thousand-pounder down the stack of a Haruna-class battlewagon before he went into the drink."

"Funny thing," said Travis. "That war—I'd go again."

. . .

"Another drink, Commander Ledbetter?" asked Craig the bartender.

"No thanks. I promised the kid lunch."

As we headed over to our table, the glaring woman followed his every step.

"Damn, I do miss the wartime navy," he said wistfully as we sat down at the table. "They asked little enough . . . just that you showed up as ordered and didn't complain when they sent you off to kill somebody. Of course, it's different now, as you'll soon find out."

"How is it different?"

"Back before Pearl Harbor, guys like me were looked at as losers who couldn't get a good civilian job. To the so-called successful men of my generation, we just wasted their tax dollars playing war games," he said. "But after Pearl Harbor, those same people looked at us like we were saviors. All of a sudden we had value, like the doctor down the street you take for granted until the epidemic breaks out."

A young waitress hustled up to take our orders. The old man ordered a rare porterhouse with French fries and a bottle of Frascati. "As cold as Valley Forge," he added. I ordered the same meal.

"But Vietnam is different," he said. "For one thing, Johnson is worried the Chinese will come in again like they did in Korea and then we'll be fighting World War Three against a billion little yellow men. So he's got us fighting this war half-assed."

The waitress came back with the cold bottle of wine and opened it with ritualistic fanfare. Travis waved her into the first pour without sampling it.

"Another big difference between my war and yours," he said. "Back then, people knew there was a war on. Every family was part of it in some way. Today, most people aren't invested because they don't know any of the men coming back in body bags. And men in uniform are becoming a target for contempt. Who knows what's around the corner?"

He took a healthy slug of his wine and leaned back in his chair.

"Enough blood and guts . . . so how's your love life?" he asked.

"I have a problem," I said.

"What's her name?"

"Kate Kurshan," I said.

"Sounds Jewish," he said matter-of-factly.

"She is."

"What's the problem?" he asked.

"She loves Tommy."

He looked perplexed.

"Your brother? Saint Thomas Aquinas Ledbetter?"

"Yeah."

"That's rugged, Ricky. This girl definitely isn't for you."

"She is. At least I think she is."

"I'm no authority on Jewish women," he said. "They have been banned here on the Gold Coast or I might have met a few along the way."

I was about to respond when the lifeguard who had been wearing the NAMATH jersey suddenly loomed up behind him. She was now wearing a long white tunic cinched at the waist with a brass buckle. After glancing at me for a moment, she placed her index finger to her lips. Snaking her hands around my father's head, she covered his eyes.

"Guess who?" she exclaimed, smiling.

"Liz Taylor," he said without pause.

"No," she said.

"Then it's my darling wife. You've seen the error of your ways and have come to bring me home."

"Oh, you knew it was me," she said, dropping her hands.

"Yes, Michelle, I knew it was you. I smelled the chlorine."

Without invitation she sat down at the table. All his attention immediately shifted to her. It was like I had disappeared.

"Michelle," he said solemnly, "I'm going to tell you something that I've never told another living soul."

"What is it?" she asked.

His lazy bedroom eyes locked on hers.

"I truly admire you, Michelle."

Her air of concern disappeared. "I admire you too, Travis," she said.

"You do?" he asked.

"Yes I do," she said, "in a kind of grandfatherly way."

I laughed.

"Michelle, I'd like you to meet my son Ricky."

She looked at me, then back at him, not sure whether to believe it.

"I was adopted," I said with a hangdog expression. "Travis was only twelve when he came to pick me up from the orphanage."

"No," my father jumped in. "No. Ricky's mine, all right. I was racing to Huntington Hospital when he arrived in the front seat. He's been a pain in the ass ever since."

"Why do you call him Travis?" she asked me.

He flashed me a warning signal.

"It's a family secret," I said, as the waiter came back with our steaks.

"Are you in a good mood, Michelle?" the old man asked.

"Yes," she said, grinning. "I've had a wonderful day."

"Will you come sailing with me this afternoon?"

"Oh, I can't, Travis," she said with obvious disappointment.

"You're not in a good enough mood."

"Maybe you're right," she said. "But I'd love to go. Really."

A few tables away, I noticed the same woman still glaring at him as Michelle looked at her watch.

"Travis. I'm going to be late. Please ask me again, okay?" She patted my father on the head like a teddy bear and got up. We both watched her walk across the room. At the door she turned and waved.

"Jesus," said Travis. "Whenever I'm around this girl it's like I've stuck my finger in an electric socket."

"I've heard you say that about twenty times," I said.

"We're talking two hundred twenty amps here."

"How old is she?" I asked.

He looked a little pained.

"A couple of years out of college. Twenty-four," he said. "Twenty-three anyway."

"Damn, Travis. I'm twenty-one."

"You can't measure anyone's age chronologically."

"That's for sure," I agreed.

"Try not to be too critical. You're going to be at the portals of the golden age yourself someday." He poured another glass of wine for both of us.

"There are a lot of things I can teach that girl," he added.

"Yeah, I've seen a few of those lessons."

"I'm not only talking about that. There's just no reason for her to make some of the mistakes the rest of us do."

"Then why didn't you teach me?" I demanded.

He stared at me for a few seconds and then looked down at the table.

"I taught you some things," he said.

"Yeah," I said.

When he wanted to, Travis could make you feel like the most important person on earth. He could even be a good listener, particularly when he was on the make. But for all his magnetic charm, there were a number of things he wasn't good at. Like traditional family values. Or marriage. Or being a parent. After all these years, I realized it was ridiculous to start holding him to account as a father.

"You didn't do so badly," I told him.

"Right," he said, finishing another glass of wine.

"How did you meet her?" I asked, hoping to change the subject.

He brightened at the recollection.

"She was giving a swimming lesson to a group of kids," he said. "She was bent over the edge of the pool with that gorgeous ass arching toward the heavens. When she turned and saw me staring at her, she gave me that innocent smile and my knees almost buckled."

"Then what happened?"

"She asked me which of the kids was mine."

"Un-hunh."

"So I told her that none of the kids was mine, but that I was afraid of the water and wanted to engage her in some private lessons."

"What did she say?"

"She asked if this was a recent development since she happened to know that I swam two miles every day even in a hurricane."

Which was the truth. For as long as I could remember, my father indulged a daily habit which was treated by our family as ordinary behavior, but which most other people found fairly amazing.

His daily routine, no matter how much he had drunk the night before, was to put on his bathing suit, walk down to the beach, and plunge into the bay. Winter or summer, regardless of the weather, he would swim out for a mile or more and then come back.

And she was right about the hurricane, too. It became the stuff of local legend after Dave and I spread the word about what he'd done. I don't think my mother ever really forgave him for it.

TEN

In 1954, Hurricane Carol descended on Long Island after causing death and destruction all along the eastern seaboard. The evening before its arrival, the Ledbetter family went to work lashing down our small boats above the high-water line, storing the porch furniture, filling the bathtubs with water, checking the kerosene lamps, and crisscrossing the picture windows facing the bay with three-inch-wide masking tape.

The next morning, my mother made each of us promise that we would retreat down to the basement at her command. I was secretly looking forward to riding out what was being called the most dangerous hurricane in fifty years. As we were completing our preparations, the first rain squall hit. The wind was already gusting to forty miles an hour. The bay began to boil over in a seething mass of angry waves. Breakers as high as our dock pilings started pounding the beach. As the minutes passed, the noise of the wind grew progressively louder.

That's when Travis came downstairs. All he was wearing was his bathing suit. He was at the door to the front porch when my mother intercepted him.

"Darling, please don't do this," she pleaded. "Travis, this is crazy! We need you here with us."

"It looks more rugged than it really is," was his response.

"Travis. I'm begging you. Stay here with us."

It was the only time I ever heard her beg him to do anything.

"I swim every morning—you know that," he said, as if the plea was over whether he needed to shave or not.

When he opened the door, the wind blew it back and opened a cut in his forehead. It only seemed to add to his resolve. Stepping out onto the porch, he dragged the door shut behind him.

"I hate you!" my mother yelled through the door while the rest of us raced upstairs to get a better view. I can see him now, striding over the dunes with the rain pummeling his body, howling the rebel yell over the roar of the wind. For a moment, he stood at the edge of the pounding surf, looking up at the blackening sky. Then he dove into the breakers. We lost him for a few seconds.

"There he is," yelled Dave, and I could see him again, now in open water, churning powerfully through the buffeting waves. My mother joined us at the window, her eyes following him too.

"Is Daddy going to try to kill the bad storm, Mommy?" Hope cried.

My mother stood there in tight-lipped silence. When she finally spoke, it wasn't to Hope or any of us.

"The sea is just another battleground," she said.

We watched him until he disappeared into the turbulence of the roiling waves.

By ten that morning, tree limbs were flying through the air, the roof of our house was leaking in a dozen places, the electricity was out, and we could barely see one another in the gloom. Tommy and I huddled around a transistor radio and listened to news accounts of people who had been injured by downed power lines and falling trees. There were no reports of anyone drowning. But where was he?

The eye of the hurricane passed over us at around ten thirty. The sun came out and the wind died to no more than a light caress. We ran down to the beach to find the water still raging unabated. Fifteen minutes later, the calm eye disappeared and we retreated again to the house. Through my bedroom window, I scanned the bay with binoculars. Hearing a tremendous shriek, we watched as the roof of our neighbor's boathouse detached itself from the walls and began a flight toward Connecticut. All of us were immediately ordered to the basement. By then my mother was wrapped tighter than a golf ball.

At around eleven, Hope complained about being hungry and we cautiously crept upstairs to the kitchen. The house wasn't shuddering anymore, and my mother heated some soup on the gas stove. She was about to serve it when the door to the mudroom crashed opened and my father staggered in, still wearing only his bathing suit. He had a dumb grin on his face, and his chest was scraped raw in several places. A rivulet of blood was running down his left leg. I watched it drip onto the kitchen floor.

"Did anybody miss me?" he called out heartily.

He held out his arms inviting a hug and we all jumped up from the table.

"SIT DOWN!" my mother screamed.

We sat down. The two of them stared at each other across the room without moving. Hope broke the silence, asking, "Did you kill the storm, Daddy?"

She was too young to know her place in these situations.

"No, honey. King Neptune was too strong for me," said my old man. "But I did enjoy a little arm wrestling with the Big G."

My mother slowly walked over to him. He was still giving her that shit-eating cocky grin when she hauled off and belted him in the nose with her clenched fist. He took it without moving. It did knock the grin off his face, though. As we all looked on wide-eyed, he limped out of the kitchen.

"Why did you hit him, Mommy?" Hope asked.

"That was for the Big G," she said, serving the soup.

The old man always had confidence. It was the kind of serene self-assurance that nothing could snuff out his light. It was the same confidence that one of his family ancestors, General Nathan Bedford Forrest, had. Custer had it too, when he led the Seventh Cavalry up to the Greasy Grass above the Little Big Horn River.

. . .

"Are you feeling all right?" Travis asked me across the remains of our lunch.

I wasn't exactly drunk. Just flying high. It was one of those rare times when I knew that I had just hit my peak and that one more drink would push me off the cliff.

"More wine?" asked the old man. I shook my head no.

"So where do you stand with Michelle?" I asked.

"I'm not sure yet. Her interest may be daughterly . . . or a sense of gratitude."

"You earned her gratitude?" I asked skeptically.

"I was leaving the club one night several weeks ago and encountered Maurice Haggerty groping her out in the parking lot. She probably could have handled him herself, but I grabbed what's left of Maurice's hair and made him take a good look at himself. Now let's get back to this Kate Kurshan."

I launched into an objective analysis of her qualities until he cut me off.

"Let me see if I understand," he said with a grin. "She is the reincarnation of Bathsheba, straight from Jerusalem."

"Yeah . . . but she says she loves Tommy."

"Are they making it together?"

"I don't know."

"I'd say it's doubtful," said Travis. "In fact, it's hard for me to believe he's from my seed. Now you . . . you have a full dose of the Ledbetter blood. And that's usually a big advantage in matters like this."

"She thinks I'm worthless."

"Any girl who loves Tom certainly would. I'll let you in on something. For many years I was convinced that your brother was put on this earth to make me feel perpetually guilty for all my sins."

"Mom was saying something like that last night."

"Even as a toddler, he was different from the rest of you guys," he said.

He shook his head and grinned at a sudden recollection.

"One night I was alone in my study—it must have been two or three in the morning. I looked up and there he was . . . just standing there in the doorway. He hadn't made a sound. It really gave me a jolt. Then he started coming toward me, one foot in front of the other, very deliberately, his hands using the furniture for support as he came on. He was actually walking with . . . I don't know . . . dignity. How many toddlers have you ever seen with dignity?"

I shook my head.

"Well, he stood there holding himself very straight and then craned his head up until his eyes were locked on mine. I waited for him to explain the theory of relativity to me with a voice like Orson Welles, but he never cracked a smile. Finally, he turned around and walked back out of the room. In recent years I've come to realize he has bigger fish to fry than his old man."

Looking over his shoulder, I saw the woman who had been glowering at him through lunch approaching the table. She had a narrow face like an Afghan hound, with her hair cut into bangs. She came up to us and stopped.

"Hello, Marie," he said congenially. "Would you like to join us?"

"Travis Ledbetter, I just wanted you to hear this from me instead of a third party. I've asked the board of directors to convene a special meeting in order to have you removed from this club. What you're doing with that child is despicable," she said in a voice that carried across the room.

"I'd like to thank you for telling me personally, Marie," he responded with another grin. "And please give my best to Maurice when you see him."

I remembered the name from his story about Michelle.

"Maurice is her husband," said Travis.

ELEVEN

It was almost four o'clock by the time I managed to make it home. When I came through the mudroom, the entire family was sitting around the big plantation table in the kitchen. I put every ounce of concentration into walking across the room without knocking into something while maintaining an air of studied nonchalance. I was going up the back stairs when I heard my mother's voice.

"I'll give you one guess who he spent the afternoon with."

Her words were followed by an eruption of laughter.

I slept like the dead until a bloodcurdling scream caused me to bolt off my bed. Through the window, I saw it was dark outside. Something fell with a great thud on the floor above me. When I heard the voices, I realized it was Dave's kids fighting at the Ping-Pong table in the attic playroom upstairs.

"It bounced twice! It bounced twice!" Miles shouted.

"Did not! Did not!" Kristen screamed back.

"Did so!" he yelled.

Another generation of Ledbetter sportsmanship in the making.

Still logy from my afternoon with Travis, I went downstairs and then walked outside to clear my head. It was a black starry night, and a brisk wind was driving heavy rollers into the shoreline. Sitting down in the gazebo, I thought about the old man, and whether he was going to get kicked out of the club. I heard a noise behind me, and Flash, his old mastiff, slowly lumbered up the gazebo steps, dropped down heavily next to me, and produced a loud fart.

"Seen any hunters lately?" I said, rubbing his scarred ear.

Flash's glory days of going after hunters on our beach were all over. A vivid memory of him chasing them brought to mind another memory of Travis. For a guy who supposedly couldn't put the war behind him, he owned no guns and detested hunting. When Flash was a puppy, Travis trained him to attack anyone carrying a rifle, and over the years, the big mastiff had run off a lot of duck hunters, to the old man's delight.

I heard the sound of a piano. At first I couldn't tell where it was coming from. After helping Flash onto his feet, I followed the haunting melody back toward the house. Mounting the steps to the front porch, I stopped short.

Through the brightly lit windows of the living room, I could see the family watching in rapt attention as Tommy sat at the piano and Kate stood next to him. Together they were singing a verse from the old ballad "Barbara Allen."

Kate was wearing a beige silk blouse over a brown-and-white-plaid skirt. The blouse had a deep V-neck and I could see just a hint of lace between her breasts. Her face was surrounded by a little halo of reflected light from the piano lamp.

I had forgotten how talented a musician Tommy was. He was a good guitar player, but his best instrument was the piano, and he was self-taught. Purely by ear, he could play anything from classical to jazz or boogie-woogie. I remember one Methodist Youth Fellowship retreat on Shelter Island when he played for a couple of hours straight, the music reaching all the way out to the lilac bushes where I was making out with Maureen Rhatigan.

I stood there in the shadow of the porch listening to the purity of the sound they created together. I knew what she saw in my brother. Maybe I had always known it and had forgotten it. There was a gentle power to him, something intensely charismatic.

When they finished the last verse of "Barbara Allen," there was a moment of silence. Then everyone was applauding like Richard Burton had just finished performing *Hamlet*. Tom gave Kate a hint of a smile. As I watched, she gently pulled his chin toward hers and kissed him full on the lips. That's when I took off.

Grabbing an open bottle of wine from the pantry, I found a blanket on the porch and headed out to the dunes, curling up in one of the hollows that offered good protection from the wind. I pulled the cork out of the bottle and sipped the wine while thinking about what the old man had said about living on the edge, exactly where I wanted to be. To finally know what war was like and what it did to the men who fought it.

I thought about why I was drinking so much. Part of it came from Travis's example. And there were all the movies. I thought of Bogie sitting in Rick's Café waiting for Ilsa to come back as he knocks off a bottle of the hard stuff. *One in . . . one out. I bet they're asleep in New York. I'll bet they're asleep all over America.*

The smell of the sea was tangy and raw and I felt at one with it.

I imagined the South Pacific still bathed in sunlight, the skeletons of all the ships and sailors who lay at rest miles beneath the ocean surface. I drank to them all. To the *Lex* and the *Yorktown*, the *Repulse*, and the *Prince of Wales* off the coast of Malaya, and to all the sunken Allied ships in Iron Bottom Sound off Guadalcanal. And to the souls of those who had crashed into the sea and died and were never found—to Glenn Miller and Torpedo Squadron 8 and Leslie Howard. Then I saluted the dead ships of the P.Q. 17 convoy to Murmansk strung out on the bottom of the sea from Archangel to Bear Island. In my mind's eye, Victor Laszlo and Ilsa Lund were taking off from Lisbon on the Pan American clipper to America.

Finishing the bottle, I hurled it out beyond the surging breakers and pulled the blanket over me.

TWELVE

My hair and face were covered with a gritty film of sand when the morning sun found me in the hollow of the dune. A gray-backed gull was flapping its wings a few feet above my perch, screeching as if the British were coming.

Heading back to the house, I tried to remember what day it was. It had to be Sunday, I decided, Easter Sunday—a time to celebrate the resurrection, a time for bonnets and Easter eggs. And the Ledbetter family tradition of milk punch before dinner. As a family we only went to church on Christmas Eve and Easter. Except for Tommy, my mother, and Grandpa Sprague, that was enough religious indoctrination to last us for the rest of the year.

Back in my room, I swallowed four aspirin before shaving and taking a long hot shower. Putting on an old tennis shirt and jeans, I went downstairs. Kate and Laura were sitting at the kitchen table, sipping coffee and talking. Pouring myself a cup of coffee, I joined them at the table. Kate was wearing a white organdy dress with a collar trimmed in ivory lace. Her hair was wreathed in a headband of white baby's breath. A small puffed golden Star of David hung at her throat from a delicate chain.

"You sang beautifully last night," I said.

She glanced up and said, "You weren't there. How would you know?"

"I was there. You just didn't see me."

"You must have been invisible," she said with sarcasm.

I tried to think of something witty and self-deprecating to say in response. But as I looked into her eyes, nothing came to me.

"He was there. I saw him," said Laura, getting up to leave. "He and Flash were standing out on the porch where they belong."

I waited for her to leave.

"Where is Tommy?" I asked.

"Reverend Carpenter asked him to be the lay reader for the service," said Kate, "and he's gone on ahead."

I sipped my coffee and waited for my head to regain its normal shape.

"You also look very beautiful this morning," I said.

She frowned into her coffee cup.

"I meant beatific. Very beatific."

For a moment she seemed bemused.

"In a little while I'll get to hear you sing," she said.

"I'm sorry?"

"At church," she added.

"Oh, yeah. Right."

"Are you going like that?" she asked.

"No. I was about to get dressed."

I stood up and headed toward the back stairs.

"I never miss Easter," I said.

. . .

Ten minutes later I was in my navy suit, starched white shirt, and Friends Academy tie, and smelling like the Old Spice windjammer. Kate looked up at me as I came down the back stairs.

"Beatific. Very beatific," she said solemnly.

My mother was attending to the coffeepot. She looked up with astonishment.

"You're going to church?" she asked.

I poured myself another mug of coffee and went back to the table. By then, Kate had walked to the alcove off the kitchen where my mother had set up a little office. She was gazing at a charcoal sketch on the wall above the desk. It was a full-face portrait of my mother.

"This really captures you well," said Kate, looking at the badly scrawled initials of the artist. "Did Tom do this?"

"No," said my mother, pointing at me with her cigarette holder. "Believe it or not, this clod at the table is the one with artistic talent."

As she turned away from the sketch, Kate's eyes betrayed no reaction. A few minutes later, we all piled into Dave's station wagon in the driveway and headed across the peninsula to the village.

The Cold Spring Harbor Methodist Church is a white-shingled firetrap with a high-peaked roof and wide-plank pine floors. The building has stood in the same spot since the Revolutionary War. There is a secret chamber under the pulpit where Nathan Hale supposedly hid before he was captured a few miles away and hanged as a traitor. As kids, Tommy and I had a lot of fun exploring all the nooks and crannies.

That Sunday the place was packed. Parishioners like us who hadn't attended a service since Christmas greeted one another like we hadn't missed a Sunday since. There was a sea of outlandish bonnets. The Sprague side of our family has had a pew there since the British retreated from Long Island. It was empty and waiting for us. At the front of the sanctuary, I saw Tommy in a flowing blue robe talking with a member of the choir. As we waited to file into our pew, I worked my way into position behind Kate.

The Reverend Rod Carpenter welcomed the congregation after we sang the hymn "Be Still, My Soul." Somewhere in the middle of the first verse, I turned to look at her and she briefly returned my glance. The nearness of her almost made me dizzy. Reverend Carpenter then invited Tom to read the scripture lesson. Tom stood up and greeted the congregation, telling us that more than one of his old Sunday school teachers out there must surely be shocked to see him standing at the pulpit. It generated a sprinkling of laughter. If they had really wanted a shock, I would have been standing there.

When Reverend Carpenter got up to deliver his sermon, I could tell he was pissed about something from the way he angrily shuffled his notes together. With his unruly hair and turkey jowls, it was hard for me to believe he had won the Silver Star as a Marine Corps private during the Korean War.

When I once asked him about it, he almost seemed ashamed of the medal. I tried to get him to tell me what he had done at the Chosin Reservoir, but all he said was, "Richard, all that took place in a past life. Now, did you study the parable of the lost sheep for confirmation class?"

The first thing he told the congregation that Easter morning was that most of us were pretty lousy Christians. As if we didn't know that already. The rest of the sermon was so controversial that *Newsday* printed it a few days later from a tape recording made by someone in the congregation.

"Before Holy Week," he began, "Jesus gathered his disciples and said to them, 'Behold, we are going to Jerusalem and the Son of Man will be delivered to the chief priest and scribes and they will condemn him to death and deliver him to the Gentiles to be mocked and scourged and crucified.' But on the third day after he will be raised into heaven."

"Not very comfortable words, are they?" he added, scanning the congregation with combative eyes.

"What Jesus was saying is that in order to get to Easter, it is necessary to go through Good Friday—to go through the horrible death of crucifixion. As the hymn writer put it, we can only trace the rainbow through the rain. This is true of all the Easters there have ever been. It is true of this Easter today."

I noticed a quick, darting movement on one of the ancient cross-beams far above us under the roof over the sanctuary. A small bird crept silently to the edge of the beam and gazed down at us. I was about to point him out to Kate, but she was too enthralled by the minister's words.

"Our world today is a Good Friday world. Laid upon our nation is a cross. A war in a far-off land has created great divisions among us. Some would say we stand on the brink of losing our soul as a nation."

I looked down the pew at the rest of our clan. Miles was already asleep, and Kristen was scribbling with a pencil stub on the back of a pledge envelope. Hope had her hand on her boyfriend's thigh. There was an empty spot in the pew between my mother and Grandpa Sprague. It had always been Travis's place until he stopped coming. I remembered the time my mother tried to get him to come back, saying how important it was for him to set a positive example for us.

"We should live and die just like the animals we are," he had said.

"Evil isn't something locked up in the attic of a haunted house," said Reverend Carpenter from the pulpit. "The capacity for evil is inside the soul of every one of us. General Westmoreland is quoted as saying, 'This is Christ's war we are fighting in Vietnam.' Yet we also have young men refusing to fight in it because they believe that Christ's teaching demands this action."

With Kate hanging on every word, I had the chance to observe the fine glossy texture of her hair where it joined the back of her neck. In the amber light of the stained-glass windows, it seemed to be of two different hues, the larger mass like dark mahogany, with the tendrils next to her skin a light tawny red.

"Jesus taught us that war as a way of settling differences is not just," the minister went on. "The burning of other human beings with napalm is against everything He has taught us."

At the end of the pew in front of us, an old guy with a cane between his legs began to mumble to himself.

Carpenter lowered his voice and repeated, "Well, there is no Easter without a cross. There is no rainbow without the rain."

Kate turned to look at me, her dark brown eyes filled with emotion. A stream of parishioners was now making its way down the side aisle to the rear of the sanctuary. I watched as two members of the choir disappeared through a door behind the pulpit.

" 'Pastor,' you say, 'marry us, baptize our children, bury us, but don't lay a cross on our backs.' By remaining silent in the face of this Good Friday world, you are like those who stood by while the crowd yelled out, 'Crucify him.' No, my friends, there is no rainbow without the rain."

More than half the congregation had left by the time he finally sat down. On our way out of the church, he was standing by the front door alongside Tom, shaking the hands of those few parishioners who chose to offer him one. Mrs. Carpenter was standing alongside him with a look of fierce pride and loyalty on her face. I felt a sliver of memory of her riding Travis on the throne up in our attic on my twelfth birthday.

Outside, I stood with Kate as Dave went to get his car.

"What a magnificent sermon," she said.

"I thought you were Jewish," I said.

"I don't have to believe in the resurrection to know that Jesus was a great man with a message for all people to live by," she responded. "It is so sad that it has been distorted to wage war."

I remembered all the times over the years we had sung the hymn "Onward, Christian soldiers, marching as to war, with the cross of Jesus going on before." For the first time, I thought about the contradiction in those words.

We rode back home with Dave and Laura. Tom stayed to talk with Rod Carpenter. As we pulled out of the parking lot, the two of them were walking together toward the parsonage.

"One more sermon like that, and that guy's going to be preaching in Outer Mongolia," said Dave. "He couldn't have cleared people out of there faster if he'd sprayed them with tear gas."

"I think he's one of the most impressive men I've ever met," Kate replied.

Dave craned his head around to see if she was kidding.

"Well, Carpenter was right about one thing," he added. "I want the rainbow without the rain, and we're going to find a new church if he puts up a fight about resigning."

"At least you won't have to worry about the decision until next Christmas, Dave," I said.

Kate couldn't suppress a smile.

THIRTEEN

When we got back to the house, I wolfed down a donut and coffee in the kitchen and then went up to change. Heading back downstairs, I saw that the door to Kate's room was open, her Easter dress folded neatly on the bed. After making a quick circuit around the house, I realized she must have gone outside. I stepped out onto the porch to hear a bout of muffled giggling. Hope and her new boyfriend Cliff were lying together under a blanket on one of the wicker couches. They were too busy to notice me.

Hope had been through a bad time. She had enjoyed a golden childhood. Always a character, she had been a little knockout with raven hair and impudent blue eyes. Even as a kid she was able to mimic everyone in the family. She declared that she was going to be an important actress someday and began writing and staging her own plays.

Her first professional break came when she was chosen to play the starring role in *The Children's Hour* at a local summer theater. "A born actress," the *Newsday* critic wrote. She was maybe eleven at the time. Hope went from one local triumph to another, playing Emily in *Our Town* and then the title role in *Peter Pan*. Later, she was selected from hundreds of kids to play a lead in a Broadway production. That's when she decided to quit school and move into the city. My mother tried to change her mind, but Hope was adamant.

That proved to be the end of her golden run. After that, she didn't get another good part. For two years she auditioned for shows and never got hired. She decided to try Hollywood, convinced it was easier to break in out there. About six months later, she had a nervous breakdown. My mother flew out to Los Angeles to bring her home. After she was released from the hospital, she hung around the house for almost a year. Then she took a trip to visit some friends in London. She came back with Cliff St. Charles.

From the porch I heard raised voices out at the tennis court and tried Kate there first. A doubles game was in progress with Dave and Kristen playing against Laura and Miles. Dave hit a shot that landed near the baseline.

"Long!" screamed Miles.

"Cut it out, son," Dave demanded angrily.

"Really, Dave . . . I think it was out," said Laura.

"This is too much," my brother yelled. "I'm trying to raise that boy to never cheat."

"Don't bring Miles into this," she came right back. "The ball was out."

I left them bickering on the court and followed the gravel path down to the bluff overlooking the beach. A freshening breeze had turned the whitecaps into good-sized waves, and I could see a squall line farther out in the sound. Above the gazebo, a lone seagull was cutting a series of dazzling down and out patterns.

Kate was sitting in the gazebo, looking out across the bay. She had changed into blue jeans and a white turtleneck, and was wearing Tom's old windbreaker. I sat down on the railing facing her.

"Tommy still at church?" I asked, and she nodded before turning back to gaze at the waves rolling in toward the beach.

"I was wondering . . ." I began uncertainly. Her eyes slowly came back to mine. "I was wondering if you and I could start over again. You know . . . a clean slate."

The coolness in her eyes reflected her obvious suspicion.

"Really," I said.

Apparently deciding to give me the benefit of the doubt, she said, "All right."

"Would you like to take a walk?" I asked.

She thought about it for a moment and nodded. The beach was deserted as we descended the wooden steps that led across the dunes. In the distance, I could see that the squall line was slowly moving our way. Kate slipped her hands into the pockets of Tom's windbreaker, and we began to walk.

As I felt the grainy sand under my sneakers, it suddenly occurred to me that I had never had a conversation with a girl that wasn't built around a snow job designed to get into her pants. Kate was right. I was nothing more than a role player. It was not a pleasant discovery.

“What an amazing place this must have been to grow up,” she said over the stiffening wind.

“Yeah . . . it was.”

“What’s that?” she asked, pointing to a rectangular opening in the dune behind us. The plywood walls were caving in and it was half-filled with sand.

“It’s a duck blind,” I said. “Some hunters built it into the dune a long time ago. Tommy and I converted it into a desert outpost of the French Foreign Legion.”

“You were Beau Geste, I gather,” she said.

“Yeah. Tommy was Digby, his younger brother.”

I had a vivid recollection of the day the hunters constructed the blind all those years ago. I decided to tell her about it.

“At the start of duck-hunting season, local guys would often come around asking for permission to hunt from our dunes,” I said. “Travis always said no. One year a group didn’t bother to ask. When my mother told Travis that men were building something out there, he waited until the sound of the hammering ended and then went down to the beach. Tommy and I snuck over to watch. There were five men and they were all armed with shotguns.

“ ‘This beach belongs to all of us,’ said one of them after my father told them to get off our property. The guy had red hair and was built like a sumo wrestler. He had a double-barreled twelve-gauge braced against his knee.

“ ‘We’re putting out our decoys,’ he said. ‘If you don’t like it, you can call the Fish and Wildlife Service.’

“Travis stood with his hands on his hips, looking at their blind as if it was an engineering marvel. They had put a lot of work into it. It had five gun mounts and a cushioned bench against the rear wall. So Travis walked over to the big guy and said, ‘You want to go bang-bang? I’m heading home, but I’ll be back in fifteen minutes. If you’re still here with that gun, you had better use it on me, because otherwise you’re going to eat your decoys.’ ”

Kate was looking at me expectantly.

“Tommy and I were hiding right above the dune, and we watched him walk back up the beach toward the house. As soon as he was gone, they all started talking at once.

" 'That's bullshit. He's bluffing!' said the red-haired one.

" 'Did you see those scars on his neck?' said another one.

" 'There are five of us and one of him,' came back the first one.

" 'I heard he got kicked out of the navy for killing someone,' said the third guy. 'He's fucking nuts!'

" 'I told you we shouldn't build it here,' said the second one as he started packing his equipment into a duffel bag.

" 'Phil, where are ya going?' demanded the red-haired one.

" 'I like the taste of roast Long Island duck, not my decoys,' said Phil.

" 'Well, I'm staying here,' said their leader. 'I got fifty bucks sunk into this blind, and nobody's going to run me out.'

" 'Fine—you stay,' said the third hunter, assembling his gear.

"The red-haired man was the only one left when we heard the front screen door on the porch slam. Tommy and I watched Travis heading back toward us. He was carrying the driver from his golf bag over his right shoulder. A few seconds later the guy was running down the beach after the others. By the time Travis got there, Tommy and I had taken over the blind and were making plans to convert it into Fort Zinderneuf."

Kate laughed out loud.

"I'm curious to know more about your father," she said, stooping to examine a dead horseshoe crab.

"That could take a month or two," I said.

"Why not give it a try?" she asked.

I decided to tell her what it was really like.

"When we were little, Travis wasn't around that much," I said, recalling the endless succession of lazy summer days on the beach with just my mother around, swimming and learning how to sail.

"I don't remember when he finally decided we were old enough to appreciate him, but suddenly he was there and planning whole batches of activities. Early on, he taught Dave, Tommy, and me how to box. We learned how to take a punch and give one back."

"Tom learned how to box?" said Kate, incredulous.

I nodded.

"Mmmm," she replied.

"Later on, no weekend was complete without a family round-robin tennis tournament or swimming races or touch football. We competed at everything, and all of us outdid each other trying to impress him. There was no quarter given and no allowance for hurt feelings."

"Tom competed that way?" she asked.

In my mind's eye I could see the family circus. At the beginning he was there. Then he wasn't.

"No. By then he had kind of dropped out."

I realized that the transformation might have followed the incident at St. John's Pond.

"Why?" she asked.

"I'm not sure . . . but another thing," I added, suddenly remembering one of the most important of the old man's creeds. "Travis taught us all to ignore physical pain—to just will it out of our minds. If we got hurt, there could be no whining. You played through it. You were oblivious to it. Travis had this saying. It went 'Don't worry. It won't last. Nothing does.'"

"Remarkable," said Kate, but it didn't sound like an endorsement.

"It wasn't always about competition," I said. "One weekend we rode horses around Fire Island. Another time we camped at Bear Mountain and searched for bears. One time he set up an archaeological dig."

"A dig?"

"Yeah." I chuckled. "Travis was convinced there was an Indian burial mound in the stand of woods behind our house. He got his hands on some old historical papers from colonial times that proved Indians once lived here. He even tracked down a Shinnecock Indian chief who said the burial mound might hold a valuable cache of ancient artifacts. Travis began comparing it to King Tut's tomb."

She was staring at me intently now.

"After dividing the burial mound into sections, he had the whole family begin to sift the dirt very carefully through a screen of chicken wire, examining every little find as if it might be one of the Romanov jewels. My sister Hope was the first one to bail out after declaring there was nothing there."

"'It's down there,' Travis kept saying. 'I can feel it.'"

"So tell me," demanded Kate. "Did you find anything?"

I nodded.

"Yeah. When we got down around five feet, we hit the mother lode," I said.

"What was it?"

"A nineteen twenty-four Dodge pickup truck," I said, reliving the moment as if it was yesterday.

Kate began laughing again. I felt like I had just won Wimbledon.

"Very rare," I added.

Her eyes turned quizzical.

"Why do you call your father by his first name?"

I saw Mrs. Carpenter again on my twelfth birthday. I debated whether to tell Kate what had happened in the attic and decided against it.

"I don't remember," I said finally.

"Oh, well," she said. "I'm definitely looking forward to meeting him."

"What is your father like?" I asked.

"He was a high school history teacher," she said. "He taught me . . . among other things, he taught me the love of learning. When I was eight years old, he and my mother were killed in an airplane crash. I was raised by my grandmother. She was German born and smuggled out of Germany in nineteen thirty-eight in the secret compartment of a wine cask. She used to say that was why she aged so well."

I laughed.

"And your grandfather?" I asked.

"He didn't make it out of Germany," she said.

We came to a rock-filled breakwater that ran from the dunes down to the waterline. As we started to climb over it, I took her hand. She didn't try to pull it away. When we were on the other side, I let it go.

"From my grandmother I learned Yiddish," she went on, "and something far more important. She always believed in the innate goodness of the American people. It was an almost mystical faith until the day she died. I would like to believe it is still true."

"What is a *yentzer*?" I asked, remembering what she had called me on the footbridge.

She actually blushed.

"It involves the frequent use of one of your glands," she said, picking up a clamshell and artfully skipping it across the water.

"As for me, let's see," she went on. "I never needed braces. I wrote bad poetry and had cats instead of dolls. I would dress them up in baby clothes. I guess that's about it."

As we continued walking, another darker memory caused her to stop short.

"I matured early. Boys started hitting on me when I was thirteen. At Stanford I made the mistake of thinking I was in love with one particular guy. The one I told you about. We stayed together for the sole reason that I knew what would happen to me if I tried to break up with him."

She stopped and looked up at me.

"What would he have done?" I asked softly.

"He was violent to anyone who showed the slightest interest in me. I did whatever he told me to do . . . so take me off that pedestal you built."

"Tell me why you stared at me when you first saw me at the Chapter House," I said.

She chuckled.

"It was because you looked so familiar," she said. "I actually thought I knew you. Later, when that girl said your name, I realized it was your resemblance to Tom. You look the same in certain ways, and yet you're so different. Like opposite sides of a coin."

"Cain and Abel," I deadpanned, and she grinned.

"Rick?" she said, stopping again.

"Yes?"

"I want to apologize for some of the things I've said to you. You have one or two redeeming qualities."

"Thanks," I said.

"You're just very different from Tom," she said. "And me."

"I know."

"We are so committed against the war, and you're probably going over there."

Behind her shoulder, I saw the squall front sweeping toward us, and immediately turned to start back down the beach. We hadn't gone twenty yards before the first drops began pelting us.

"Come on!" I said, taking her hand again and starting to run toward a row of scrub pines that fringed the beach. Just inside the tree line, I found what I was looking for. It was an old outhouse covered with weathered shingles and a tin roof. The door had been missing for as long as I could remember.

"A privy?" she said as we took shelter inside.

"Yeah—but I doubt anyone has used it since Teddy Roosevelt."

There were two well-worn holes cut into the bench. We sat down between them.

"A two-seater," she said with a childlike smile. "My grandmother had one of these in her backyard."

"In those days I guess families did everything together."

My shirt was dripping wet. Kate's windbreaker had given her a little more protection.

"Here. Take Tom's jacket," Kate said.

"No."

"No, really. My sweater is dry underneath and you've only got your shirt. I'll be fine."

She draped the windbreaker around my shoulders.

"As soon as this lets up, we can run back," I said.

"Okay."

Maybe it was the cold wind knifing through the cracks in the walls. Or the fact that she was sitting so close to me. I meant to say something casual, like "I love a good storm." That's what I intended. Honestly. I thought I had traveled a few steps up the path toward decency.

Instead I found myself saying, "I can't stop thinking about you, Kate. I know you don't want to hear that, but I can't help it. I'm sorry."

Her face was inches from mine. Her brown eyes were examining me with skepticism and maybe vulnerability too.

"Do you have the slightest idea what could happen to you in Vietnam?" she said over the wind.

Instead of answering, I kissed her. I regretted it as soon as I saw her reaction. She looked stricken. A moment later she was on her feet and out into the rain, moving fast through the pines down to the beach.

FOURTEEN

Dave began mixing the milk punch at around five o'clock. The closely guarded recipe had supposedly been concocted by Travis's great-grandfather as a toast to Sam Houston for winning the Battle of San Jacinto over General Santa Anna. Now that Travis was no longer part of most family gatherings, the responsibility had fallen to Dave as the eldest son. After making a full pitcher, he began circulating the drinks in the Ledbetter family's old cut-glass goblets.

Tommy had returned from the parsonage and was sitting near the television set in the living room leafing through the latest issue of *Life*. Rather than decline Dave's offer of the punch, he took a polite sip and set it on the table next to him. The TV was tuned to one of the major networks but the volume was turned off. When the evening news came on, I saw that the first story was about Vietnam. The visual images showed a rural village with several huts on fire. Two Vietnamese women were running away from them.

Dave came over with his drink and said, "Christ, the goddam liberals can't even give us a day off on Easter Sunday."

One of the women was silently screaming. Something was lying on the ground near her that was giving off a small cloud of black smoke. It was barely human and writhing back and forth.

"Napalm," said Tom as we all stared at the figure on the ground. "The Vietnamese call it fire rain."

As the news story ended, Cliff St. Charles sat down next to me on the couch. In his late twenties, he had shoulder-length blond hair, blue eyes, and a lantern jaw. He was wearing what looked like loose-fitting white cotton pajamas.

"Rick, have you ever thought about flying?" he whispered in a conspiratorial tone.

"I used to think about trying it," I said. "Hope probably told you that our old man was a navy flier."

"No. I don't mean that," he said, staring at me intently. "Would you like to learn to fly? You know—by yourself?"

I was on a second glass of punch and wasn't sure I had heard him correctly.

"What do you mean, by myself?" I said.

"I can teach you how to fly," said Cliff. "Have you heard of the Maharishi Mahesh Yogi?"

I shook my head.

"How many people is that?"

"Just one," he said. "But he is the greatest leader in the world today. As a result of his personal guidance, I can fly. Hope is about to learn in the next few months at his ashram in India."

I couldn't help laughing out loud. Cliff took it in good spirits, and laughed right along with me. When I calmed down, the intent look came back into his eyes again.

"So what do you say?" he asked.

As I tried to figure out how to answer him, I heard the front door slam. A few seconds later, Travis swept into the living room. I had to hand it to the old man. You never would have guessed he had been banished from the house. From the way he greeted us, you might have thought he had been upstairs taking a nap for the last four months. He wouldn't have been there if my mother hadn't agreed to it. Dave and I took it in stride. After what the family had witnessed in the last few years, all of us knew when to keep our heads down. Travis disappeared into the butler's pantry and emerged with his Annapolis goblet. He filled it with Dave's family concoction.

"You've learned well, son," he said after tasting it. "The torch is passed."

Laura came out of the kitchen to say that dinner was ready and we all filed into the dining room. Travis took his traditional place at the head of the long mahogany table. My mother sat at the opposite end. I sat next to Travis, with Laura and Cliff to my right. Hope and Grandpa Sprague were sitting across from us. Tom and Kate were at the other end of the table with Dave and the kids.

The tablecloth was covered with our traditional favorites, including roast turkey, baked ham, rack of lamb, cranberry soufflé, mashed potatoes, pearl onions in cream sauce, chilled asparagus vinaigrette, sausage stuffing, giblet gravy, and bottles of red and white wine. As Travis carved the turkey, Dave opened the conversation by asking me how I was faring in my last term. My mother began shaking her head as I told him I was doing pretty well, although it was hard slogging.

"I understand the faculty is planning to convert some of the courses to a pass-fail plan," he said with an air of skepticism.

"Yes, and it's a good idea, too," said Hope, who had recently enrolled at Nassau Community College. "Everything is too competitive."

"Competitive?" said Dave. "These days you can buy detailed outlines for every major course. They had a survey a few weeks ago where some professors reported they often get the same word-for-word answers on essay questions."

"Well, you might be interested to know that they had those things in my time," said Grandpa Sprague, as if he was talking about the Middle Ages.

"Yeah," said Dave. "But it wasn't a big business on campus. According to the survey, these companies advertise that you can buy everything up to a master's thesis for three or four bucks a page."

"Five," I blurted, without thinking.

Thankfully, Grandpa Sprague took up the slack.

"I don't believe that laziness is characteristic of today's college students," he said. "The young people that I meet and talk to at church are far more serious and committed to changing this world than my generation was. Just look at all the young people involved in the demonstrations against the war."

"Yeah, look at them," came back Dave. "If they don't get their way, they announce they're ready to destroy the country, and then they whine like spoiled brats when it comes to facing punishment for breaking the law."

"May I say something?" asked Kate.

She had raised her hand like she was sitting in class, as if that would ever get you the floor in a Ledbetter family conversation. I saw Travis eyeing her with a speculative look as Dave continued.

"They talk so easily about violence and guns and offing the pigs—that's the latest thing ... The next minute they're weeping about police brutality."

"Are you finished?" asked Kate.

"No, I'm not," he said, plowing on, "and I'll tell you this about the people in SDS, the so-called Students for a Democratic Society. What a joke! The 'D' is supposed to stand for 'democratic,' but if someone disagrees . . ."

"David," my mother said sharply. "I believe that Kate has something to say."

Kate glanced over at Tom as if for moral support. His hand slid over hers and he smiled at her reassuringly.

"I'm not a member of SDS, but I think we're being lied to about the war. Those of us who believe this have to take a stand against it and try to change the policy."

"Exactly right, Kate," said Grandpa Sprague, "exactly right. We need a lot of changes down in Washington."

Cliff St. Charles chose that moment to weigh in.

"I'd like to talk about an important change that's already taking place throughout the world," he said. "It's called inner consciousness—the knowledge that we all have boundless potential if we can find a way to harness the deepest levels we each possess."

Travis leaned toward me and whispered, "Your brother's girl is everything you said she was, a knockout with brains. Very dangerous."

"So why are you here?" I whispered back to him.

"I need to talk with your mother," he said.

It had to be about money. That was the only thing that could have gotten him there under the circumstances. And that meant my mother must have been open to the idea.

"Most of us are operating at about ten percent of our full mental capacity," Cliff went on. "With proper training and study of the Maharishi's teachings, a person can reach unparalleled levels of knowledge and power."

Grandpa Sprague's nose wrinkled up like it did when he was confused.

"What can you do that I can't do?" asked Dave.

In the pause that followed I said, "For one thing, Cliff can fly."

Hope threw an angry look at me.

"What do you mean he can fly?" demanded Dave.

My mother saw the potential for danger and tried to head it off.

"I'm sure Cliff was speaking in figurative terms, David."

"No, he's right Mrs. Ledbetter," said Cliff, beaming. "I can fly. And that's only one of the powers that can be yours if you follow the Maharishi."

"The what?" asked Travis.

"I want to fly!" shouted Miles.

"You mean without technical assistance of any kind you can make yourself airborne?" asked Grandpa Sprague.

Cliff nodded. "And Hope will soon share this power too."

"Forgive me for being ignorant about this development," said Travis with a straight face. "I rarely read scientific journals, but I would have thought a breakthrough like this would be more widely circulated."

"I know what you mean, Mr. Ledbetter, but there are very good reasons why it isn't," replied Cliff. "First, it can be extremely dangerous. I'll be candid with you. Right now, it's even dangerous for me."

"Dangerous? How so?" demanded Dave. "Low-flying aircraft?"

"That's enough," Hope came back.

"Yeah," I added. "He has to get clearance to land from the tower at La Guardia,"

"You bastard," Hope hissed at me.

Cliff was still oblivious to what was happening.

"There are many other rewards aside from flying," he said.

"Stop, Cliff," said Hope, her eyes tearing. "Can't you see? They're just trying to make you look ridiculous. I told you they wouldn't understand."

"What did I say?" I asked innocently.

This was the standard follow-up line in our family after ruining someone's day.

"You are hateful. Cliff knows more about life than all of you put together. You're so jealous you can't stand to just learn from him. You have to drag him down to your level. We're leaving."

Cliff gazed down at his plate heaped with roast turkey, cranberry soufflé, buttermilk biscuits, and pearl onions in cream sauce. My mother tried to salvage the situation.

"I'm sure that those who said anything to offend Cliff will be happy to apologize," she said.

This seemed to enrage Hope even further.

"Oh, *you*. You're worse than any of them, Mother," she declared angrily.

Dragging Cliff to his feet, she hustled him out of the dining room. As she ran him upstairs, Tom folded his linen napkin and got up from the table. He didn't have to say anything. We all knew he was on his way up to try to calm the waters.

My mother seemed unruffled.

"More cranberry soufflé, anyone?" she asked.

Grandpa Sprague got to his feet and declared he wasn't feeling well and asked to be excused. He didn't have much stamina for what he knew was coming after seeing the family in action for so many years.

Dave couldn't get off the subject of Vietnam.

"The other night on the evening news they actually showed a captured enemy soldier being tortured by a Green Beret. If that wasn't bad enough, they ran it again in slow motion. I mean who wouldn't get sick of the war with the TV networks putting the worst face on it? The reporter always says, 'This may not be appropriate for children,' and everybody rushes in to watch it. They're going to lose it for us, I tell you. And if Vietnam falls, we can write off the rest of Southeast Asia."

"What does that mean?" asked Kate.

"We lost Laos because we weren't willing to fight. Now we stand to lose Vietnam."

"You talk about Vietnam as if it was ours," said Kate. "It isn't ours. The truth of this war is that it's a revolutionary war. The North is fighting to get rid of a colonial power just as we did with the British. Except now we're in the British role. We're not only on the wrong side, we created the wrong side, and now we're desperately trying to prop it up. The South doesn't have the will to fight this war because they have no stake in it."

Dave twirled his wineglass. One side of me was pulling for him to keep going. Obviously, we had to stop them in Vietnam or the dominoes would start falling. This was the battleground. The best and the brightest around JFK had told us so.

"I don't know what you've been reading in *Pravda*, honey," said Dave, "but you're not looking at the same pictures I've seen. Did you see today's *New York Post*—the photograph of the twelve-year-old Vietcong kid chained to his machine guns? That's a proven fact. These bastards keep their hold on the people by torture and murder. They murder schoolteachers, missionaries, anyone who opposes them. They murder Christians. I mean, just for being Christians for God's sake."

"What does that have to do with my point?" Kate responded.

Miles and Kristen were the next to be excused until dessert was served. Laura sent them off.

"I'll tell you the real problem," said Dave. "We're fighting with one hand tied behind our back. We could win that war in a week with a total commitment. We could wipe the whole stinking country right off the map."

"I think you're wrong, Dave," said Kate. "The reason we're not winning this war and why we'll never win this war is that deep down, the American people know it's wrong. That's why so many young people are refusing to serve in it."

"Well, that's fine," Dave responded. "I'm glad you've cornered the market on morality, Kate. And as a woman, you can also enjoy the luxury of not having to worry about serving your country. I might add that we could probably count the number of Jews serving over there on one hand. Your people always seem to find a way to avoid service."

That's when my relationship with my brother ended.

"Well, that's rich," I began. "I mean that's rich coming from you, Dave."

"What does that mean?" he demanded.

I glanced over at my mother. She could have shut me down with one furrow of her brow, but she didn't. *Screw it,* I thought.

"Every year you get more and more warlike—talking about how everybody else is afraid to fight. The further you get away from the draft yourself, the tougher you talk. I remember when some of your friends called you the Artful Dodger. Where the hell were you when the country was looking for a few good men?"

"Wait a goddam minute, Rick."

"Do you remember when your law school deferment expired? Within two weeks you were standing at the altar with Laura, and nine months later, Miles came along. As I recall, that was double-barreled protection back then. Face it. When you had the chance to serve, you didn't want to waste two or three years of your life. If you're so hot and heavy to fight, why don't you volunteer right now? How about it?"

I looked at Travis. He was focused on his plate and didn't look up.

Dave didn't say a word. I had put him down for the count. He just sat there with his knife and fork in his hands, looking at me with undisguised loathing. Laura said what he was thinking.

"You're really a bastard, Rick, do you know that?"

She threw her napkin on the table and stalked out of the dining room. Dave got up and followed her. Most of the food on their plates was untouched.

"I'm sorry, Kate," said my mother. "You've seen us at our worst, if that's any consolation."

"We've all been wounded by what's happened in this war," she said.

"Kate, why don't you go see if you can help Tom," said my mother. "Hopefully, we'll get back together for dessert."

The chances of that happening were about the same as LBJ deciding to stop the bombing of North Vietnam, but Kate nodded and followed Tom upstairs.

So then we were three.

. . .

I was sure my mother knew exactly why Travis had asked to come for dinner. She knew him better than anybody. Money was the sole measure of control she had over him. That was obviously why he had sat silently through the whole family debacle with a smile on his face like old Fezziwig in *A Christmas Carol*.

In truth, money never meant anything to him, which is the principal reason he could never hold on to any. I'm sure he didn't have a dime in the bank, nor would any bank have been stupid enough to lend him one. I could only imagine how much pride it had cost him to come over and ask for it. Whatever the amount was, he obviously wanted it badly. My mother was smiling cordially at him from her end of the long table.

She took a sip of her wine and said, "How much do you need, Travis?"

The old man leaned back in his chair.

"It's the Pearson, the one I'm living on, Edy," he said. "I have a chance to steal it for two hundred thousand. It's worth around four. I'm not here to ask you to lend me the money. It's actually an investment. Within two years, I can guarantee you will double your money."

"That sounds like quite a lucrative opportunity," she said. "And it has your ironclad guarantee. What is your own interest in the venture?"

"I'd like to live on the boat until you sell it, maybe take her across the Pacific to revisit some of my old stomping grounds. That's all. I'll keep it in immaculate condition for you."

"Immaculate," she repeated amiably.

It was so cordial that I knew she was setting him up. I guess he wanted the boat so badly that he was oblivious to the familiar warning signs. My mother never displayed warmth when it came to spending part of the Sprague fortune.

"I assume you're a little short on collateral right now," she said.

"As you well know," he responded affably.

"Yes, of course. So when would you be able to pay me back?"

"As soon as it's sold," he said. "I'll handle it through the brokerage, but without charging you any commission."

"That's very generous, darling."

She fitted a fresh Salem into her ivory cigarette holder and lit it with her Ronson. Taking a deep drag, she made the smoke eddy out of her nostrils before giving him another Greer Garson smile.

"Considering how wonderful this investment sounds, why don't you take it to Sue Livingston? Why not enrich Grace McVicker?"

"I haven't seen either one in a long time," he said, some of the color beginning to drain out of his face.

"How laudable of you," she said, no longer smiling. "Well what about Sharon Prentiss, or Dawn Mackesy, or Sally Amarell?"

"Edy, I didn't come here to dredge up old skeletons," he said. "I've brought you a sound investment. If you want to consider it, fine. If not, that's fine too."

You could have cut diamonds on the edge of her voice when she answered him.

"You come swaggering in here with your phallic strut on Easter Sunday and I'm supposed to welcome you with open arms and give you a fat check and send you back to your love nest. Is that it?"

Travis slowly pushed back his seat. "I think I get the picture."

"Yes, and I've got it too," she said. "The owner of that sailboat is selling it out from under you. You have no place to live, right? Well, let me give you a suggestion. Why not try that sleazy room at the Anchorage Motel where you used to service your lunch hour conquests."

"Not a bad idea," he said, working up a rueful smile.

Truthfully, I don't believe he ever looked at a woman as someone to be conquered. It wasn't the thrill of the hunt. He never had to hunt. They were usually all over him. It was like some magnetic force. It was elemental. I might add that he had been asking my mother for a divorce for three years. Up till then she had refused to give him one.

"Tell me, Travis, isn't Michelle a little old for you?" she asked. "Isn't it time for another cherry for my big handsome conqueror of the skies and oceans?"

"It was you, Edy," he said quietly.

"What was me, sweetheart?"

"You're frigid, Edy. I've always wondered what might have caused it. It sure as hell wasn't me."

I went out to the butler's pantry and brought back the open bottles of Smirnoff and Jim Beam. I poured a stiff one for the old man and topped up my mother's glass. They acted as if I wasn't there.

"For you, having sex was like getting a tooth pulled," he said.

"It's amazing. That's exactly what sex with you was like," she replied.

They were like a Broadway flop that refused to die. As horrible as the words were, they had lost the power to hurt.

"If they gave out a Nobel Prize for trying to bring your wife to an orgasm, I'd have been in Oslo a dozen times," he said.

"Ahh," my mother came back. "Such sensitivity from the hero of Midway and Leyte Gulf. Part of the problem is that your Nobel Prize–winning technique consisted of rutting between my legs like a feral donkey."

"The man you really wanted in bed was your father, Edy," he said, draining his goblet.

"He's twice the man you are, in or out of bed."

"I should have expected that from someone who once said that Adlai Stevenson was the sexiest man you've ever met."

"Adlai was also twice the man you are, in or out of bed," she said, waving her cigarette holder at him like a rapier.

"It really isn't your fault," went on the old man. "It's in the blood. I've always suspected your mother was frigid, too. And we both know your father is as neurotic about sex as an inbred rabbit. On one of those rare occasions when they were groping at one another in mutual disgust in the darkness, I imagine they made you."

"I think the war years were best for us," said my mother. "You know I enjoyed the company of a dozen different men during the years you were out in the Pacific. They were the best years—when you were five thousand miles away. The problem was you came back, darling."

She stood up from the table.

"I'm never coming back," he said.

"Well, it was lovely getting caught up," she said as if saying good-bye to one of her old sorority sisters at Cornell. "And thank you for making it such a special Easter for all of us. I'm sure there's someone back at your boat wondering what's become of you."

Pivoting gracefully, she strolled out of the dining room.

Travis seemed to deflate as soon as she was gone. I figured he probably wanted a few minutes to regain his confidence. Getting up, I went to take a leak. When I returned, he was gone.

FIFTEEN

It might seem strange that Tommy hadn't chimed in at dinner, but through the years of verbal bloodshed, he was always the one who remained above the fray, tending to the wounded when we were finished.

If the Ledbetters weren't fighting over politics, we fought over whether someone had been tagged in two-hand touch, or whether one of us had really landed on Boardwalk with two hotels, or whether "gordian" was a legitimate word in Scrabble. It's what finally inspired me to draft the Ledbetter Code at the end of one of our family vacations at the Sprague Lodge on Lake Champlain. After days of swimming races, waterskiing contests, and nightly grudge bouts of Hearts and Pitch, none of us were speaking to one another. Except for Tom, we were all seeking revenge. I wrote out the Ledbetter Code on the back of the plain brown wrapper that had enclosed the latest issue of *The New Yorker,* and pinned it to the kitchen wall near the percolator so no one could miss it in the morning.

The Ledbetter Family Code

1. If you're enraged at the loss of a game or family athletic contest, use the rest of the family as a whipping post. That's what they're there for.
2. If you aren't feeling well, drag the rest of the family down with you. Make them suffer as much as you are.
3. If someone in the family is actually having fun or enjoying himself, bring him or her back to earth.
4. If you are hopelessly behind in a game, spoil the winner's victory by upsetting the card table or accusing that person of cheating.
5. If you are fortunate enough to win, be sure to taunt your opponent and humiliate him as much as possible. After all, that's what he would do to you.

6. In a family conversation, never admit that you have been bested even though you know you are wrong. Just move on to the next subject.
7. Above all, keep asserting that you are the best at whatever it is you are doing.

The rest of the family got a pretty good laugh out of it at the time, even Tommy. But it didn't change the way we treated one another.

. . .

Dave left with Laura and the kids early Monday morning. It was overcast and chilly, matching the general mood. I watched them from my bedroom window as they packed up their station wagon and headed off down the gravel driveway. By then, Hope and Cliff were already long gone.

After showering, I went downstairs to find Rod Carpenter sitting at the kitchen table with Tommy, Kate, and my mother. They were deep in discussion of what would happen later that morning at Tommy's draft board hearing. I poured milk into a bowl of Cheerios and stood eating at the center island. My mother was still urging Tommy to apply for status as a conscientious objector.

"Bill Mott is the chairman of the draft board," she said, "and he's known you most of your life. He'll endorse your application if you'll only apply. He is confident that a majority of the board members will go along with him once they've met you."

"I really appreciate everything you've done, but after talking this through with Rod, I think I have a greater responsibility," said Tom.

"But, darling, you can accomplish so much more by actively fighting for your goals than if you are sent to . . ."

Her voice stopped in mid-sentence, and it wasn't hard to know why. They were handing out three to five years in a maximum-security federal prison for resisting the draft.

"I know this is really tough," said Tommy, his hand wrapped in Kate's. "It's hard to talk about these things without sounding like a plaster saint. I don't want to go to prison, but hundreds of young men are going across the country so that the American people will sit up and take notice. And each time one of us goes to prison, there will be a hundred more who will say, 'Set him free or take me too.'"

I didn't tell him that most of the guys I knew were so busy dodging the draft they couldn't care less what happened to anyone else. They were all looking out for number one. I could have told him about Pete Demetropolis using the exemption for orthodontic care. Then there was Jimmy Camaratta, who stopped bathing a month before his physical and showed up with shit smeared all over his balls. I could have mentioned Ted LaFreniere, a friend of mine from Friends Academy, who had recently won local fame as the Kool-Aid Kid. When the board rejected his petition, Ted picked up a pitcher of fruit drink and threw it at the hearing officers. They charged him with "assault with Kool-Aid." He won an exemption for being a manic-depressive. I could have told Tom to move to Seattle, where the local draft board separated draftees into two groups: those who had letters from psychiatrists and those who didn't. Everyone with a letter received a medical exemption.

It was hard to imagine any of them saying, "Set Tom Ledbetter free or take me too."

But none of it would have made any difference to Tommy. He was going forward because he believed he could help change the world through the force of his conscience and character, like his hero Martin Luther King Jr. He was going forward to put his body on the line.

Tommy was never sanctimonious or evangelical about his views. He wasn't out to become the leader of a movement like so many of the radicals who are against the war and love all the attention they receive on television. But there was something about him that made people naturally follow him. I hate to use the word "goodness," but I think that was part of it. He just thought through each personal decision he felt he needed to make and then acted. In his own way, he had the same kind of self-confidence that Travis had. They were totally different, but they each put their body on the line.

I guess it was like Davy Crockett, or at least Fess Parker playing Davy Crockett in the Disney TV series we watched when we were kids. He would always say, "Be sure you're right. Then go on ahead." Of course, Davy went to the Alamo, which wasn't the brightest idea in the world.

We drove over to the draft board hearing. Three of the five board members were already there when we arrived. One of them was the tennis coach at Huntington High School. Thinking I might be able to do some good, I wandered over to the table. He looked up as I approached and he recognized me.

"Richard Ledbetter, right?"

"Yes, sir," I said.

"You're playing at Cornell now, aren't you?"

"Injured," I said, and he nodded sympathetically.

"You have a hearing today?"

"No. Actually, it's my brother Tommy. I'm going into Navy OCS in June."

"Good show," he said, sounding like the British colonel in *The Bridge on the River Kwai*. "I went through Navy OCS in fifty-seven—spent two years on a tin can in the Med—God, those Italian women—loved every minute of it."

"What happens here?" I asked.

"The kids who can get into college have a two-S deferment," he said. "We're mostly drafting blue-collar kids and dropouts."

"You have draft evaders coming through?"

"We get a few oddballs," he said. "This one fairy . . . he told us he couldn't harm any living creature. He said if a fly was cruising around the room, he'd go get a cup and capture it and take it outside and let it loose."

"What happened to him?"

"He's probably on his way to Vietnam," he said, chuckling. "We get our jollies once in a while."

I laughed along to keep him in a good mood as Mr. Mott sat down in the chairman's seat and tapped his gavel to start the proceedings. An elderly clerk was sitting next to him. She reached over to turn on the tape recorder on the table in front of them.

"The first case we'll hear this morning is that of Mr. Thomas Ledbetter of One Bay Crest Lane in Cold Spring Harbor. Mr. Ledbetter, are you prepared to proceed?" asked Mr. Mott, as if he hadn't known Tommy since he was five years old and hadn't pinned the Eagle Scout badge on him.

"Yes, sir, I am," said Tom.

Mr. Mott invited him to take the chair in front of the table.

"Are you represented by counsel?" he asked.

"No, sir, I'm not," said Tommy.

"Mr. Ledbetter, it is my understanding that you have returned your draft card to our office along with this letter that I have in my hand. Will you please examine the letter and confirm that you sent it to the board?"

The clerk took it from Mr. Mott and carried it over to the chair. Tommy briefly looked it over.

"Yes, sir, I sent this letter," he said.

"Then I will now enter it into the record that will accompany the transcript of this hearing. I cannot speak for other members of this board, but I would like to ask you this. Considering your opposition to the war in Southeast Asia, which you have so eloquently expressed in your communication to us and through your religious beliefs, I would like to ask if you wish to apply for status as a conscientious objector."

He was lobbing up the fat pitch. It was as close as anyone could come to an engraved invitation to sit out the war.

"There are many young Americans who deserve that status and who are being denied it by law," Tommy replied, his voice steady.

"That may be true," said Mr. Mott, "but at this hearing we cannot be interested in anyone else except you."

"I understand, sir."

"I appreciate your concern for the other young men who oppose this conflict on religious grounds," said Mr. Mott. "However, I'm pursuing the strong possibility that you are entitled to conscientious objector status."

His face took on a slightly pained expression as he again offered Tommy the out.

"I've considered that option," said Tommy, looking at each board member in turn. "But I want the board to know that I am not seeking this status, nor will I accept it."

Mr. Mott had gotten the message. He gave a brief glance toward my mother, who was sitting in the last row, and said, "Mr. Ledbetter, in spite of your views, this panel must make its judgment under the laws as we know them to be, not as you would like them to be. Do you have any further comments to add for the record?"

"No, sir."

"Very well," concluded Mr. Mott. "The board will take your case under advisement. This hearing is adjourned."

Outside, we all gathered in the parking lot. Kate embraced him.

"What happens now?" asked my mother.

"I'll be hearing from the U.S. attorney's office pretty soon," said Tommy. "They have to indict me."

That evening, Tommy told us he wasn't going back to Cornell to finish the spring term. There were too many more important things he needed to do, he said, before the warrant was issued for his arrest.

"And when will that happen?" my mother asked, her voice an octave higher than usual.

"Based on what I've been told, it could be a few weeks or as long as several months," he said.

Rod Carpenter had already found him a job at a church-based antiwar organization in Washington, and Tommy was to become the full-time assistant to its director, helping churches to organize local demonstrations throughout the Northeast.

Tommy looked at me and said, "Maybe by the time you finish Officer Candidate School, there won't be any reason to send you to Vietnam."

"Yeah," I said, knowing that there wasn't a prayer of a chance.

"What are your plans?" I asked, turning to Kate.

"Tom and I agreed that I should finish up this term and then I'll join him in Washington."

From the way she said it, I was willing to bet she had wanted to quit school too and he had talked her out of it. I politely offered to drive her back to Ithaca, and she politely replied that she had already arranged a ride back with a friend of hers in the city. It was all very polite.

SIXTEEN

In late April I was notified by official letter that thanks to my grade of F in Professor LaFrance's history course, I would be two credits shy of the number I needed to graduate, and would not be allowed to participate in the graduation ceremony. If I didn't graduate, I wouldn't be able to become a naval officer or join the swift boat program after being commissioned. My class at Naval Officer Candidate School in Newport was scheduled to begin a few days after graduation.

The situation looked hopeless. I made an appointment to see Professor LaFrance at his office on the third floor of Sibley Hall. Although he seemed to take no pleasure in my failure, he was adamant that my "work" had not earned a passing grade. I sensed that any attempt to humiliate myself by begging him would only produce the same result and I didn't try.

Next, I went to see my faculty adviser, Professor Dong. He was a visiting scholar from National Taiwan University and a leading advocate for international human rights. I had originally chosen him as my adviser because he was a recent arrival to the Cornell government department and spoke very little English. I assumed correctly that he would never bother to raise a challenge to some of my unusual course selections.

Our conversation about my problem was frustrating. He didn't appear to remember who I was or that I was one of his advisees. At one point he brought in a Chinese graduate student to assist us. When I explained my problem in English, she posed the issue to Professor Dong in Chinese. He consulted a folder and pronounced in Chinese that only the chairman of the government department had the authority to issue a waiver on credit hours, and only under extraordinary circumstances. The Chinese girl translated his answer for me.

This was definitely an extraordinary circumstance, at least from my point of view, but it led to an even bigger problem because the chairman of the department was Professor Karl Wagner. I had as much chance of getting in to see him as I would the Beatles.

In the years since my arrival on campus, Karl Wagner had become a meteoric star in foreign policy circles and was now an adviser to the National Security Council. A week still doesn't go by when he isn't being interviewed on the evening news looking like Kirk Douglas, with his Brylcreemed hair combed straight back from his forehead, the dimple in his chin, and the trademark speckled bow tie.

I took his comparative government course freshman year and it was one of the few times I toed the line from start to finish. He has that kind of take-no-prisoners personality. By my senior year, his schedule was so packed that he taught courses only on Monday and Tuesday. He spent the rest of the week in Washington, assuring LBJ that saturation bombing would bring the North Vietnamese to their knees. When it comes to Vietnam he is a fully committed hawk.

With time running out, I called several times to ask for an appointment and was always rebuffed. Possibly at the end of the semester, I was told. I decided to take matters into my own hands. There was nothing to lose. His office was on the top floor of Goldwin Smith Hall. On the afternoon I went to see him, there was another protest demonstration against the war going on, this one closing down Goldwin Smith. Maybe a hundred protesters were massed around the statue of Andrew Dickson White in front of the building. One of them was sitting on his lap as a student protest leader harangued the rest about shutting down the university.

I caught the reek of marijuana as I approached the crowd on my way to Goldwin Smith. I noticed that the hair on the male protesters seemed to be getting longer by the week, and was now accompanied by desperado mustaches and scraggly beards. Seeing that the front doors of the building were chained shut in the now familiar manner, I walked along the promenade toward Lincoln Hall. One of the basement windows was cracked open, and I dropped over the transom to get inside. When I finally reached Professor Wagner's office on the top floor, his secretary was on the phone in his outer office. She motioned for me to wait.

"I'm calling to confirm his flight reservations on Mohawk from Ithaca to Washington . . . first class," she said into the phone. "That's right, Wagner."

She cupped her hand over the phone.

"Can I help you?"

"My name is Richard Ledbetter. I'm hoping to see Professor Wagner."

"That won't be possible," she said. "He's leaving in ten minutes."

"It's very important," I said, giving her the Redford grin as she waited for confirmation.

My eyes were drawn to the wall of photographs behind her desk. Wagner with JFK and Jackie in a White House receiving line, Wagner with McGeorge Bundy wearing tennis whites, Wagner and General Maxwell Taylor conferring over maps on a conference table, Wagner with LBJ in the Oval Office.

"You may have to hold the flight for a few minutes," she said into the phone. "He's running a bit late."

The secretary continued looking up at me as she waited for the response. She was probably in her forties and a very attractive redhead. I could tell she liked me. I know it sounds conceited but it's true. Hanging up the phone, she smiled and said, "I'll see if he might have a minute to see you."

She opened the door to the inner office, went in, and closed it behind her. She was back thirty seconds later.

"One minute," she said with another smile as I went inside the inner sanctum.

He was sitting behind a heavily carved mahogany library table. A purple and gold Chinese rug covered most of the hardwood floor. There were floor-to-ceiling bookcases crammed with leather-bound books. Life-size busts of Lafayette and Washington stood on marble pedestals in the corners of the room.

"Are those jackoffs still holding the building?" he asked without looking up at me. A stack of essays lay on the table and he was scanning the words at the rate of about three seconds a page.

"Yes, sir," I replied.

He finished reading the essay, scrawled a grade on the last page, and looked up at me.

"What's your problem? Cynthia said it was important."

"I need a waiver of two credit hours in order to graduate with my class."

He was on to the next essay.

"A waiver is only issued under extraordinary circumstances, Mr. . . . what is your name again?"

"Richard Ledbetter."

"Ledbetter," he repeated as he graded the next paper. "Not our tennis phenom who is supposed to be the next Tony Trabert."

"Uh . . . yes, sir."

He punched his intercom.

"Cynthia, bring me the academic record on Richard Ledbetter."

I silently groaned and continued to stand there while he knocked off the papers at a rate of about thirty seconds apiece. I had forgotten that since I was a government major, they would have a copy of my academic record on file. Two minutes later, she came in with my folder and put it on his desk. He looked at the first page through his half-moon reading glasses.

I heard the blast of a bullhorn followed by a raucous cheer.

"We're going to put the fear of God in those people very shortly," he said without looking up from my folder. "What is Introductory Apiculture 201?"

"Sir?"

"Apiculture 201. You're taking it this semester for four credits, it says here."

"Sir, that's an applied science course I'm taking in the Agriculture School."

"I can see that for myself, dammit. What the hell is it?"

"It's about the . . . uh . . . world of bees. We work right there in the hives, harvesting the honey and . . ."

"You're a government major, Ledbetter? In my department?"

"Yes, sir. Very much so, sir."

"Professor Dong advised you to take this beekeeping course?"

"Sir, we agreed it could provide me with a broadening experience."

"Dong used the word 'broadening'?"

"Well, not exactly, sir."

He began chuckling at me contemptuously as he continued to look over my academic record.

"Ledbetter, I've seen students squander four years of college, but never before on your scale. You've really worked at it. I'm impressed."

"All those courses . . ."

"Save it for your parents. Get out of here."

I watched him scrawl a large "F" on someone's paper.

"Sir, if I graduate, I'm going into the navy as a line officer. I've been accepted for the swift boat program as soon as I complete Officer Candidate School."

He paused in speed-reading the next paper and looked up at me again.

"If you're being honest with me—which I very much doubt—I'll see what I can do for you. We need Cornell men over there to set an example."

"Yes, sir," I agreed as I headed for the door.

"I want to see your acceptance papers before I do a damn thing."

"They'll be on Cynthia's desk in twenty minutes," I said, closing the door behind me.

She was standing in the outer office with his luggage.

"Was he able to help?" she asked.

I nodded and thanked her for getting me in to see him.

He was as good as his word.

. . .

The remaining days before graduation went racing by. There were pre-graduation parties almost every night, but I didn't go to any and I wasn't dating anyone. My thoughts were with Kate Kurshan. I called her several times at her rooming house, but she never responded to the messages I left with her housemates. By then I knew better than to try to see her without an invitation. I spent a lot of time packing up or selling four years' worth of accumulated junk and furniture. My plan was to drive straight to Newport after graduation weekend.

On June 5, the Six-Day War began in the Middle East. In the days that followed, I was riveted by each breaking story as Israel first defeated King Hussein's Arab Legion and then captured East Jerusalem on the seventh. Two days later, the Israeli army in the Sinai destroyed the massive Egyptian armored forces and reached the Suez Canal. It was truly a strategic miracle, and their feat of arms thrilled most of the world, including me.

Of slightly less importance was my graduation a day or two after the Arab forces quit on the eleventh. As proof, I received an impressive piece of sheepskin that declared I was a bachelor of arts "with all the rights, privileges, and honors pertaining thereto."

. . .

The morning of June 12 dawned hot and humid. The graduation ceremony was held in Barton Hall, the field house in the middle of the campus, with the thousands of graduates sitting in folding chairs, and our families and guests crammed in the bleacher seats that ringed the massive room, the roof held aloft by steel beams.

I had spent many happy hours in Barton Hall over my four years at Cornell. I had seen Eric Burdon and the Animals perform there, the best concert I have been to in my life. In 1965 I watched Blaine Aston drop a seventeen-foot jumper with just three seconds left to beat Bill Bradley and the Princeton basketball team, 70–69. We carried him off on our shoulders.

I didn't expect graduation to be as much fun as that, but I had looked forward to it. After receiving my cap and gown, I tried them both on. They fit me fine, but when I glanced into the mirror before leaving to join the procession over to Barton Hall, I felt a vague uneasiness. It only got stronger when I joined my fellow graduates from the College of Arts and Sciences in our corner of the arts quad. You could see actual joy in their faces, all the hard work yielding the final triumph before they set off on their careers.

I wasn't part of their world. I had lived in a kind of parallel universe, a member of the Cornell community but not part of it. I was frankly feeling embarrassed to be there. It might have helped if I could have walked the processional with Pete Demetropolis, but he was graduating with a horticulture degree from the Ag School and they were assembling up there.

It wasn't like I had to perform for anybody. No one had come to see me graduate. Travis was broke and searching for another place to live. My mother was in Europe with a couple of her old sorority sisters. Tommy was working in Washington. The rest of the family wasn't talking to me.

The procession line slowly wound its way around campus until we approached Barton Hall. Family members along the route would shout out to their children, and they would step out of line to take photographs. I didn't recognize a single person in the procession. The whole thing began to feel like a gigantic fraud.

When we came through the big entrance doors on the west side of Barton, I remained part of the procession until we reached the top of the stairs that led up to the main floor. There was a side corridor off to my left that led to the army ROTC offices. I stepped out of the procession line and walked down the empty corridor.

Barton Hall had originally been a training center for the hundreds of Cornell men who had joined the Army Expeditionary Forces in World War I. Grandpa Sprague had trained there before heading over to France. It had been a ROTC training center ever since. I found echoes of the past in a glass case that was bolted to the painted brick wall at the end of the corridor. Behind the glass was a faded black-and-white photograph of a young man wearing boxing gloves, boxing trunks, and a Cornell T-shirt. Beneath it were the words:

Lt. Col. Matt Urban
Cornell '41 (BA History)
Boxing, Track and Field
U.S Army (WWII)
Congressional Medal of Honor
Silver Star (2)
Bronze Star (3)
Purple Heart (7)

Someone with a red marking pen had scrawled the words *"STOP ROTC"* over Colonel Urban's face. The artist had added some red teardrops that were supposed to signify dripping blood beneath the scrawled letters.

As the long procession line continued to snake its way past the side corridor to the seating area inside, I took off my cap and gown and left them by the glass case. Walking back down the corridor, I watched as the procession finally came to an end.

It had to be eighty degrees in there by then, and I was glad to be down to my polo shirt and shorts. I watched the ceremony from the entrance to the hall. At its conclusion, the thousands of delirious new graduates sent up a thunderous cheer and hundreds of them tossed their caps high into the air.

I headed back down the main staircase and outside, past the big white tents set up for the celebration parties. I walked over to the Royal Palm in Collegetown. The bar was completely empty aside from me and the bartender, who was setting up for the crowd to come.

I ordered a vodka and tonic and went over to the jukebox. There was very little I wanted to hear. I finally found Procol Harum's "Whiter Shade of Pale" between Bobby Vinton's "Please Love Me Forever" and "Snoopy vs. the Red Baron." I pumped in four quarters and it played four times.

I was still there when the Palm shut down at four the next morning.

SEVENTEEN

I began my naval career in Newport, Rhode Island. It came to an end in the same place. It started at Officer Candidate School and ended a quarter mile away at the Newport Naval Hospital.

A couple of lifetimes happened in between.

I reported on a cool, cloudless, sunny morning. As I surveyed the license plates in the visitors' parking lot, it was clear that my fellow officer candidates came from all over the country and that most of us drove the same kinds of cars. Everywhere I looked, there were Triumphs, Jaguars, Corvettes, MGs, Healeys, and Mustangs. I was pulling my bag out of the trunk when a petty officer in starched khakis approached me and asked for my name.

"Richard Ledbetter," I said, not sure whether to come to attention as he flipped through the pages of names on his clipboard.

"Ledbetter. You're in Kilo Company," he said. "Over there."

He pointed to a crowd of several hundred young men forming up on the parade ground next to the parking lot. They were clustered in small groups next to company flags staked into the ground at twenty-foot intervals. Arriving at the flag marked with the letter K, I felt totally relaxed, ready for the training that would prepare me for the test of war. A young officer with a lieutenant's bars strode up to our group.

"Gentlemen, I'm Lieutenant Shields. I want you to form up in ranks, the first line of four beginning right here."

Listening to the chatter as we assembled, I heard regional accents from all over the country, but we were die cast from the same mold. For one thing, we were all white. Most of us had been cradled from the family to the college fraternity and from there to the coziness of Alpha Company, or Bravo, or Tango, or Delta. The only black face I saw on the parade ground belonged to an enlisted man in fatigues who was policing the area for cigarette butts.

A navy captain in dress whites emerged from the mass of men now assembled on the parade ground. Several officers followed in his wake. Reaching the center of the line, he squared around to face us, glancing up and down the ranks for a few seconds.

"I am Captain Joe Johnston," he called out in a voice that needed no bullhorn, "and I want to welcome you to the United States Navy Officer Candidate School. All of you stand at the beginning of a rigorous challenge. The navy has a fine tradition of service, and your role as future officers will help keep it so. For each one of you accepted here, more than three hundred were rejected. You can be justifiably proud."

"Yah, boy!" someone bellowed exuberantly farther down the line.

The company officers glared sternly down the ranks.

"The importance of your service as a naval officer has never been greater or more urgent," went on Captain Johnston. "We as a nation and a free people are engaged in a grave struggle that challenges the free world. Our adversary is communism, gentlemen, an atheistic form of dictatorship that is bent on world domination. Only we in the military services stand in the way of its growing empire. As the communists work toward this goal, their stock-in-trade ranges from pious protests for peace to guerrilla warfare against our allies in Vietnam. You are now taking your place in the forefront of the effort to make our nation safe from this threat. May your seas be calm, your storms brief, your battles victorious, and your accomplishments grand."

Pivoting to his right, he strode quickly back down the front of the line. As soon as he was gone, Lieutenant Shields herded us toward a modern brick building at the far end of the parade ground. It was six stories high and looked like a new Holiday Inn. A sign over the front entrance read NIMITZ HALL. We took an elevator up to the sixth floor.

"This will be your home until the day you are commissioned," said Lieutenant Shields as we clustered around him in the corridor.

He glanced at his watch.

"Along with Chief Petty Officer Hatcher, I will serve as your military instructor and your counselor in the event that life for you here becomes a trial. I will teach you how to salute, how to wear your uniform, how to render honors, and the other things you'll need to know as a commissioned officer. Right now, I only want to find out if you can successfully locate your room. To help you in this quest, we have put three-by-five cards on the doors of your assigned billets. Take thirty minutes to meet your new roommate. At oh nine fifty, I want everyone back here in a straight line organized in alphabetical order. Dismissed."

The rooms along the corridor were about twelve by fifteen feet, with two closets, two bureaus, two desks, two desk chairs, and two beds. A stocky guy with sandy hair and an easy smile was sitting on one of the beds when I found the door with my name on it. He got up and stretched out his hand.

"Garland Gentry," he said, the words coming out like pancake syrup.

"Rick Ledbetter," I replied, shaking his hand.

Garland said he was from Natchez, Mississippi, and had just graduated from Ole Miss with a degree in mechanical engineering. Six feet tall, he had kind of naïve blue eyes and a cherub's face. The eyes were deceptive. I soon discovered he was good at whatever he did.

Our first day was spent outfitting ourselves at the supply depot with uniforms and other gear, including insignia, brass buckles, shoes, handkerchiefs, T-shirts, undershorts, and caps. We were then issued textbooks on navigation, seamanship, engineering, and weapons systems.

By supper we were wearing khaki shirts and pants, and our hair was the same depth as a putting green. Chief Hatcher marched us in a ragged double column over to the dining hall, which looked like a franchise steak house.

"Hell, they've even got a salad bar," said one of the guys.

"I can't wait to get my girl up here," said another.

A sweating enlisted man in a white chef's hat was grilling sirloin steaks to order behind the counter. On the steam table, there were bins of mashed potatoes, asparagus tips, and corn on the cob. Another enlisted man was serving pie à la mode for dessert. During the meal, a petty officer came over to the table and asked us if everything had been prepared to our satisfaction. We assured him that he was running a tight ship.

Given all the war movies I had seen about basic training, the whole thing seemed pretty strange. I wasn't expecting to be frog-marched through ten miles of swamps, but it was clear they were making a determined effort to keep us happy, and I wondered why.

Garland and I spent that first evening learning how to polish our shoes. I tried to convince him that there was no point in polishing them since they were already the shiniest shoes I'd ever seen. He assured me that we were expected to do better. As we buffed away at them, Garland told me that he had married his sweetheart, Janet, at the end of his junior year at Ole Miss. As soon as his three-year hitch in the navy was over, he planned to join the family cotton brokerage, just like his father and grandfather before him. His life plan included a lot of children.

He asked me what I was going to do after the navy, and I realized that I hadn't given the matter any thought. I had no other goals aside from going to war. That was the moment when one of the officer candidates in the room across the hall leaned in from the hallway. Short but heavily muscled, he was wearing a white towel cinched at the waist and plastic shower slippers. His upper body and legs were covered with a thick pelt of curly black hair.

"Chad Montgomery," he said, his slow drawl similar to Garland's. "At dinner I thought I heard the voice of our All-American running back at Ole Miss. Your touchdown run against Auburn was just beautiful."

Garland nodded, not getting up from his chair.

"Yeah—the only thing I don't miss about Mississippi is what I like most about this outfit."

"What's that?" said Garland, tight-lipped.

"No nigguhs," he came back with the same wide grin. "You know what I'm talkin' about."

Garland put his shoe brush on the table and stood up.

"Yeah, I do," he said, slowly heading toward him. "And just so we understand each other, from now on every time I hear you say that word, I'm going to knock you flat on your ass. You know what ah'm talkin' about?"

The last line was perfectly mimicked. I could feel the hairs pricking up on the back of my neck. It was my first day at OCS and I was probably going to be in a fight.

"What's your problem, buddy?" said Montgomery, the grin gone.

Garland stopped a few inches away from him.

"I guess that's why this country has had to fight all its wars," he said. "So assholes like you have the freedom to say what you please. Now—you want to say that word again?" asked my new roommate.

Montgomery was staring up at him with a look of stunned confusion. Shaking his head, he turned around, crossed the hall, and shut the door behind him. Garland came back and sat down. Picking up his wallet, he opened it to the plastic photograph folder.

"This is my wife, Janet," he said.

The girl was wearing a white cotillion dress. She was strikingly beautiful, with almond-shaped eyes, a narrow sculpted face. Her skin was a rich mocha.

"Well, you're full of surprises," I said.

"Yeah," he said, staring at the picture before closing the wallet and putting it back on the desk. "We had to get married in Maryland. It's still a secret."

"Why?"

"It was illegal for us to get married in Mississippi."

"You've got to be kidding. This is 1967 not 1867."

"In some ways," he said.

I suddenly heard footsteps running down the hall.

"Hey, everybody," someone shouted. "Check out what's happening on the drill field."

Garland and I looked out the window. The parade ground was still lit up from evening drill, and a man was running across it toward the far end. He was being chased by two military policemen, but they were too far behind to catch him. As we watched, he disappeared into the darkness.

"What is that all about?" asked Garland.

My eyes were drawn to a big cardboard sign that was now taped over the brick-lined entrance to the drill field. It hadn't been there when we walked back from dinner. Under the drawing of a red-painted clenched fist, the words on it read POWER TO THE PEOPLE.

I guess we weren't viewed as part of the people.

EIGHTEEN

It was still pitch-black outside our window when the door to the room swung open and a hulking figure filled the doorway. A moment later, the ceiling light was turned on by Chief Petty Officer Hatcher.

"Reveille," he said.

He sounded almost apologetic. Garland and I followed him into the hallway to see the rest of the company forming outside their rooms, wearing our newly issued white T-shirts and boxer shorts. Lieutenant Shields was standing at the head of the corridor.

"Okay, gentlemen, just a few words about exercise," he said. "You wouldn't be here if you weren't in shape, and the navy leaves it up to its officers to get the exercise they need. In the next few days, we'll be setting up intra-company touch football and basketball teams. There's also tennis, boxing, and the swimming pool."

"Jesus, this is fantastic," I heard someone whisper.

"The navy doesn't plan for you men to be humping through the boonies with a seventy-five-pound pack," he went on. "That's for the pecker heads in the army and marines."

We laughed.

"Being a naval officer means three things. Number one—the best women. Number two—the best food. Number three—the best women."

We all cheered.

"Okay. Shave, shower, and let's go to breakfast," he said.

At breakfast I polished off two orders of blueberry pancakes with bacon and sausage patties. Then it was on to the battalion morning formation. After thirty minutes of close order drill, the American flag was hauled up on the drill field at precisely 0800.

The first class was communications, in which we were expected to learn the phonetic alphabet from alpha through zulu, then the sixty-eight signal flags commonly used by ships at sea. Garland and I used flash cards to quiz each other until we had it all down.

Then there was the navigation class.

"You'll find that navigation can be a difficult challenge," said the officer in charge of the course.

He had just spent an hour explaining how to use a sextant, and Garland still had no idea what to do with it. "For most of you, the day will come when navigation is suddenly the easiest thing in the world."

Garland wasn't so sure, but it came easily to me, maybe because I had grown up on the water and handled boats from the time I was eight years old. Over the years I had sailed all over the Northeast from Long Island Sound to Maine.

After lunch, we had a course in seamanship. It was taught by a short redheaded petty officer with six red hash marks on the sleeve of his uniform blouse. He didn't take any chances when it came to our ability to absorb the fundamentals. The first thing he did was to write his name in block letters on the blackboard behind him. Then he picked up a three-foot-long pointer from his desk.

"My name is Dinorvic," he said. "The first thing you should know is that I ain't trying to be no infant ensign. I'm just here to teach you basic seamanship."

Picking up an empty pickle jar from the floor, he hocked a big glob of brown tobacco spit in it.

"The smallest naval vessel in the entire fleet is the naval punt," he said, using his pointer to spear the big photograph of a dinghy on the wall behind him. "The naval punt is a twelve-foot double-square-ended craft that is used while painting the sides of larger naval vessels. Do you know who rides the naval punt?"

No one said a word as he hiked up his pants and spit into the jar again.

"Do ya think an ensign rides the punt?"

"Noooo!" I found myself saying with most of the others.

"Very good," said Dinorvic.

He then pointed to the red hash marks on his sleeve.

"Do you think a bosun's mate rides the punt?"

"Noooo!" we echoed back.

"No," agreed Dinorvic, using his pointer to tap another picture that was taped to the blackboard. It showed a young enlisted sailor. "This fellow right here rides the naval punt. The seaman apprentice."

He hiked up his trousers again. "Now, there's always one or two of ya that won't listen to Dinorvic. And when they kick your ass out of here 'cause you won't learn seamanship or navigation, ya know where ya gonna end up?"

We sat there waiting for the obvious answer.

"That's right. You'll be riding the naval punt," he said. "And when yer down there chipping the paint off those steel plates with your naval utensil until your fingers look like hamburger, you'll wish you'd listened to yer old chief. And when they flush the scuppers and that slimy shit lands on your head, you'll kick yourself for not paying more attention to all the things I'm here to teach you."

He definitely had our attention.

Once a week we had to complete an obstacle course that consisted of a broad jump, sand trap, tire maze, scaling wall, and rope climb. Aside from that, Kilo Company competed against the other companies in basketball, water polo, volleyball, softball, and touch football. In some ways, it was like a summer camp for new college graduates. Being a good athlete, I had no problems with any of the physical aspects of our training.

My third week into OCS, I found out why we were being treated like junior congressmen. Garland and I were sitting in the bar at the Hotel Viking in Newport after receiving a pass, when I saw John Dusenberry come in. He was no longer wearing his OCS uniform. John had been a member of Kilo Company, but in the section that arrived a month before we did. A strapping ex-tackle from Penn State, he loved to play jazz trombone. The only reason it didn't drive the rest of us crazy was that he was so damn good. It was like having Tommy Dorsey in the dorm.

One morning he disappeared, and no one seemed to know where he had gone. A week later, two more guys vanished. One of them was from our own section. Lieutenant Shields acted like the guy had never been there. We walked over to John's table and asked him what had happened.

"I got out."

"Why?" asked Garland.

"I don't know. I'm not against the war or anything, but when I applied for OCS, the recruiter told me I could go right into the navy band after I was commissioned. They play at Arlington for the president. The son of a bitch lied to me. After I got here, I found out they don't allow officers to play in the band. That's when I decided to get out."

"What are they going to do to you?" asked Garland.

"Nothing," he said with a grin. "Not after I came up with my plan."

"What plan?" I asked.

"It was a plan to end the war. After writing it up, I sent it to President Johnson, the Joint Chiefs of Staff, and every member of Congress from Pennsylvania. I gave my return address here at OCS."

"What was the plan?" I asked.

"I proposed a law where one quarter of the House of Representatives and one quarter of the U.S. Senate would always be on combat duty on the front lines in Vietnam on a rotating basis with ninety-day tours of duty. There would be no exception, and any member who didn't feel qualified would have to resign from office."

He flashed us another grin.

"So then what happened?"

"A week later they moved me out of OCS. The secretary of the navy ordered me separated from the service."

"Jesus," Garland and I said in unison.

It wasn't just John Dusenberry. Guys were quitting all over the place, and the navy obviously didn't know what to do to stop the hemorrhaging. A few weeks later, they started making examples of them.

The quitters were forced to work around the OCS complex wearing khaki jackets that had the letters D.E. stamped on the back. The letters stood for DISENROLLEE. We would look out our windows and there they would be, emptying a Dumpster or riding around in the back of an open pickup in the rain.

In some ways we were cut off from the outside world. There was no television lounge and no newspaper stand. We were discouraged from reading newspapers or watching the television news. It was only by accident that I picked up an old copy of the *New York Times* at the dining hall and learned that the boxer Muhammad Ali had been sentenced to five years in federal prison for avoiding the draft.

Out of boredom I decided to organize a company poker game. After lights out, Garland and I would erect a blackout curtain. Talking was kept to a minimum. The one common denominator was that most of the guys couldn't wait to shovel their money into the pot. They chased their hands like greyhounds running after a rabbit.

Some guys seemed to view poker as a test of their masculinity. A few gave themselves a nickname. Fast Bobby. Cool Hand Fred. There was no point in trying to bluff them out. In retrospect, the principal attraction of the game was that many of us realized we would soon be going overseas. Beyond that, we were each earning one hundred and forty-five dollars a month and there was nothing to spend it on.

I can still see their faces in the darkened glow of that dorm room, sweet-natured guys fondling their hands while silently praying to whatever deity looks down on card games. Their open expressions so obviously saying, "Just this once. Oh, please, fill me just this once."

NINETEEN

After two months, I had one of the better cumulative scores in the battalion and hadn't cheated to get there. I realized it was probably the first time I ever really applied myself, and it felt good. I had also become a marksman with a .45 Colt pistol and, being a good swimmer, qualified at water survival in a submersion tank as big as a farm silo.

In August I was ordered to undertake an additional training course in Melville, Rhode Island, in order to qualify for the swift boat program. By then, Garland had decided to change his status as an undesignated line officer to join me.

"I decided you bear watching out for, Ricky," he said in that slow Mississippi drawl.

A petty officer instructor named Hurd began the process of introducing us to the vessel we would eventually be commanding in Vietnam. The first thing he did was to run a ten-minute silent movie on a projection screen.

"Don't mind the way the picture's jerking all over," he said. "This is actual combat footage."

The first sequence showed a swift boat engaged in a firefight, its machine guns blazing toward an unseen enemy. The boat wheeled around in a tight turn and began streaking toward the camera.

The petty officer approached the screen with a long pointer.

"When you take command of a PCF Mark Three swift boat, you become the most dangerous animal on the river," he said, raising the pointer to the screen.

"Your armament consists of this mortar, three fifty-caliber machine guns here, here, and here, and a forty-millimeter grenade launcher here."

I imagined a young Jack Kennedy sitting in this same classroom in 1943, getting his first introduction to the PT boat. On the screen, a

Vietnamese junk was chugging along a river with what appeared to be a group of people wearing cone-shaped hats aboard.

"This is not the *Nina*, the *Pinta*, or the *Santa Maria*," said the instructor. "It's a well-camouflaged Vietcong gunboat. You make a mistake with this guy and Charlie'll give you a real hosing."

One morning we were driven over to some dock facilities at the edge of Narragansett Bay. The sky was dark with a steady rain. After being given slickers, we were met on the dock by Lieutenant Commander Shane Connell, who had recently commanded a swift boat flotilla in Vietnam and was now a senior instructor in the training program.

A Mark III swift boat was tethered to the jetty beyond him. He welcomed us and we all filed aboard. After introducing the crew and conducting us on a brief tour belowdecks, Commander Connell fired up the engines and we headed out into the bay. The instructional course was about two miles long, with a lot of twists and turns between marker buoys that were arranged like the poles in a slalom ski race. The first time through the course, Commander Connell concentrated on showing us how fast he could thrash the boat along while the rest of us held on for dear life. Its maneuverability was astounding.

When we returned to the start of the course, he spent several minutes telling us about a gun battle in which one of his flotilla's boats had been sunk by enemy fire from a fortified redoubt along the My Tho River. Pointing to a target float that was anchored about a half mile down the instructional course, he told us that his crew would now demonstrate the effectiveness of an 81 millimeter mortar to help suppress such an attack by harassing the enemy's position. To actually hit the target from a moving boat would be a lucky bonus, he said.

The mortar tube on the fantail of the boat was a four-foot-long cylinder about as big around as a drainpipe and bolted to a revolving steel turret. Mounted on the same turret was a .50 caliber machine gun. Standing at attention in front of the weapon was a young enlisted man wearing a combat helmet over his rain gear. An open crate of mortar rounds lay on the deck beside him. The mortar projectiles had metal fins at the base and looked like miniature versions of a Jules Verne rocket ship.

"Unlike mortars used by the army," said Connell, "naval mortars aren't launched by dropping a round down the muzzle of the tube. They are inserted the same way, but the naval gunner controls the actual firing with a trigger."

He spent five minutes showing us the basic operation of the elevation gauge and direction finder before going over the loading and firing procedures using the trigger mechanism. The rain began coming harder as we slowly cruised toward the target.

Garland and I were standing together on the starboard side of the boat, holding on to the steel cable railing that ran along the edge of the deck. As the boat picked up speed, the small American flag mounted on the fiberglass mast above our heads began to snap in the wind.

"Already feels like Mississippi winter up here," said Garland with an involuntary shudder.

We were still quite a long way from the target when Commander Connell turned from the wheel and looked back toward the stern.

"You may load and fire, Mr. Rodney," he called out over the roar of the engines.

With practiced motions, the enlisted man made quick adjustments to the elevation gauge and direction finder on the swiveling turret. He stooped to pick up a mortar round using both hands and slid it base first into the end of the tube. A moment later he squeezed the trigger. There was a loud *crump* and the projectile was on its way. I turned to look at the distant target float and was astonished when the round exploded within twenty feet of it.

"I believe we can do better than that, Mr. Rodney," called out Connell, swinging the wheel hard to port.

"Aye, aye, sir," said the enlisted man.

As we came around for another run at the target, Seaman Rodney adjusted his gauges, deftly inserted another round into the barrel, and squeezed the trigger mechanism again. Instead of a loud *crump,* however, there was an odd-sounding kind of gasp and the mortar round came floating out of the mortar tube as if in slow motion. Rising no more than four feet in the air, it fell straight back as dead weight, striking the edge of the cable railing a few feet away from us and toppling sideways onto the deck.

I didn't think about what I did next. If I had, I probably wouldn't have done it. I reached down and picked up the mortar round with my right hand. It was heavier than I thought, and the casing was so hot that

I had to shift part of its weight to my left hand as I hustled toward the stern. Reaching the transom, I hurled it as far as I could away from the boat. It disappeared into the foaming wake. When I turned back toward the bridge, Commander Connell was angry.

"Real dumb, Ledbetter!" he shouted. "Those mortar shells can't explode until they reach their maximum speed, and even then . . ."

There was a loud explosion behind us. An eruption of turbulent water jumped fifteen feet into the air. Stopping the engines, Commander Connell rushed back to the stern. Grabbing my wrists, he turned my hands palm up. Although I wasn't feeling any pain yet, the fingers of my right hand were already swelling up like overstuffed sausages.

"Fill a bucket with ice from the galley," he ordered Rodney before turning back to me. "We'll get you over to the base hospital right away."

Resuming his place on the bridge, he gunned the engines and swung the boat around in a tight turn. The swift boat handled so beautifully that in spite of my injury, I couldn't wait to get my hands on the controls of one myself. In the meantime, I immersed my fingers in the bucket of ice water. We were nearly back to the base when Connell came over again to see how I was doing.

"Look," he said. "There's a firing device in those things that prevents each round from exploding until it has achieved a certain rate of speed. That's the way they are designed so they can't explode prematurely."

He was obviously feeling lousy about the whole thing.

"Just bad luck," I said.

"Maybe the casing was cracked," he suggested.

"Yes, sir," I said, as he began shaking his head.

When we reached the hospital, the doctor used a freezing spray to dull the pain in the nerve endings of my fingers. He promised that as soon as the swelling went down, the burns would heal very quickly. In the meantime, I was relieved of all duty that required the use of my hands.

That was really frustrating for me. For the first time in my life I was doing something as part of a team, and I was doing it well. My biggest concern was that the injury would prevent my graduating with the rest of my company.

Garland and I were back in our room and preparing for bed when I happened to look up and saw him gazing at me.

"Ricky, they should give you a medal for what you did on that boat. You may have saved our lives out there."

"You don't get a medal for a training exercise," I said, although his words gave me a jolt of genuine pride.

"Yeah . . . I guess you're right. And if I've learned one thing up here, it's that the navy doesn't like to advertise its screwups."

He gave me another long look with those lazy blue eyes.

"It's a good thing I'm going with you. As I said, you bear looking out for."

TWENTY

I was sitting in navigation class at Spruance Hall when Lieutenant Shields came in and motioned me to join him out in the corridor. As soon as we were alone, he told me it was urgent that I call my mother.

Using the phone in his office, I reached her at home a few minutes later. Her voice was trembling as she updated me about Tom. He had been arrested for the fourth time since joining that antiwar religious outfit in Washington. While still waiting for his federal indictment for resisting the draft, he had led a group of peace activists in a demonstration outside a munitions factory in Massachusetts, that was making napalm bombs.

My mother had received a call that morning from a deputy in the Worcester County sheriff's office who told her that Tom had gone on a hunger strike in the jail and they were no longer taking responsibility for his health. An hour later, Kate had phoned my mother to say that she wasn't being allowed to visit him and that Tom had supposedly been beaten by another prisoner. My mother stopped in mid-sentence. The silence was followed by a low, guttural moan. Then Grandpa Sprague was on the line.

"We need your help, Richard," he said.

"What can I do?" I replied.

"Could you secure emergency leave and drive to Worcester to find out whether Tom is all right?" he said. "Based on the map I'm looking at, you can't be more than two or three hours from the jail where he is being held."

"All right, I'll try," I said.

"Call us as soon as you know anything," he said before hanging up the phone.

. . .

When I told Lieutenant Shields it was a family emergency, he authorized an immediate twelve-hour pass. I was on my way thirty minutes later. Driving into Massachusetts, I tried to think through everything that had happened since Tommy had left school after Easter break.

First he had been arrested outside a Selective Service induction center in Albany for publicly advocating resistance to the draft. Two more arrests followed at other supposedly nonviolent protests. As the miles passed, I found myself increasingly angry at what he had done. Our nation was at war. It might not have seemed like it as I drove through the small New England villages with their white-painted colonials bordered by tall oaks, but men were fighting and dying halfway across the world to protect us from communist aggression.

What Tommy was doing was a betrayal of the millions of young men who were serving in the war. A lot of them didn't have any choice in the matter because they had gotten drafted. Others went because they thought it was their patriotic duty to go. If what Tommy was saying about Vietnam being an immoral war was true, then I and a lot of others must have been acting immorally in helping to fight it.

I didn't believe that to be the case. And what about the thousands of young Americans who had already died over there, I wondered. Shouldn't their lives count for something? I was sure about one thing. If we were to cut and run now, North Vietnam would win. And all those men would have died in vain.

The picturesque villages gave way to the grim industrial landscape of central Massachusetts. Arriving in Worcester, I saw that many of the downtown buildings were boarded up. A neighborhood bar stood on almost every street corner. Stopping for gas, I got directions to the jail. It turned out to be a five-story redbrick building that looked like the Massachusetts factories my great-grandfather had shut down when they were no longer profitable. I parked the Healey in a lot across the street from the jail entrance.

Before leaving Newport, I had changed into my dress blues in the hope that the uniform might lend some form of official stature to my visit. Squaring away my cap, I walked into the waiting room.

The air reeked of stale cigarette smoke and disinfectant. A reception counter on the far wall was enclosed in bulletproof glass. Three rows of scarred wooden benches sat in front of it. A kid in a Dodgers baseball cap was slumped in one of them, his eyes closed.

As I came up to the counter, an elderly black woman was talking to a uniformed officer through a metal vent in the glass. He said something to her and she slowly turned around to face me, her eyes without focus. She looked like she was about to collapse, and I helped her over to one of the benches before returning to the counter. Through the glass partition, I saw several officers seated at metal desks. They all wore tan uniforms with brown piping at the pockets and seams. The officer who had been talking to the black woman watched me approach.

"What do you want?" he said, taking in my uniform.

"My name is Richard Ledbetter and I would like to visit my brother Thomas Ledbetter, who I believe is being held here," I said.

He grinned at me.

"You mean our famous war protester?" he said.

"I don't know what he's charged with," I said.

"You'll need to get permission from Sheriff Lopata on that, and he is in a meeting right now. Take a seat," he said.

When I sat down next to the black woman on the bench, tears were flowing silently down her cheeks. Apart from the sound of typewriters clacking on the other side of the glass, it was quiet. No one else came in or out of the building. After waiting fifteen minutes, I got up to walk off my nervousness.

The kid in the Dodgers cap in the third row hadn't moved on the bench. He sat slouched over, his chin almost resting on his chest, his legs crossed in front of him. On my next circuit around the room, I thought I recognized something vaguely familiar about his face. The third time around I realized it was Kate. She had cut off her hair. Barely an inch of it extended below the back of the baseball cap. Her skin had an unhealthy pallor to it, and there was a purple bruise on the back of her right hand. I knelt down on one knee next to her.

"Kate?" I whispered.

Her eyes took me in and widened. She opened her arms to embrace me and buried the side of her face in my chest for a few moments before pulling away.

"They won't let me see him," she said. "I've waited here for two days. Because I'm not a relative, they say I have no right to see him."

"I'll get in," I said.

"Rick, I think they've hurt him. One of the other prisoners got a message out through his wife that someone had beaten him."

"What is he charged with?"

"He was arrested with eight Holy Cross students. The charge was demonstrating without a permit."

"Why are they still in here? That doesn't sound like a serious charge."

"Tom is the only one still here. The parents of the college students paid their fines and they were released."

"Why wasn't his fine paid?"

"It was. I paid it. But by then they had charged him with assaulting a fellow prisoner. Now he's facing a felony charge."

"Tommy would never assault anyone. That's ridiculous," I said.

"I know," she said, blinking back tears. "They're lying, Rick."

Her eyes took in my still swollen fingers.

"What happened to your hands?" she demanded.

"A long story," I said.

"Are you Ledbetter's brother?" asked a raspy voice behind me.

I stood up and turned around. A short thickset man wearing a tan uniform was standing at the heavy-gauge steel door next to the reception counter. He looked about fifty and had an iron-gray crew cut.

"Yes," I said.

"You got identification?"

I showed him my military ID card. He scanned it for a moment and gave it back to me.

"I'm Sheriff Lopata," he said. "I already lost one son in Vietnam, and you can tell your goddam brother that if he wants to starve himself to death that's fine with me. He just isn't gonna do it in my jail."

A young deputy was standing behind him. He looked like a carbon copy of the sheriff, except thirty years younger. The name badge over his left breast read LOPATA too.

"Your brother's being fed right now. He'll take you back there," the sheriff said, gesturing to his son.

The deputy walked me through the steel door next to the reception counter, and I followed him down a narrow brick-walled corridor into the first cell block. The doors to the cells were solid metal with small

Plexiglas windows cut in at eye level. We went up a flight of stairs and along another brick-lined passageway. At the end of the block, the last cell door stood open. An officer was standing in the doorway with his back to us, chuckling as we came up.

"Is he cooperating?" asked Lopata as the officer turned around to face us.

"See for yourself," he said with a grin.

The cell was about eight feet square and lit by a dim bulb recessed into the concrete ceiling. Tommy was lying on his back on a thin mattress. His long legs extended several inches past the foot of the iron bedstead. Three leather belts were strapped around him, one across his torso, the other two confining his upper arms and legs.

They had inserted a plastic tube down his throat and fastened it in place over his mouth with a wad of duct tape. Some sort of liquid was being fed to him from a plastic bottle suspended above the bed on a metal stand.

"He's just finished our blue plate special," said the other officer without looking up.

Tearing the tape away from Tommy's mouth, he extracted the tube from his throat and removed the leather straps. I stood back as they wheeled their equipment out of the cell. Deputy Lopata lingered at the open cell door, the hint of a smile on his face.

"Are we allowed any privacy?" I asked.

"You got ten minutes," he replied, closing and locking the cell door behind him.

. . .

I knelt down next to the cot. Tommy's once straight nose was bent crookedly over to one side. There were bruises under both eyes. His jaw looked slightly misshapen, and a raw patch was starting to scab over on his chin. When Tommy looked up and saw me, he gave me a lopsided smile and I could see that one of his upper teeth was missing. His right hand rose slowly from the mattress and gently grasped my hand. Bringing it back down to his mouth, he kissed it.

"What have they done to you?" I asked, shocked at his condition.

He opened his mouth to say something but produced only a harsh, racking cough. When the spasms subsided, he said, "My mouth . . . very dry."

There was a tin mug on the little porcelain sink in the corner. I filled it from the water spigot. Lifting his head from the mattress, I held it to his mouth while he took several swallows.

"Thanks, Beau," he said.

"We only have a few minutes Tommy. Tell me about this assault charge."

"When . . . when the police arrested us and brought us here, I refused to walk," he said. "That made a couple of the officers mad. After we were processed and heading to our cells, Deputy Lopata forced my head down and ran me into one of the other prisoners. Another officer said, 'Why did you push that man?' and I said I didn't. Deputy Lopata said, 'Don't lie to me,' and hit me in the mouth."

My first reaction was pure anger.

"That's when I refused to cooperate," he said.

I took his hand again and held it tightly in mine. Lifting the lower edge of his undershirt, I saw more bruising around his stomach.

"I dreamed last night about that time Dad let you and me camp alone in the High Peaks of the Adirondacks," he went on, "when we hiked to the summit of Whiteface in the dark so we could be there when the sun came up."

"Yeah," I said, remembering the sun emerging golden from the mist. On the way back down, we promised each other we would climb all forty-six High Peaks together.

"Well, I was there again, Beau. It was beautiful."

"We don't have a lot of time," I said. "We need to figure out what . . ."

"At times in here . . . it gets pretty bad."

"Yeah," I said.

"And then—I know this sounds kind of strange—but I sort of feel like the lily of the fields, you know—they neither toil nor spin?"

After everything they had put him through, I wondered if he even knew what he was saying. I felt another deep surge of anger at the thought of what they were doing to him. I checked my watch.

"Listen, Tommy, as soon as I get out of here . . ."

"Did you know Mickey Schwerner?" he said then.

"Who?" I came back, confused.

"Mickey Schwerner—at Cornell," he said.

I remembered the name then. Schwerner was one of the three civil rights workers who had been murdered down in Mississippi in the summer of 1964. He had been at Cornell. I hadn't known him.

"No," I said. "I never met him."

"I did," said Tommy. "I knew all three of them down in Mississippi."

He was fourteen or fifteen when he went down there with Grandpa Sprague to become Freedom Riders. That was the summer I won the club tennis championship.

"I was in Neshoba County the night they disappeared," he said next. "A lot of us were being harassed by the police. Usually we were arrested and then let go. I called the jail to see if they were being detained there. One of the deputies told me they had been released."

I vaguely remembered the television coverage of their disappearance.

"But they were there—in that jail," said Tommy. "If I had asked to be driven there to find out for myself, they might still be alive," he said.

"You couldn't have known," I said. "Listen, Tommy . . ."

He shook his head back and forth.

"I thought he was lying when he told me they weren't there," he said. "But I didn't do anything about it."

"You did all you could," I came back. "You were only a kid."

I lifted his head again to give him a few more sips of water, desperately trying to think what I should do next.

"Hey . . . hey . . . you in there," came a voice behind me.

We were alone in the cell, and the voice gave me a start.

"Hey . . . hey," the voice repeated.

It appeared to be coming from the back of the cell. There was only a brick wall there. Stepping around the edge of the bed frame, however, I noticed a small iron grille cut into the base of the rear wall.

"Who is it?" I whispered toward the grille.

"I'm in the next cell," said the voice. "You the kid's lawyer?"

"No, his brother," I said.

"Well, you better do something goddam fast to get him out of here or that motherfucker Lopata is gonna kill him."

"The sheriff?"

"Naw—the son. He comes early in the morning when no one's around. You oughta hear what he does to your brother just for kicks . . . He's nuts. Is your brother retarded or somethin'? Why ain't he screamin' bloody murder? I keep askin' him but he don't say nothin'."

Now I understood the bruises. What I couldn't understand was why he was letting it happen. Even with the weight he had lost, Tommy still outweighed the deputy by thirty pounds. And he knew how to box from when were kids. It didn't make any sense.

"Why don't you fight back?" I demanded.

"You wouldn't understand," he said, struggling to raise himself up to a sitting position.

"What is there to understand? He hates you, and he'll keep doing this until you're dead."

"It's a test of faith," said Tommy.

"What the fuck does faith have to do with it?" I shot back.

"Matthew five thirty-nine," he said, looking up at me with feverish eyes.

"Oh, shit," I said.

I knew he had religious convictions, but how could letting himself get beaten to death be part of them? A moment later I heard the key moving in the lock of the cell door. It swung open behind me.

"It's over," said Deputy Lopata.

I leaned closer to Tommy and whispered, "Kate's outside. She's been waiting here for two days. I know how strongly you feel about your principles, but please don't do this. She loves you, Tommy."

Looking at me through his bruised eyes he said, "There's nothing she can do here, Beau."

I looked up at the deputy sheriff. He was staring down at Tommy with a hint of a smile again, and I knew he was just waiting for his next session. I was consumed by such a feeling of rage it was all I could do not to go after him right there.

Instead, I walked out of the cell. Behind me I heard Lopata lock the door and then heard the sound of his boots tapping as he came toward me. I had no idea what to do. If I turned on him, I would probably end up in the cell next to Tom for assault and battery.

We needed a good lawyer. That was the first thing.

The little deputy passed me and strutted ahead like a bantam rooster. We were walking down the first flight of iron stairs when in my mind's eye I could see him torturing Tom. I knew I couldn't let him do it again. I didn't plan what happened next. It was like I was outside myself, watching from a distance.

As we reached the bottom of the staircase, I could see there was no one in the passageway ahead of us. Grabbing the back of his shirt, I jerked him toward me. While he was off balance, I ran him into the brick wall and rode him to his knees. I got my left elbow under his chin and lodged it against his throat. He tried to reach for his pistol, but I dragged his hand away and twisted it behind his back. I had to stop myself from breaking his arm.

"Listen, you perverted little piece of shit," I said hoarsely. "I know what you're doing to my brother. And it stops now or else I'm going out there right now to tell your father what a cowardly scumbag he has for a son. If you lay one more hand on my brother, I swear I'll come back here and kill you."

Before letting him go, I hit him as hard as I could in the kidneys and he grunted in pain. As he struggled to his feet, the hatred in his eyes was almost tangible. He stared up at me. I stared back at him with no less loathing

I watched him unclip his hip holster. He was pulling the gun free when I heard footsteps coming toward us. The two guards who had force-fed Tom emerged from the gloom.

The gun was back in Lopata's holster as I walked back with the other two to the visitors' entrance. He walked behind us. I didn't turn around and I didn't stop until I was outside in the waiting room.

Five minutes later I was on the pay phone at a bar across the street, calling home. Kate was by my side, more frightened than ever for Tommy's safety, but reassured by the fact that we were finally doing something.

When my grandfather came to the phone, I told him about Tommy's physical condition. Kate began to weep silently as I went through the list of his injuries. I said that Tommy had been beaten regularly by Deputy Lopata and that there was no time to lose in getting him released. I didn't mention Tommy's silent acceptance of the beatings. Grandpa Sprague said he would set things in motion and told us to wait outside the jail. An hour later, two men in suits arrived in a Cadillac. Seeing my uniform, the first one walked over to us.

"Are you Richard Ledbetter?" he asked, and I nodded.

He gave me his card.

It read "Stephen Matheson, Attorney at Law."

He looked to be in his fifties with a shock of gray hair and penetrating blue eyes. He said he had been hired to represent Tommy. I quickly told him everything I had done, including my attack on Deputy Lopata. I watched Kate's eyes as she visibly reacted. We followed the men inside. Matheson immediately demanded to see the sheriff.

"What are you doing here, Congressman?" the sheriff began with a grin when he saw who it was.

It turned out Matheson had represented the area in Congress for ten years before retiring to resume his law practice. Lopata was obviously surprised when the lawyer told him he was representing Thomas Ledbetter. Twenty minutes later, my brother was officially released from the jail. The other man had already called an ambulance, and it was waiting outside when they rolled Tommy out on a metal gurney.

Just before she got into the ambulance to go with him to the hospital, Kate turned to me and said, "What you did to the deputy. It was a terrible risk to take."

"I didn't think about that," I said.

"I know," she said gently. "You never think."

Smiling, she held me close for a moment.

"I'm proud of you, Rick," she whispered. "Thank you."

On the long drive back to Newport, I couldn't get the image of Tommy absorbing those beatings out of my mind. I wondered whether it might have stemmed from his guilt over the deaths of the civil rights workers. When I arrived back in my room, I grabbed Garland's Bible and looked up Matthew 5:39. It read: *But I say unto you, That ye resist not evil: but whosoever shall smite thee on thy right cheek, turn to him the other also.* I remembered my mother telling me that he made all his personal decisions on the basis of his faith. He was paying a terrible price for it.

TWENTY-ONE

Unlike Travis, who crossed the Pacific in an aircraft carrier to reach his war, I went to mine in a commercial passenger jet. We were in the middle of the largest American military buildup since World War II. Troop levels in Vietnam had climbed to five hundred thousand, and there weren't enough military transport aircraft or ships to ferry us over to seal the final victory.

That was how Garland and I found ourselves sitting in an airport bar in San Diego drinking margaritas and waiting for our flight to be called by a private charter operation called Golden Eagle Airlines. Our flight had already been delayed several times. Since we had been sitting there, hundreds of military families had gathered to say good-bye to their husband, father, brother, or son, and they were piling up together in the confined space.

On someone's portable radio, Bobbie Gentry was singing "Ode to Billie Joe." A hippie at the table next to us was breast-feeding her baby while reading a paperback novel. Long lines stretched out of the restrooms.

"I'm beginning to think the navy wouldn't miss one ol' boy from Natchez over there," said Garland.

"Sorry—you're stuck with me," I said. "We're going."

A USO volunteer was handing out free coffee and donuts from a rolling cart when I saw two men slip through the service door behind her into the departure area. The first one was wearing sandals and a long white ankle-length robe. He had curly red hair, and there was a circlet of thorns around his head. The man behind him was wearing a rainbow-colored outfit. They were each carrying cardboard signs on wooden stakes.

THOU SHALT NOT KILL, read the sign carried by the red-haired Jesus.

I poked Garland in the ribs and pointed him out as the second guy raised his sign to the crowd of soldiers in the departure lounge.

It read, YOU BE BABY KILLERS.

"Bad grammar," I said to Garland. "And they're mixing their messages."

As we watched, a burly security guard came up and moved them along to the nearest departure gate, shoved them outside, and slammed the door. A cheer went up as he walked back to his post.

"An obvious case of police brutality," I said, sipping my margarita.

"Yeah—well, you never met Sherriff Bull Connor," said Garland.

I was feeling pretty mellow by the time a voice came over the public address system and announced that our flight would begin boarding in a few minutes. It set in motion a chain reaction that spread across the waiting area. Wives and daughters fought to hold back tears as they hugged and kissed their men good-bye. Children were wailing in concert with one another. It was a relief to finally get aboard the plane and into our seats. As soon as we were strapped in, a brunette stewardess wearing a pink miniskirt came down the aisle.

"Well, how are my young naval heroes doing?" she asked, leaning over the armrest until her breasts were a few inches from my nose. "My name is Angela and I want you to know that serving as a stewardess on these Vietnam flights is the most important thing I've ever done in my life," she said. "I want to make it a beautiful memory for you."

It might have meant more if she hadn't repeated the exact same words to the men in every row. An hour later we were out over the Pacific, and she came back with a plastic menu card.

"What can I bring you for lunch?" she asked with a perky smile.

There were two choices on the menu, and Angela recommended the charcoal-grilled savory chicken. As she took the orders, I offered to help her at the barbecue pit. She told me that the entrees were "pre-frozen" and had to be warmed in her little galley oven. They arrived a few minutes later.

"This tastes like old squirrel," Garland said after the first bite.

"I thought you people ate a lot of squirrel back in Mississippi," I said.

"We do," he said gravely. "But only young squirrel."

After Angela took our trays away, the two of us passed the time recalling our favorite World War II movies, dividing them by military branch. I started with the navy and *Run Silent, Run Deep*, *The Caine Mutiny*, *They Were Expendable*, *The Enemy Below*, *The Fighting Sullivans*, *Destination Tokyo*, and *Away All Boats.* Garland knew them all. It was like we were talking in shorthand. Both of us had grown up on war movies. They were the way we defined war.

After Angela brought us a selection of complimentary splits of wine, Garland moved on to the army, and we compared notes on *The Naked and the Dead, Battleground, A Walk in the Sun, Back to Bataan, Battle Cry, The Young Lions, Objective, Burma!, Merrill's Marauders, Between Heaven and Hell,* and *The Story of G.I. Joe.*

"Great early Mitchum," I concluded, and Garland nodded sagely in agreement.

Then it was on to the Army Air Corps, with a boozy comparison of *Twelve O'Clock High, Air Force, Thirty Seconds Over Tokyo,* and *Command Decision*. By the time Angela brought us our complimentary splits of Courvoisier, we had discussed every branch of military service except the Marine Corps.

"*Sands of Iwo Jima*," offered Garland.

"Forrest Tucker—that cowardly son of a bitch," I declared.

"Right there, buddy," Garland agreed as we finished our brandy.

"*Pride of the Marines*," I intoned grimly. "Ol' John Garfield."

Garland gripped my arm.

"Who did he play?" he asked, drawing a blank.

"Al Schmid," I came back. "Guadalcanal . . . Hell, he wiped out just about every Jap on the island with that machine gun."

"Didn't he get the Navy Cross?" asked Garland.

"Yeah," I said, "but he came back blind."

"Well, here's what I'm coming back for," said Garland, pulling his well-worn pictures of Janet out of his rucksack and spreading them out on the tray table. She truly was beautiful. I told him so for the fiftieth time.

A few minutes later, I was asleep.

. . .

We awoke to the hard bounce of the plane wheels hitting a runway. When I checked my watch, I knew it was impossible for us to be anywhere near Vietnam. For one thing, the sky was full of stars, and we were supposed to get there around midday. Through the cabin window, a broad swath of ocean stretched into the distance, dark against the white sand beach next to the runway.

"Where are we?" I asked sleepily when Angela came down the aisle.

"Midway Atoll," she said.

"Midway?" I replied, feeling an immediate shiver of excitement.

"Did she say Midway?" asked Garland, his interest as aroused as mine.

"What's going on?" I asked.

"A problem with one of the navigation instruments," she said. "We'll be on the ground here for about an hour while they fix it."

A few minutes later, Garland and I were standing at the edge of the ocean, staring north into the darkness where the most important naval battle of the Second World War had been fought. Over the wind I could almost hear the roaring engines of the TBF Avengers and B-26 Marauders as they took off to attack the Japanese fleet.

As the gleam of the stars reflected off the churning sea, I felt closer than ever to Travis, and silently vowed that I would live up to my duty, just as he had. An hour later, we were on our way again. Garland and I agreed that the unscheduled stop in that hallowed place was a good omen for what awaited us in Vietnam.

TWENTY-TWO

Our jetliner arrived at Tan Son Nhut Air Base in Saigon in the middle of a thunderstorm. As we came in to land, the intersecting approach paths were clogged with military traffic waiting for clearance to take off.

Once we were down, it took ten minutes to taxi across the vast concrete airstrip, zigzagging past dozens of planes in the process of unloading men and equipment. When we finally came to a stop, the ground crew wheeled a mobile exit ramp to the forward compartment door. A wave of moist, suffocating air swept through the cabin.

After getting our hand luggage from the overhead bins, Garland and I made our way to the front of plane. Angela was standing by the entrance to her little galley with tears in her eyes. Wishing us good luck, she kissed each of us on the cheek as we went past. An American military policeman was standing at the top of the exit stairs.

"Say hello to Vietnam," he said with a smile as we emerged into the pouring rain.

The reek of jet exhaust fumes clogged the air as we boarded a shuttle bus that took us to the replacement officers' depot. A Vietnamese flag hung in tandem with an American flag at the entrance to the building. Inside, it was like a steam bath. I felt the sweat soaking through my uniform shirt.

"Man, this reminds me of home," said Garland with a contented smile.

"Remind me never to visit home," I said.

"Don't worry. You'll get used to it."

After waiting in another line to have our orders approved, we took a shuttle bus over to the helicopter terminal. The rain had stopped by then, and the lush tropical flowers that ringed the entrance were glistening red and pink in the brilliant sun.

An hour later, we boarded a Chinook helicopter that was headed south to resupply several American and ARVN military units in the Mekong Delta. It felt hotter than ever, but when the big machine picked up speed, the steady stream of air pouring in through the open gun ports dried my sweat.

Through the shimmering heat waves, the Mekong Delta unfolded below us like the crooked fingers of a man's hand, each finger a major river flowing down to the South China Sea. Joining the rivers were hundreds of smaller streams and manmade canals, along with miles of mangrove swamps, green paddy fields, groves of palm trees, and tiny villages of thatched buildings. The pilot made stops to deliver the mail to two small U.S. Army outposts before descending again over a small peninsula jutting out from a broad copper-colored river.

As we dropped toward a well-marked landing pad, I caught a quick glimpse of a compound studded with tin-roofed buildings, tents, and sandbags. It adjoined a small lagoon, and I could see eight swift boats tethered to floating piers attached to the riverbank.

A yellow cloud of dust swirled around the pad as we landed. When we jumped from the open gun port, a marine carrying a sawed-off shotgun waved us toward one of the buildings located in the middle of the compound. It was a wooden shack with unpainted plywood walls and a corrugated tin roof. Inside, a window-mounted air conditioner was struggling noisily to keep the temperature below a hundred degrees.

I followed Garland down a narrow corridor and through an open doorway. Inside the room there were two gray metal desks with folding chairs and filing cabinets. A thick coating of fine, powdery dust covered every surface. A chief petty officer was standing at an electric hot plate and measuring coffee into a blue enamel pot. Through another open doorway, I could see the backs of two naval officers talking quietly in front of a briefing map. The chief looked over at us and began wagging his wrinkled bald head back and forth.

"Just what we need," he said, "two more infant ensigns."

"Welcome to the brown-water navy, gentlemen," came a voice from behind us.

I turned to see a tall blond officer with the collar tabs of a lieutenant commander.

"My name is Jack Rosenthal," he said extending his right hand. "I command River Support Squadron Nine. You can call me Jack."

In his thirties, he was wearing jungle fatigues with the sleeves rolled up to his elbows. A Colt .45 bulged out of a leather shoulder holster strapped across his broad chest. The Star of David hung from his neck next to his dog tags.

"Things are a little hairy here right now," he said. "Last night the VC ambushed one of our patrols about five clicks up the river at a charming spot they call Blood Alley. We had two KIA, including the exec on *PCF One Twelve*. One of you guys will be replacing him. You have your personnel jackets with you?"

"Yes, sir," said Garland as we dug them out of our travel bags.

"Call me Jack," he repeated, wearily raking his fingers through his thick crew-cut hair.

Pulling a pack of Camels out of the breast pocket of his fatigues, he lit one with a cigarette lighter engraved with the Annapolis crest. He opened the folders and quickly scanned them while we stood there.

"Forget everything they taught you back there except how to drive the boat," he said, leading us back across the hall into the other office with the briefing map.

He pointed to one of the curving fingers of the delta.

"We're right here," he said. "This whole area is a designated free-fire zone. There are no standard rules of engagement. If you're outside this compound and something moves on the river after dark, assume it's the enemy. At night, the Vietcong control most of the villages, rivers, and streams, and a lot of the countryside in between. Our job is to recapture control of it all and deny them the ability to infiltrate and resupply their forces. Our intelligence guys believe about forty thousand enemy troops currently occupy the delta, so it's a big job."

His eyes roved speculatively from Garland to me and then back again.

"Almost ninety percent of the country's rice crop comes from down here. That's what makes it strategically important. We have to deny that rice to the enemy. He knows every square inch of this territory and every ambush point. He is very tough, and he rules through terror. He can come in all shapes and sizes—from a twelve-year-old kid to a ninety-year-old man."

Glancing at his watch he said, "Tonight I want you both to relax, have some chow, and get acquainted with the base. Tomorrow I'll assign you to your boats. Report back here at oh seven hundred."

The chief was still wagging his bald head at us disdainfully as we headed outside. We were stowing our bags in the tent that served as the bachelor officers' quarters when Garland drawled, "Never met a blue-eyed Jewish guy before."

"Paul Newman," I said, as we began to wander around our new home.

"I never met him," said Garland.

With each step around the compound, our shoes raised small clouds of dust from the fine, silt-like soil. As the setting sun beat down on us, the smothering heat made me feel almost lightheaded. Garland was completely at home.

The base was in the shape of a crude rectangle, bordered on one long side by the lagoon that was fed by the river. The squadron's swift boats were tethered to small finger piers. The neck of the inlet into the lagoon was protected by two anchored World War II–vintage LSTs, equipped from fore to aft with machine guns and mortars.

The base was bordered by dense mangrove swamps at each of the shorter ends of the rectangle. The rear perimeter consisted of a five-foot-high bulldozed earthen wall that ran the length of it and was protected by sandbagged machine gun emplacements. Beyond the earth wall were three courses of barbed tanglefoot and concertina wire.

An open field of elephant grass stretched inland past the other side of the barbed wire for about fifty yards to a grove of palm trees. A large wooden sign in the field warned in English that it was loaded with land mines.

In the middle of the compound, a defense bunker had been dug into the powdery soil and reinforced with sandbags. Cyclone wire covered the air vents and exit passages to protect the base personnel from rocket-propelled grenades in the event of an attack.

"Looks pretty safe to me," I said.

"I just hope all these marines can shoot like Marshal Dillon," said Garland.

A dozen other plywood structures dotted the rest of the base area. The first proved to be the communal latrine. Inside the open doorway, flying insects as big as my thumb were dive-bombing the walls and floor.

The next building was the sleeping quarters for the enlisted men in the marine defense detachment. It had a Confederate battle flag waving above it and was jammed with rough-cut bunk beds covered by mosquito netting. There was also a spare parts storage shed and a repair shop with fabricating tools. Beyond that was the base shower facility.

Only two structures were guarded and padlocked. The first turned out to be the beer and liquor shed. Through the narrow slits between the plywood wall panels, I could see there were wooden pallets containing hundreds of cases of beer. The second building was the largest on the compound and located inside a separate enclosure surrounded by an eight-foot-high chain-link fence. The entrance was guarded by two heavily armed men who I thought might be Korean. Unlike the other buildings, it had walls made of cinderblock, and a large air-conditioning compressor was rumbling away alongside it. A light observation helicopter was warming up on a separate concrete pad.

"They got some important generals in there?" Garland asked one of the guards.

He looked at us for several seconds without saying anything. Then he spat a wad of tobacco juice onto the ground at our feet. Over his shoulder, I saw the front door of the building swing open and a man came out. He was a chubby white guy wearing an African safari jacket and a straw planter's hat. He was followed by two more Korean men. Both were wearing standard-issue American camouflage uniforms.

"Good hunting!" I heard the chubby man call out to them as they headed for the helicopter.

The pilot revved his engines and took off, leaving us coated in a film of yellow grit.

"How about some shrimp cocktail and a couple of rare prime ribs along with a vodka and tonic?" I suggested.

"Sounds good," said Garland. "I just hope they're gulf shrimp."

The officers' mess was a large open tent with cafeteria tables and folding metal chairs. After going through the serving line, we sat down to a dinner of canned minestrone soup, Spam sandwiches on rye toast, and dust-covered chocolate sheet cake.

"Not quite the Hotel Viking, I'll admit," said Garland, although he finished everything on his plate.

Pushing back my tray, I agreed with him.

It was completely dark by the time we unpacked our bags in our tent. Since officers already assigned to the swift boats slept aboard, we had the tent to ourselves. Unlike the mess tent, it had a plywood floor to keep out crawling insects, and four sturdy cots. Mosquito nets hung from metal grommets stitched into the canvas roof.

Turning up the Coleman kerosene lamp next to my bed, I removed a picture of Kate from my wallet. It had been taken outside church on Easter Sunday, and originally included the family. I had cropped it down to just her, and then paid to have the tiny image enlarged to wallet size. Using a piece of duct tape, I fastened the photograph to the netting above my head so that it would be the first thing I saw when I woke up.

I soon discovered that the problem wouldn't be waking up. It was going to sleep.

Both Garland and I were completely wrung out from the twenty-hour flight across the Pacific and everything since. It affected us differently. Garland went right off like a contented child and was snoring peacefully within five minutes.

I was wide awake. There was no breeze to stir the fetid night air, and the tent fabric seemed to retain the sunbaked heat. Even without a top sheet, it was stifling under the netting, and sweat was pouring off my forehead and chest in a steady trickle, soaking the cotton bedding beneath me. Then there were the birds. I had always assumed that birds slept at night. In the Mekong Delta, some of them screech all night, cackling and shrieking at one another from their perches in the mangrove swamps. It was two or three in the morning before I finally fell into a fitful sleep.

TWENTY-THREE

I awoke to the smell of hot shit. Literally. The noncoms in the marine defense detachment had picked that morning to burn the massive pile of excrement in their latrine pit with gasoline. The stench permeated the whole compound.

"Don't tell me it reminds you of home," I warned Garland as we stirred out of our cots and headed over to the showers.

It was another brutally hot day and I felt my energy flagging before sipping my first cup of hot coffee in the mess tent. Garland pulled a small plastic bag out of his breast pocket, removed two pills from it, and placed them on my breakfast tray.

"What are those?" I asked.

"Salt tablets," he said. "Trust me, you'll need them."

After breakfast, we reported back to Jack Rosenthal. He spent an hour showing us the areas on the briefing map that we would be responsible for patrolling that morning.

"In the next few weeks, we'll be part of joint missions with both American and ARVN infantry units to stop the enemy from moving rice out of the delta," he said. "We'll have the assistance of a helicopter attack group to level the playing field a bit. They'll patrol above us with additional firepower if we need it."

As Jack continued with the briefing, the old chief brought in three mugs of black coffee, the best I've ever tasted, before or since.

"As execs, your work week will be around eighty hours," Jack went on. "When you're not out on patrol, you'll be responsible for cleaning, refueling, and maintaining your boats under the direction of your skipper. Snatch some sleep whenever you have time to get it. You'll be way ahead of the rest of us if you can sleep all night in this place."

I looked over at Garland and he just smiled back at me as Rosenthal removed the Colt .45 from his shoulder holster and held it loosely in his palm.

"Last point: the single most important thing we have to worry about here is the possibility of an attack by a Vietcong assault team," Rosenthal began. "I'm talking about well-trained sappers who aren't afraid to sacrifice their lives to penetrate the perimeter and blow us all to kingdom come. About a month ago, they got through the security at Vinh Long and our guys paid a big price. Wear your forty-five at all times, and keep a live round in the chamber."

He then assigned Garland as executive officer to *PCF-59* and gave me *PCF-112*, which was commanded by a Lieutenant Maddox. Pulling me aside, Jack told me that I would be replacing the executive officer who had been killed two nights earlier.

"Doug Maddox is a good man," he told me, "but he's seen a lot of rugged shit over the last couple of months. Try to give him a lift."

We met all the squadron skippers later that morning as they returned from the morning patrol. I noticed that Doug Maddox was the only one still wearing a flak jacket over his khakis when he came ashore, which surprised me because it was so goddam hot. I wondered if he had just forgotten to take it off after the patrol.

Doug was one year out of Notre Dame and had gone through OCS at Newport six months before Garland and me. Short and soft-spoken, he had Saint Bernard eyes in a long, narrow face. He walked me back to the pier to introduce me to the rest of the *PCF-112* crew. There were four. The most senior was Petty Officer Second-Class Harmon Posey. I soon learned that his Baptist faith was as deep as Doug Maddox's Catholicism.

Posey enjoyed quoting long passages from the Old Testament. The other crewmen called him "Pastor." The crew also included Jeff Hazelbrouck, who was from Alaska and was working on his second stripe. The last two were high school dropouts who had volunteered for the navy to avoid being drafted. Mickey Kaufman was from the South Side of Chicago and wanted to race motorcycles when he got home. Bobby Krusa was from Pittsburgh and sported a Mohawk haircut. Both of them were short timers counting the days they had left in Vietnam.

When Garland and I got back together for lunch, I told him that Lieutenant Maddox was from his neck of the woods—Baton Rouge, Louisiana. Garland laughed and said his new skipper had grown up near me on Long Island.

"Ol' Jack sure has got a sense of humor," said Garland.

. . .

We made our first patrol the following morning. Jack Rosenthal believed in the adage of safety through numbers, and that first patrol was no exception. It consisted of seven swift boats and two PBRs, which were similar to the PCFs but had aluminum hulls. Jack led in the first PCF.

We moved out from the base at dawn. Following Jack's standing orders, I wore a helmet and flak jacket over my summer tans. On my web belt I carried a .45, two extra clips of ammunition, a bag filled with battle dressings, and a KA-BAR knife. It felt really uncomfortable to be weighted down like that in the brutal heat, but I soon got used to it.

Maddox invited me to take the wheel as we moved out. With easy precision, I maneuvered the boat away from the dock and found our position in line with the others. We left the protected inlet and headed down the river in two columns. Above us, the sky slowly turned a startling blue. The wide expanse of the river was already alive with a steady stream of vessels moving in both directions. They ranged from small skiffs to forty-foot sampans, and carried every sort of cargo from rice and hogs to construction materials.

"The morning rush hour," said Doug. "Sampans and junks are like delivery trucks down here.

He reached down under the steering console and pulled out a bottle of Pepto-Bismol and took a long swig.

"Start the show-and-tell," came the voice of Jack Rosenthal over the radio, and I watched the lead boat in each column peel off to block the two broad traffic lanes of Vietnamese river craft.

A second later, I heard Mickey Kaufman, Jeff Hazelbrouck, and Bobby Krusa charging the .50 caliber machine guns. Almost as one, the gun mounts swung around on their turrets and were trained on the first sampan in front of us.

"Are we going to search every one of them?" I asked Maddox.

"No, the skimmers will do that," he said. "Our job is to provide them cover."

Before he finished answering, four Boston Whalers came zooming out of the wakes of the PBRs that were cruising behind us and closed on the first sampan. A young navy seaman with a sawed-off shotgun leaped from one of the Whalers onto the deck of the first sampan and disappeared below.

Taking another long swig of Pepto-Bismol, Maddox turned to me and said, "My wife, Barbara, wrote that she had a miscarriage last month."

Although I had seen the wedding ring on his finger, he hadn't mentioned his wife until that moment. I wasn't sure I had heard him correctly over the noise of the engines and didn't say anything.

"Did you hear me, Ensign?" he asked. "I said my wife had a miscarriage last month."

"Yes, sir," I replied. "I'm sorry."

"Well, does that tell you anything?"

At that moment, I was focused on keeping the boat in the right position for the machine gunners in case the men in the Whaler needed fire support. Out of the corner of my eye, I could sense he was staring at me.

"I'm going below," he said.

"Yes, sir," I said.

Harmon Posey was standing right behind us. He stepped aside as Doug disappeared through the open hatchway. Posey's eyes met mine for a second, but I couldn't read anything in them. An air horn blared from one of the Boston Whalers, signifying that it was moving on to the next sampan.

For the next hour, our flotilla continued searching vessels for contraband goods and weapons. Only one search resulted in a seizure. It followed the discovery of several cases of cosmetics that had apparently been stolen from an army PX in Saigon. The river traffic began thinning out by late morning. I kept expecting Maddox to return to the bridge. He never reappeared. On the positive side, my taking over the conn for that first patrol, helped to build my confidence.

Before we returned to the base, Jack Rosenthal brought the flotilla close to shore near a riverside hamlet. The enclave was protected by six-foot-high spiked bamboo walls, and there was a fortified gate that led into it from a prefabricated steel pier. A sign on the pier read CONSTRUCTED BY THE U.S. ARMY CORPS OF ENGINEERS.

A large group of people were waiting on the pier. Along with about twenty Vietnamese men and women, there were a dozen uniformed American soldiers and several American news crews filming our arrival with television cameras.

Jack brought his swift boat alongside the pier, while the rest of us were ordered to kill our engines and stand offshore in a semicircle around the pier. When Jack stepped off his boat, he was greeted by a delegation of Vietnamese dressed in colorful brocade tunics. The man in front was apparently the mayor. He presented Jack with a proclamation and several baskets of fruit.

A gray-haired American wearing a white linen suit then delivered a brief speech in which he congratulated the village officials for their participation in the strategic hamlet program, which was fostering closer cooperation between the rural Vietnamese and the government in Saigon. The ceremony lasted about twenty minutes, after which we started our engines and returned to base. Doug Maddox never came on deck for it.

. . .

In the days that followed, I learned how to navigate through a lot of different obstacles as we chugged up and back along the curling river as it made its way to the South China Sea. The boat's compass would gyrate crazily back and forth as the river meandered in one direction and then another.

There were no good charts of the smaller rivers and tributaries, and we always had to be prepared for hidden shoals and sandbars. Many of the channels were cluttered with fish pots and fallen tree limbs. Mangrove jungle covering both banks would occasionally open up long enough to reveal farmers on water buffaloes pulling their wooden plows across rice paddies.

At first, my nerves were always on edge as I scanned both sides of the river, fully expecting an ambush to be sprung on us at any moment. As the days passed without incident, my mind began to wander. Mostly I thought of Kate on the other side of the world. Glancing at my watch,

I daydreamed of where she might be at that moment and what she might be doing. From a letter my mother had written me, I knew that in the months since I had last seen them, Kate had left Cornell too. I assumed she was probably working with Tommy.

I heard raised voices behind me. Bobby Krusa and Mickey Kaufman were having another petty squabble. They could sometimes be quite entertaining in an idiotic way, and it took my mind off the fact that Doug Maddox rarely showed up on the bridge anymore.

Mickey was jawing loudly about his prowess on a motorcycle.

"I was one fast dude on that Harley, man. I made it from Jacksonville down to Lauderdale in two hours, man."

"Mickey, your brainpan is dripping. Nobody could make it in two hours," said Bobby.

"I made it man . . . That baby could fly."

"That's about three hundred miles, numb nuts!"

"I know . . . and I made it in two hours."

"I spose you averaged a hundred and fifty miles an hour."

"I don't know about that, man. All I know is I made it!"

"Right, Mick, and you made it with Ann-Margret, too, you dumb shit."

I ordered Bobby to bring up coffee from the galley as we passed a patch of shoreline that looked like it had been hit with incendiary bombs. An orange residue covered the dying mangrove vines at the edge of the bank.

"They're using this new kind of insecticide stuff," said Harmon Posey when I asked him what had happened there. "They drop it from the air on Charlie's favorite ambush spots. It burns out the jungle like acid."

By the time we were ordered to turn the boats around and head back upriver, we usually had checked dozens of sampans, barges, junks, and lighters. The most aromatic discovery we made was a full bargeload of pink hibiscus flowers that was on its way to the street market in Saigon. As far as finding illicit rice shipments or Vietcong arms and munitions, we weren't having any success at all.

We were back at the base and securing the bow and stern lines at our finger pier when Doug emerged from down below and came up to the bridge. Looking over the log entries I had written, he signed them without a word, stepped down onto the pier, and headed over to the compound. He was still wearing his sweat-stained flak jacket. It didn't take Sigmund Freud to know there was something strange about his behavior, and I decided to ask Garland's advice about it. In the meantime, I ordered a work detail to clean and refuel the boat.

At supper, I described what had happened over the previous days to Garland. He just shook his head and laughed. "You should meet my Long Island guy," he said, describing the quirky behavior of his new commanding officer. "Maybe they've all got a dose of jungle fever."

When the mail was delivered from Saigon, I saw that one of the letters was for me. It was from my mother, and I wasn't at all sure I wanted to read it. I shoved it in my pocket. Showering ashore, I headed back over to the officers' club.

After drinking a cold Schlitz, I pulled out the letter again. In one short paragraph she expressed the hope that I was doing well in my new job and then reeled off two pages on Tommy. He was in jail again, charged in a new federal indictment with "willfully interfering with the administration of the Military Selective Service Act" after leading a twenty-four-hour vigil outside a draft board office in Baltimore. He was facing another possible five years in federal prison in addition to whatever sentence he was going to receive for resisting the draft.

Sitting there in the sweltering darkness and surrounded by officers carrying .45 Colts, I thought it all seemed so far away. Garland showed up as I finished reading the letter. My reaction to it must have registered on my face.

"Bad news?" asked Garland.

"My brother's in jail again," I said, before remembering that I hadn't told Garland anything about him or what he had done.

"Your brother's a criminal?" he asked, as if Tommy might be a convicted axe murderer.

"I guess it all depends on how you define the word," I said.

TWENTY-FOUR

After my first two weeks in the Mekong Delta, the only part of Vietnam I had really come to know was inside the concertina wire. Aside from the nightly booze sessions in the officers' shack, amusements were few and far between. The base library consisted of a few dozen well-thumbed paperbacks and an assortment of magazines. It was housed in an empty refrigerator crate nailed to the exterior wall of the main defense bunker.

Once a week, a helicopter would bring down a first-run American movie along with frozen meat in big coolers. The movies were on 16 millimeter reels, and at night they were projected onto a screen made of bedsheets strung together in the middle of the compound.

On the assumption that fighting men would probably enjoy war movies, we were treated to pictures like *Tobruk,* in which Rock Hudson takes on Rommel's Afrika Korps, and *The Dirty Dozen*.

One evening we were ordered out to provide fire support for ARVN ground troops that were seeking to eliminate a Vietcong strong point that military intelligence had identified in our sector. After spending several hours searching unsuccessfully for the ARVN troops, we were told they had canceled the mission, and we were ordered back to the base. By then I had taken to sleeping topside in the deck space directly behind the bridge of our boat. I woke one morning at dawn to a fog so thick I couldn't see across the finger pier to the next boat in line.

Jack Rosenthal sent a detail to warn each skipper that fog provided perfect cover for sappers, and we were ordered to post an extra man on watch as long as it lasted. The marine defense detachment sent out men in the Whalers to toss hand grenades into the narrow passage leading into the lagoon. When the fog finally cleared, the local fishermen came out to harvest a tremendous bounty of dead fish.

The reason I had taken to sleeping on deck was Doug Maddox. We had been sharing a compartment aboard the boat, but every time I went down there, it smelled like the lion cage at the Bronx Zoo. I don't know which smelled worse, Doug or his flak jacket. He never took it off, even to sleep. To my knowledge, he hadn't showered since I had joined the crew. At night he would sit in the galley reading the Bible and fingering his rosary beads while occasionally making notes in a spiral notebook. He kept a small framed photograph of his wife and kids propped on the table in front of him until he went to sack out.

The smell had driven the other crew members topside too, and one evening before chow I went down to the galley to talk to Doug about the situation. He had just received a letter from home and was sitting there with tears running down his cheeks, bare-chested under the flak jacket, the sweat pouring off him onto the plastic seat cushions.

He looked up to see me standing in the hatchway.

"Father O'Brien wrote to say that the children in our parish planted a rosebush in my honor behind the sacramental garden," he said.

"That's pretty special, Doug," I said.

"Those children don't know me," he came back angrily.

I turned around and went back up on deck—mission failed. Most of the crew was over at the compound watching a movie. Jeff Hazelbrouck was standing watch. I told him I was heading over to the mess tent and would be there if he needed me.

"You never goddam know, sir," he said.

I spoke to Garland about the problem again as we ate our hamburger and noodle casserole with canned corn and then headed over to the officers' club to rinse out our mouths. The long plywood bar was packed with officers, as were the surrounding tables.

"We're talking about Captain Queeg here," I said, after detailing Doug's latest nutty behavior. "He may not have the steel balls in his fingers, but I'm telling you the guy is certifiable."

"You need to talk to ol' Jack. He'll know what to do."

Jack came into the club shack twenty minutes later. He ordered a double bourbon and socked it back as I came up and asked to speak to him. After he ordered another round, I told him I thought Doug was having a nervous breakdown. From the way Jack stared back at me, I wondered whether he thought I was angling for a quick promotion.

"Listen," he said. "You already know that he lost his first exec. Well, two months ago, we were in a firefight upriver. It was a night action. He ordered in a strike on a ground target from the helicopter gunships and gave them the wrong coordinates. We lost a dozen ARVN troops and two American advisers. He's still down about the whole thing. We all are."

"I can understand his being down about it," I said, "and I don't want to undermine a fellow officer, but I'm not sure he should remain in command of the boat right now."

"Look . . . I'll keep a closer watch on him," he said. "Meanwhile, give him all the support you can."

It was hazing night at the club for newly arrived officers like Garland and me. At one point each of us was ordered to stand on a chair to sing our college's fight song. Garland did a credible job of screaming, "Rebels you're the Southland's pride, Take that ball and hit your stride, don't stop 'till the victory's won for your Ole Miss." When I started singing, "Give my regards to Davy, remember me to Tee Fee Crane, tell all the pikers on the hill that I'll be back again," I was hooted off the chair before I could finish the song. I announced they were all too stupid to appreciate sophisticated Ivy League lyrics.

Later on, I happened to glance up toward the bar and saw the fat guy in the safari jacket we had encountered on our first day in the compound. He was talking to two other guys in civilian clothes, and his voice carried across to me.

"What can you expect from people who use two sticks to eat a spoonful of rice and one stick to carry two buckets of their own shit?" he said to laughter.

"Who is that?" I asked Jack.

He looked over at him, and then back at me.

"You don't wanna know," he said.

"Don't want to know what?" I asked.

"Project Pale Horse . . . CIA shit."

"What horse?" I asked him.

"Behold a pale horse," said Garland, "and his name that sat on him was Death. Revelation six eight. And Hell followed with him."

But Jack was no longer paying attention. He was already on his way out of the tent. In the reflected glow of the club lights, we watched him weave off toward his boat, trying hard not to appear drunk and doing a pretty decent job of it. I spent another night sleeping up on deck.

TWENTY-FIVE

A few days later, the flotilla took its first serious casualties since Garland and I had arrived. They didn't result from contact with the enemy. The fight was between a petty officer and a seaman in his crew. The petty officer was white and from Alabama. The seaman was black and from Chicago.

The seaman had spent several weeks cultivating a modified Afro haircut, and the petty officer ordered him to cut it off. The seaman refused. Angry words were exchanged. No one seemed to know what they actually said. The fight took place behind the enlisted men's barracks under the waving Confederate battle flag. When it was over, the petty officer had a knife wound in the stomach and the seaman had a fractured skull. They were medevaced out together to the field hospital at Vung Tau.

The other big news was that three Vietcong suspects had been captured at a neighboring village less than a mile from our compound. The capture had been made by one of the Koreans who worked out of the CIA stockade.

At mail call that morning, I received two letters. The first was from Pete Demetropolis. His orthodontic ploy with the braces had worked out as well as he had hoped. After being rejected for induction into the army, he had bought an old roller-skating rink near the Cornell campus and turned it into a "gold mine." He wrote that he was shacked up with one of my old girlfriends and promised to give me a big welcome-home party when I got "back to the world."

The second letter was from my mother. She wrote that Tom and Kate were working together in Washington and helping to plan a major demonstration there that was to take place at the end of October. They had come to Cold Spring Harbor to raise money for the event, and had spent the night with her. Tom had lost even more weight, she said, but

Kate had assured her she was doing everything she could to help him regain his strength. I didn't bother to write back that I had lost fifteen pounds since arriving in Vietnam.

That same afternoon, Jack Rosenthal brought all the officers in the flotilla together to brief us on another night mission. According to MACV headquarters in Saigon, the Vietcong were assembling forces for a proposed attack on an ARVN unit in our sector. Our mission was to provide fire support for the assault on the Vietcong enclave by South Vietnamese marines. As the meeting broke, I saw Jack motion Doug Maddox to stay behind. Twenty minutes later, Jack walked down to our boat as I was making the last-minute maintenance checks.

"Doug isn't feeling a hundred percent," he said quietly. "I'm giving you temporary command."

I informed the crew that I would be taking over and they all looked relieved. As for me, I had no doubt I could do the job well and felt a real sense of pride in being chosen by Jack from all the execs on the base.

"We got us a brand-fucking-new quarterback," I heard Mickey Kaufman say to Bobby Krusa. "About time."

I walked to the repair facility with Harmon Posey to find a replacement part for the linkages on the bridge controls. On the way, I happened to glance over at the CIA stockade and saw the three Vietcong suspects being escorted to the unit's helicopter. The two men and one woman had their hands bound behind their backs, and they were being prodded forward by one of the Koreans. I watched the helicopter take off and head out over the South China Sea.

The chief of the repair facility told Harmon they would have to fabricate a new linkage rod and it wouldn't be ready until the next morning. I told him I was heading out on a mission, and if they couldn't make it in the next hour, I would inform Lieutenant Commander Rosenthal that our boat wouldn't be ready. He stalked back inside to make it.

No more than ten minutes later, I heard the helicopter coming back and watched it slowly descend to its landing pad. Aside from the pilot, only two people stepped out of it, the Korean and one of the male Vietcong suspects. The bound man was having trouble walking and the Korean had to half-carry him back inside the cinder block building. I wondered where the helicopter might have dropped off the other man and woman before returning so quickly.

Our night mission was a fiasco. When we arrived at our designated rendezvous point, the landing boats carrying the South Vietnamese marines weren't there. Two hours passed as our boats cruised slowly up and down the river, waiting for them to show. It was after midnight when Jack radioed us that the attack had been canceled and we were all to return to base. I was navigating slowly past a shoreline thick with mangrove vines when we suddenly came under fire.

"Three o'clock!" shouted Posey, pointing toward the bank. "Recoilless rifle."

"Return fire!" I ordered.

Mickey and Bobby opened up with their .50s, spraying the jungle where Posey had last seen the muzzle flashes. Gunning the engines, I headed out into the middle of the river at full throttle.

After radioing to Jack that we had been attacked, I ordered Posey to check for casualties and boat damage. Fortunately, no one had been hit, although one of the sniper's bullets had torn up the base of the instrument console a couple of feet from where I had been standing.

It was the first time in my life I had been shot at. After all the war movies I had grown up on, I had wondered how I would react if it actually happened. In truth, I didn't have time to think about it until we were back at the base and I was getting ready for bed. I lay there in the dark cabin wondering why I didn't feel any different until I fell asleep a couple of minutes later.

Early the next morning, I was in the middle of refueling when Jack appeared at the foot of the dock. Wiping my hands on a rag, I dropped down to the dock and followed him back to his office.

"I had to send Doug Maddox home this morning," he said when we arrived. "You were right to come and see me. He's had some kind of breakdown."

"I'm sorry," I said.

He ran his blunt fingers through his blond hair

"Well . . . do you think you can carry the load?" he asked, handing me a cup of the chief's superb coffee. "If not, I'll get a replacement from one of the other squadrons."

"I can handle it," I said.

"I think you can too, Rick," he said.

We shook hands and that was it. I became the skipper of *PCF-112*, entitling me to wear the same captain's star on my shirt collar as the captain of the USS *Enterprise*. Granted, with a carrier crew of three thousand, he might have had a shade more responsibility than me, but I wasn't going to split hairs.

Aside from the captain's star, nothing really changed. Each morning we went out on patrol. Each night we sealed ourselves up inside the security perimeter of the base compound. Between missions, Garland and I enjoyed our few hours of free time, playing gin rummy at ten cents a point down in the galley of my boat. I was looking forward to our first leave in Saigon.

TWENTY-SIX

It was maybe a day later when Jack received an urgent request shortly before dawn to provide military assistance to a local hamlet that was under attack by a strong Vietcong force.

By the time we got there, the attack was over. It was the same hamlet we had visited after my first patrol with the flotilla, the one where the American official in the white suit had led the press event celebrating their participation in the strategic hamlet program.

There was enough light beneath the rain-soaked sky to see firsthand the horror of the scene along the shoreline. Clouds of smoke were rising from the destroyed thatch-roofed buildings inside the bamboo-walled compound. The outer wall had been breached in several places, and I could see dead livestock lying all over the ground inside.

An even greater price had been paid for the hamlet's cooperation with Saigon. At least twenty of the villagers had been gutted and hung upside down from the main gate like carcasses in a slaughterhouse. Some were presumably the local officials we had seen offering gifts at the celebration ceremony, but a number were old women and small children.

"Why'd they kill the little kids?" called out Bobby Krusa.

"To set an example," I called back, but I'm not sure he understood.

. . .

It was a Saturday night and most of the off-duty men were watching a movie that had just been flown down to us. It was *For a Few Dollars More,* starring Clint Eastwood. Passing by the makeshift white screen on my way back to my boat, I looked up to see Lee Van Cleef striking a wooden match on Klaus Kinski's jaw. The men roared in appreciation.

"Man, that is so cool," I heard Bobby Krusa howl from the edge of the crowd. I didn't bother to stop and let him know it was a direct steal from *Stalag 17,* when William Holden struck a match on the cheek of Neville Brand.

Back at the finger pier, I checked over the boat and made sure that the lines were properly tied off so it wouldn't scrape the dock if there was any turbulence. The water in the lagoon was like black glass, but occasionally one of the boats would come in at high speed, leaving a good-sized wake behind it.

Garland came over at around nine and we headed down to the galley for our gin rummy game. Although the dock area had been liberally sprayed with pesticide, a small cloud of mosquitoes swarmed around the lantern on the table between us. I silently longed for a tropical rainstorm to cool things off. Even with my khaki shirt unbuttoned, the sweat was running down my chest and back.

"Man, I just love this heat," Garland said with a tired grin.

I tried to ignore the buzzing mosquitoes as I contemplated my lousy cards. With his third draw, Garland filled his hand and proceeded to nail me for eighty-seven points.

"I'm going up on deck for a few minutes," I said.

Lighting one of the cheap Dutch Masters cigars I had bought just to keep the insects off my face, I went topside and walked along the deck toward the bow. I thought about going over to the compound for a cold shower, but Jack Rosenthal's standing watch order required that three members of the crew, including one officer, be aboard at all times. I still hadn't been assigned an executive officer.

Harmon Posey, Mickey Kaufman, and Jeff Hazelbrouck were sitting at the stern on aluminum folding chairs. Posey was reeling off a chapter from the Book of Isaiah, while the other two listened in respectful silence. In the reflected shimmer of the dock lights, I watched a huge snake glide from the edge of the riverbank into the brackish water of the lagoon. Glancing up at the black sky, I hoped the clouds above us held some rain.

On one of the boats down the line, a transistor radio was blaring a live concert. Andy Williams was in Vietnam somewhere giving a performance for the troops, and he had just launched into "Moon River." The song brought back a lot of memories. I had danced to it so many times over the years. It was like a security blanket from innocent times in the early sixties. When JFK was still alive.

Oh, dream maker, you heart breaker, wherever you're goin', I'm goin' your way.

Out on our own river, a patrol craft was cruising back and forth along the neck of the lagoon, using searchlights to guard the most vulnerable access point to the base. Every few minutes, I heard the reassuring *thump* of a concussion grenade being detonated in the water.

I heard Jeff Hazelbrouck say, "Okay, so I ain't been to school since the eighth grade. I can't much read or write. I'm a stupid man . . . but I know this. We ain't never gonna win this here war."

I thought I felt a drop of moisture on my ear and lifted my face to the sky. A moment later, I felt another one on my cheek. *Thank you,* I thought. When it rained in Vietnam, it usually came down like a biblical flood.

"Ya can't have no progress without war," said Mickey Kaufman, his voice grave. "Since this war here, we now got more people workin'. And there's more jobs 'cause a lot of guys will get greased over here. This is what we call progress."

"What we really need is like an insurance corps," Jeff came back. "They talk about this Peace Corps. What the fuck do they do? Now, you take life insurance . . . If everybody had life insurance, they'd think their life was worth somethin'."

I felt another drop of moisture land on my face. A few moments later, the sky opened up and I was drenched in lukewarm water. The stern section where the guys were sitting was covered by a canvas top sheet, and they never moved out of their chairs.

The rain came harder, almost blotting out the lights from the base compound. I stood at the bow and let the downpour cool my body. In the distance, I could see the hazy glow of the patrol craft's searchlight swinging back and forth across the entrance to the lagoon.

As I was turning to head back down to the galley, I suddenly glimpsed what looked like a pale shadow on the surface of the water. Wiping the rain from my eyes, I stared out into the murky gloom. The shadow disappeared, but a few seconds later it reappeared like the crest of a small wave slowly moving across the surface. Then it was gone again.

But there couldn't be any waves in the lagoon. Aside from the raindrops roiling the surface, the water was flat calm. The power of the cloudburst was already diminishing, and I could now see almost thirty feet from the bow. Maybe my eyes were deceiving me, but the same shadowy form was there again and heading slowly away from the line of swift boats toward open water. I wondered if it might actually be a sapper, just as Jack had warned us about, but the notion seemed ridiculous as soon as it occurred to me. A moment later, the rain stopped as suddenly as it had started.

Something was definitely out there in the water. Pulling the Colt .45 from my hip holster, I cocked it with my thumb. It was a standing order for watch officers to keep a round in the chamber of our pistols with the hammer down.

I briefly considered the possibility it might be a large bird or a floating coconut and imagined the sarcastic grief I would take if that turned out to be the case. But Jack's words about sappers rang in my ears.

Steadying the gun with both hands, I fired at the shadowy form as it receded into the darkness. Little geysers of water erupted as each bullet hit the surface. One of them seemed to hit the shadowy spot as I emptied a full magazine of its rounds.

Someone on one of the boats farther down the line switched on a searchlight and trained it in the direction where I had fired. By then, the shadow had disappeared. Nothing moved in the water. Having fired a full clip, I felt ridiculous and let the .45 drop to my side.

"You win the stuffed panda bear, sir?" yelled Jeff Hazelbrouck from the stern.

One of the officers of the swift boat that shared our finger pier came up on his bridge with a pained look on his face.

"We're trying to listen to Andy Williams over here," he said with a midwestern twang in his voice.

"False alarm, I guess," I said sheepishly. "Sorry."

As I turned to head back toward the hatchway to the galley, the sun seemed to explode in my eyes, and there was an ear-splitting roar. In the white-hot glare of sudden daylight, the other boat alongside us disintegrated. I saw the officer who had just been lecturing me fly straight up into the air.

Our boat heeled over to the side as if a rogue wave had struck us broadside. A solid wall of intense heat picked me up and hurled me across the deck, slamming me into the port bulkhead. I felt a white blossom of intense pain behind my right eye and briefly lost consciousness.

When I regained my senses, our boat was canted way over. Slimy water was flushing across the deck. Still disoriented, I saw that we were settling toward the muddy bottom of the lagoon.

The air was filled with an acrid stench. A few inches from my nose, a can of Maxwell House coffee lay on its side, the metal perforated with holes. An inch-high mound of loose coffee lay next to it. I realized I was still lying on the deck. Struggling to my knees, I stared across the dock pilings at the boat that had taken the brunt of the sapper's charge. The whole forward section was on fire. The rest of it had disappeared.

I heard a ragged yell and looked back to see a man crawling along the ruins of the pier, his clothes on fire. It was Harmon Posey. Another sailor ran to him and dragged him into the shallow water to douse the flames.

Something warm was running down the right side of my face. I could only see out of my left eye. I held two fingers to the warmth and pulled them away. The fingers were bright red in the glare of the fires.

I felt a stinging pain in my ribcage and glanced down to see blood seeping through a tear in my shirt. A shard of metal, maybe a half-inch thick and an inch long, had been driven into my right side just below the ribs. I tried to pull it out, but my hand wouldn't work. With curious detachment, I noticed that a sliver of white bone had punctured the skin above my wrist. I still felt no serious pain.

I thought next of my crew. I remembered that three of them had been sitting on aluminum chairs under the canvas awning at the stern. Looking back, I saw the stern was awash in lagoon water. The awning had disappeared along with the chairs. What looked like a white potato sack was lying half-submerged in the water.

I heard the sound of machine gun fire and turned to see one of the boats up the line moving slowly out into the channel, its .50 caliber machine guns spraying the water at the end of the inlet. What I had thought was a potato sack crawled toward the transom. I realized it was a human being, but the fire-blackened face was unrecognizable. As I watched, a sailor leaped aboard the boat from the remains of the dock and bent down to help him.

My good eye took in the shadowy opening where the hatchway led to the galley. It registered in my brain that Garland was still down there. I began crawling along the slanted deck toward the opening.

The boat that had absorbed the full brunt of the charge was gone. The one on the other side of us was on fire too. Someone inside it was screaming like a tortured animal. Men were attacking the flames with hoses and fire extinguishers as I crawled down through the wrecked hatchway.

Nothing looked remotely familiar in the darkness. Shattered equipment and wood debris filled the passageway beneath my knees as I inched forward toward the first bulkhead. As my good eye adjusted to the darkness, I worked past it toward the bulkhead of the galley.

"Garland?" I shouted.

There was no response. He might have gone topside while I was up in the bow enjoying the cloudburst. Through the opening into the galley, I could see the outline of vague shapes littering the deck. My ears picked up the sound of water coursing through another hole somewhere below the waterline.

Something moved in the forward part of the cabin.

"Garland!" I called out again.

"Yeah," he finally came back. His voice was a feeble croak.

Drawing closer, I saw that his legs appeared to be trapped under a pile of debris. He was on his back, his head resting against the corner of an overturned locker. Water sloshed through a hole in the hull near his head.

Kneeling beside him, I was relieved to see that his face and upper body were unmarked. The brackish lagoon water that covered the deck around us was rising fast.

"Your right eye is gone," he said as I stared down at him.

"Don't feel much pain yet," I said. "How about you?"

"You owe me thirty bucks," he said.

I grinned and said, "The game isn't over, buddy."

He grimaced.

"My legs are starting to hurt bad."

"I've got to get you out of here," I said.

Grabbing the seat of his pants with my good hand, I started to pull him clear of the debris covering his legs. He came toward me with surprising ease. I looked back and saw why. Both his legs were gone, the left one above the knee. His head slid sideways and came to rest on my thigh.

"Is it okay?" Garland asked, looking up at me.

I had no idea how to keep him from bleeding to death. When he suddenly lifted his head to look down at himself, I turned his face back toward mine.

"A lot of pain," he said, gritting his teeth, "mostly my left foot."

With each beat of his heart, a small gout of blood erupted from the stumps where his legs had been. In the continued glare of the fires, the water around us turned a dull brown.

"Is it okay?" he repeated, his voice hoarse.

I was removing my belt to make a tourniquet for one of his legs when he raised his head far enough to look down at himself. For a few seconds he stared at the obscenity below his waist. Then his right hand moved to his groin. It was bloody mush.

"Kill me," he said very distinctly.

"You're going to be all right," I said, looping the belt around his right thigh with my good hand.

I remembered one of the lectures we had received at OCS in basic lifesaving techniques. Stop the bleeding. That was what I needed to do first. The medevac unit would take care of the rest.

"Oh, God," he said.

"You're not going to die, Garland," I came back. "Think of Janet."

It was the wrong thing to say.

"Kill me," he repeated. "Kill me, Rick."

It was a plea.

"No," I said.

"I don't want to live this way," he said, his voice shot through with agony. "Finish me."

"You're not going to die. They'll have you in a medevac chopper in ten minutes."

"Give me your gun," he demanded.

"No."

I watched his right hand move toward his own .45, which was still strapped in the holster at his hip. He tried to unclip the cover guard but couldn't free it from the holster.

"You fucking coward," he said, tearing at the holster strap as if his life depended on it.

"All right," I said, pulling his hand away.

The fury slowly died in his eyes.

"Tell Janet I loved her and . . . to find someone . . . someone good," he said.

"I will," I said, still desperate to avoid what he was asking me to do.

"Do it," he demanded.

As I held him in my arms, the water from the holes in the hull surged over him, washing away the gore that covered us both. His eyes were still looking up at me when I slowly pushed his head under the water and held it there. His body seemed to tremble for a few seconds. It finally went slack and his head got heavy in my hands. I let him go.

The water rose above my waist. I thought about staying there with him.

. . .

"Anyone down there?" a voice called from the shattered hatchway.

Looking up, I saw a dark figure crawling toward us. He appeared to be moving in slow motion, as if he was a hundred years old. When he came closer I saw it was Bobby Krusa.

"You're hit, sir," he said, but staring down at Garland's body.

I tried to get up, but my legs felt rooted to the deck. Bobby helped to raise me to my knees and began hauling me out of the cabin. As we came up on deck, Jack Rosenthal appeared over Bobby's shoulder, a dead cigar clamped between his teeth.

"Did you nail that son of a bitch?" he demanded.

For a moment I thought he was talking about Garland.

"The bastard in the water," he said next, his voice softening as he took in my right eye. "The one you were shooting at."

"I don't know," I said.

He and Bobby used their hands to form a sling between their arms and carried me to the command compound. It was now bathed in flood-lights. They laid me on the ground near the helicopter pad alongside a number of other men. Sometime later, I felt a finger opening my good eye.

"Is that a stomach wound down there, Ensign?" asked the voice above me.

"No," I said.

Raising my head a few inches, he held a canteen to my mouth. It contained raw whiskey, and I greedily took several swallows before he laid my head back down. The air was filled with engine noise, and a big transport Huey came hurtling down toward us, kicking up massive clouds of choking dust in the air.

I must have passed out. Sometime later, I awoke to a corpsman examining my eye. Rolling up the sleeve on my good arm, he injected me with a syringe of amber liquid. I felt myself sailing away again.

For most of my life I had yearned to be a hero. Now I had been to war and was going home again less than a month later. I had never led troops in battle. I had never experienced the nobility of making a heroic sacrifice for another warrior. But I did know what war was really like.

I had killed a man in combat, and he had been my first real friend.

TWENTY-SEVEN

I awoke on a rolling gurney in a field hospital. A gauze patch was taped over my right eye. Someone had removed the shrapnel from my side and dressed the wound. My broken wrist was encased in a plaster cast.

An unshaven black doctor in a white surgical gown leaned over me. After removing the gauze eye patch, he began to probe gently around my damaged eye with his finger. A red wave of pain and nausea sent me under again. The next thing I remember was the sound of jet engines. I couldn't see anything at all. Attempting to move my left hand, I found that my arms were strapped to my sides. A female voice found my ear over the engine noise.

"You're on your way to Japan, Ensign," she said. "The doctors have put medicated patches on both your eyes. Try to sleep now."

I faded in and out of consciousness, letting them do whatever they wanted, turning me one way and another, checking my blood pressure, pricking me with needles.

My only desire was to somehow disappear inside myself, to escape from any conscious thought. I came up from the haze to the bouncing jolt of the aircraft's wheels hitting a runway.

"You're in Yokota, Ensign Ledbetter," came the same low voice. "They'll take good care of you here."

I was in Yokota just long enough for the doctors to decide they had no one there who could save my eye. They greased both eyelids with petroleum jelly and covered them with gauze bandages and adhesive tape. On the plane back to the States, they put me under with a sedative and I slept most of the way.

In one lucid moment, my mind went back to the flight across the Pacific with Garland on Golden Eagle Airlines. We had talked about Al Schmid, the real-life hero of the film *Pride of the Marines*.

"Yeah, but he came back blind," I remembered saying to Garland.

Then I remembered Garland was dead. I had murdered him.

. . .

I was in an ambulance, and the patch over my left eye had somehow come loose. Through the window I could see a sliver of gray landscape flashing by as the ambulance passed between brick pillars and came to a stop. Two hospital corpsmen placed me on another rolling gurney. Then we were inside a hospital corridor.

"Where am I?" I asked the corpsman who was walking beside me.

"Ophthalmology ward," he said.

"Where?" I repeated.

"Newport Naval Hospital," he said.

So I was back in Rhode Island. Back where I had started OCS.

"You're going to see Dr. McCormick," he said next. "He's one of the best eye docs in the navy."

The doctor was waiting for me in a brightly lit examination room. Through the opening in the patch over my good eye, I could see that he was tall with brown hair and had what looked like a miner's lamp strapped to his forehead. Turning off the lights in the room, he leaned over the gurney and gently removed the bandage over my right eye. Switching on his head lamp, he focused a narrow beam of dazzling white light on it.

"Try to open it wider, son," he said.

I couldn't tell if it was open or not.

"You've got to help me here, son," he said sternly. "I don't want you to lose that eye—as wide as possible now."

He probed away under the miner's lamp until I was ready to pass out again. Finally finished, he used a hypodermic syringe to flush the area around the eye with something that immediately dulled the pain. After bandaging it, he gave me his first assessment.

"You've suffered a severe traumatic injury, Ensign Ledbetter," he said. "A piece of metal has penetrated the cornea. There was a hemorrhaging of the vitreous fluid that fills the eye itself—how much I can't tell. You have a large clot inferiorly, and your lens was shattered. The anterior chamber of the eye is too murky with blood right now to know anything more."

"Will I lose the eye?" I asked.

"Too early to tell," he said, turning off the miner's lamp.

"Will I be able to stay in the navy?"

"That isn't for me to judge. I'm only interested in saving your eye, and that will depend on whether the retinal wall is still intact. Right now there's no way to tell."

"What happens if the retinal wall isn't intact?"

"I'll remove what's left of the eye," he said. "But if the retina isn't detached, it should eventually regain its proper size and ocular tension. It's like trying to bake a soufflé, son. Let's hope it's going to rise."

I thought about the absurdity of it all.

"There's one more thing," said Dr. McCormick. "When a person suffers a traumatic injury to one eye, there is always the possibility of a sympathetic response in the other one. I'm going to keep the patches on both your eyes. You'll need to remain immobile. I'm prescribing sedatives that will help you to stay calm through most of it."

"For how long?" I asked.

"I don't know. You'll have to be patient. Would you like me to notify your parents or anyone else about what has happened to you?"

"No," I said, remembering my mother's emotional collapse after learning that Tommy was in jail. "I'll take care of it."

"Your decision," he said.

Blind again, I was wheeled outside. Cold rain lashed my face for a few seconds before we were inside another hospital building that smelled of floor wax. When we arrived where we were going, I was given another injection and slept again.

For the next several days and nights, I was sedated around the clock. I was in a single room. I knew that because there were no other sounds when the nurses left. The drugs took me through the nights and most of each day. I was kept on a liquid diet. Only one thing remains in my memory from those days and nights, and it was a very vivid dream.

I heard someone approach my bed and I turned my head to face whoever it was. Of course I couldn't see anything. I felt someone kiss my cheek.

"Who's there?" I whispered.

"How are you feeling, Beau," he said.

It was Tommy's voice.

"How did you find out I was here?"

He ignored the question and said, "Someday you'll realize this is the best thing that could have happened to you."

"Give me a break," I said.

"You might hate me for saying it, but this truly is a blessing. God is saving you for a purpose."

I felt him squeeze my left hand before I fell away again into a barbiturate haze.

When the nurse changed my dressings the next morning, I asked if it was possible I might have had a visitor the previous night.

"No one outside of hospital staff is allowed to enter this ward without a pass," she said.

Dr. McCormick came that morning to check on the progress of his soufflé.

"So far, so good," was his early prognosis. "Your eye is slowly healing."

"It's odd," I said, "but I feel more pain in my wrist and in my side than in the eye."

"Your eye was penetrated by a tiny sliver of metal. In that sense it is a minor wound compared to the bigger shrapnel wound in your side and the compound fracture of your wrist," he responded. "There won't be any further serious pain in the eye, but there is another thing to consider. In my experience, the possible loss of an eye can impact a man psychologically more than physiologically."

"In what way?"

"An artificial eye has its obvious limitations from a cosmetic standpoint," he said.

The blinds on the windows remained closed all day long. Aside from the nurses, my only companionship came from a radio that they put beyond my reach near the window. One Saturday afternoon I heard part of a Brown-Princeton football game broadcast from a radio station in Providence. As the nurses began to wind down the sedatives, I was no longer able to sleep very well. Outwardly I resembled every other semi-comatose patient in the hospital who had just come back from Vietnam, all of them grateful to be out of the killing zone.

But Garland was always there with me, lying in a dark corner of my mind, ever present, his haunted eyes gazing up at me as I pushed his face beneath the surface of the lagoon water, his head getting heavy in my hands. Like a short loop of film, it kept endlessly repeating itself in my brain. Sleep became nothing more than a few minutes of ragged oblivion until the next morbid apparition.

I tried to think of Kate, but her sweet memory held no allure against the nightmare I was living through. I began to think about the what ifs. What if I had seen the shadow of the sapper as he approached us instead of on his way back to safety? What if I had screamed out his presence as soon as I had seen the shadow? What if I hadn't spent all those hours back at OCS convincing Garland of the great adventure that lay ahead of us in the swift boat program? He would probably have ended up on a carrier or a battleship like most of our classmates, another morale officer who organized basketball games for the enlisted men.

The nurses gave me daily sponge baths, fed me, medicated me, and emptied my bedpan. They took everything in stride. Without the use of my eyes, my sense of smell became more acute. I could distinguish each of the regular nurses within seconds of their coming into the room by the perfume they wore, or didn't.

. . .

A few days after my arrival, I was helped into a wheelchair and rolled down to Dr. McCormick's examination room again. After removing my patches, he went to work with his miner's lamp.

"The good news is that there is no evidence of a sympathetic injury to your left eye," he said fifteen minutes later. "It's still too early to know anything else. However, you will no longer have to wear the second patch. You can also begin to take some light exercise."

When I got back to my room, there were two letters waiting for me on the nightstand next to the bed. Considering that I had asked the hospital staff not to notify my family, I was curious about who could have sent them. Seeing the return address in the left-hand corner of the first one, I knew it was from Janet Gentry. She had mailed it to my APO address, and it had been forwarded from Vietnam to the hospital.

It was clear from the letter that she thought I was still in Vietnam. It was also obvious she was in emotional shock. The letter was from someone trying to convince herself that her husband had died for a worthy cause. "He gave his life to help that little democracy," she wrote. "Now he is in heaven with our other great heroes."

The last line was the one I dreaded.

"Rick," she wrote, "please tell me how he died."

It struck me for the first time that I had been part of two drowning incidents in my life, with two different outcomes. I had tried to save my brother. I had taken Garland's life. I put her letter aside, not sure how I would respond.

The other letter was from Tommy and had also been forwarded to me from Vietnam. It was almost a month old. "Dear Beau," it began, and ran on for three typewritten pages, each line single-spaced with the words going right to the margin of the paper. The letter reminded me of the ones he had sent from Mississippi during his Freedom Riding summer. It was full of his impressions and word pictures, the people he was meeting, the places he had been. It was a paragraph on the last page that stunned me.

"We have received compelling evidence from the Red Cross that teams of American-led assassination squads have been organized by the Central Intelligence Agency and are now roaming the Vietnamese countryside at night, kidnapping, torturing, and murdering men and women who have supposedly been identified as Viet Cong sympathizers," Tommy wrote. "I know this may be hard for you to believe, but hundreds of people have apparently been killed in this way, many selected for death by paid informants looking to settle personal scores. It is in direct violation of the Geneva Accords."

It was no longer hard for me to believe it at all. I thought back to the helicopter I had seen take off over the South China Sea and return just ten minutes later. Pale Horse was what Jack Rosenthal had called it.

Tommy's final words in the letter demonstrated how much his attitude had changed from when he had left school just months earlier.

"I have come to abhor our government," he wrote. "In spite of Christ's teachings, I have come to hate our leaders—men like McNamara and Rusk and Bundy who have routinely ordered the deaths of so many innocent people through their own arrogance and sense of moral superiority.

There is a rising tide of protest around the world, and it grows stronger every day. In Vietnam, you may have heard that many Buddhist monks are actually sacrificing their own lives to bring the war to a quicker end."

I knew all about them, all right. But I didn't see how their actions were shortening the war. It seemed like some monk in Saigon was lighting himself on fire with gasoline almost every day.

"Rick, I pray every day for your safe return" were Tommy's closing words.

TWENTY-EIGHT

My legs trembled as I made my first expedition to the shower stalls at the far end of the ward. I was carrying my shaving kit, clean pajamas, and a piece of plastic wrap that the nurses had given me so I could take a shower without soaking the cast on my wrist. By the time I got there, I felt like I had just run a mile. I stripped off my dirty pajamas and headed over to one of the mirrors above the porcelain sinks.

It wasn't my familiar face I was looking at. A stranger stared back at me, a skid row bum. My good eye was sunk back in the socket like it was trying to hide. There were red welts where the nurses had taped and re-taped my bandages. My hair was matted down on one side. There were even some pale white hairs along my right temple. The bruises covering my chest had turned yellowish-purple. The one around the shrapnel wound in my side was an ugly green.

When I stepped onto the bathroom scale, I saw that I had lost twenty-eight pounds from my regular weight of one ninety-five. Turning away in disgust, I stepped into the shower. After letting the warm water sluice off my back and lower body for ten minutes, I put on clean pajamas and headed back down the ward. When I returned to my bed, a nurse came up bearing a sunny smile.

"Would you like to walk with me to the sunporch?" she asked, as if inviting me on a date.

She had a kind face.

"Maybe tomorrow," I said.

"The doctor thinks it's time for you to enjoy some light exercise," she said.

"Maybe tomorrow," I repeated.

A few hours later, I left the ward for the first time. It wasn't to make a visit to the sunporch for light exercise. Putting on a bathrobe over my pajamas, I waited until the nurses' shift change was under way before heading toward the lavatory. I kept on going through it to the next ward and then outside. The canteen was about fifty yards across the hospital complex. Attached to it was a small PX that sold basic items like candy, film, shaving articles, and liquor. I bought a pint of Wild Turkey and returned the way I had come, smuggling it back to my room inside my robe. I took hits on it until I finally fell asleep.

. . .

When I came awake, I was in a different room. I knew as soon as I opened my good eye and saw the changed light. During the night they had rolled my bed to another ward. A ceiling fan slowly stirred the air above me.

I heard a low chuckle and swung my head around on the pillow. A man was sitting up in the bed and gazing down at a book on his lap. Something in it made him chuckle again. Turning his face toward mine, he saw that I was awake.

"Morning," he said.

His skin was ebony black and his head was shaved. There were livid pink scars on his left cheek and forehead. The wound or injury had apparently severed a facial nerve, because the left side of his face drooped down, slightly distorting his mouth.

"Hello," I said.

A white card in a plastic holder was hanging from the headboard above his pillow. It read THOMPSON, A. R., Capt., USMC.

A stack of books stood several feet deep on either side of the headboard.

"Andy Ray Thompson," he said.

I took in deep-set intelligent dark brown eyes.

"Richard Ledbetter," I said, my eye traveling down his bed to his right leg.

It was suspended above the blanket by counterweights. Below the knee it was withered to about half the size of the other one and connected to a steel brace with metal pins.

"Where you from?" he asked.

"New York . . . Long Island," I said.

He nodded.

"You?" I asked.

"Montgomery, Alabama," he said.

"You been here long?" I asked.

"In this hospital—seven months," he said.

"What happened?"

He looked down at his shrunken leg and grinned almost bitterly.

"My leg got infected," he said, turning away from me and staring down at his book.

I remembered the unfinished pint of Wild Turkey and began searching for it under my pillows. It didn't take long to realize the nurses must have found the bottle and taken it.

"Lose something?" he asked, glancing over again.

"Nothing I can't replace," I said.

Heading to the bathroom, I discovered that my new room was one of six set aside for officers at the end of a ward for enlisted men. The enlisted men's end was one big open room with hospital beds lined up next to one another along both sides. A glass-enclosed nurses' station occupied the center of the ward like an aquarium. Walking through the ward, I saw that every bed was filled.

. . .

Over the next few days I spent a lot of time wandering the hospital grounds and stopping to rest when my strength began to ebb. The brisk fall air was filled with the familiar smell of burning leaves. I thought long and hard about how to respond to Janet Gentry's letter and her question about how Garland had died.

I would usually eat dinner in the hospital's main cafeteria and return to my room at around nine. Thompson would almost always be reading a book from one of the stacks next to his bed. He rarely looked up when I got back to the room. The night after they found my Wild Turkey, one of the nurses came through rolling a medication trolley.

"Dr. McCormick wasn't thrilled about the sleep medication you were using, Ensign Ledbetter," she said. "He thought these would work just as well."

She gave me two sleeping pills in a Dixie cup and waited until I had swallowed them with water. On her way out, she turned off the overhead lights. As I lay there waiting for the pills to click in, Thompson switched on the small lamp clamped to the headboard above his pillow and returned to his book.

I woke later that night to the sound of rain pelting the window. Thompson's reading light was still on. His head was tilted over his book, but I saw that his eyes were closed. The small electric clock next to his bed read four thirty. I heard the faint sound of whimpering from the open surgery ward down the hall. It slowly rose to a moaning wail before I heard the clicking sound of nurses' shoes moving fast on the linoleum floor. Then it was quiet again. The cry had woken up Thompson, too.

"Where did you go to college?" he asked, his eyes still closed.

"Cornell University," I said.

"Is that up north here?"

I couldn't believe he had never heard of an Ivy League school.

"Yeah," I said. "What about you?"

"Sewanee," he said.

I had never heard of his school either, even after he spelled it out.

"What did you study?" he asked.

"What do you mean?"

"You know—mathematics, literature, philosophy, chemistry. What did you study?"

"Liberal arts," I said.

"What are you going to do with it?"

"With what?"

"Your education—when you get out."

"Hell, I don't know," I said.

"Well, why did you go to college?" he asked.

Why *did* I go to college? I wondered, apart from the chance to play competitive tennis and meet girls. I thought about telling him that all the Ledbetter children went to college in preparation for spending the Sprague money. I doubted Andy Ray would understand.

"Take a look at the page I marked," he said, tossing me one of the books he had been reading.

It was a military history manual about the operations of the 101st Airborne Division after the D-day landings in France. The bookmark lay between two pages that displayed black-and-white photographs of a thick hedgerow between two pastures. Wrecked military equipment littered the field on either side of the hedgerow. There were two dead cows lying in the pasture.

"So what do you see?" he said.

"A hedgerow?" I said uncertainly.

"That's right," he replied. "They took that hedgerow at the cost of fourteen paratroopers killed."

I looked up from the pictures.

"So?" I said finally.

"That hedgerow opened up one of the pieces of ground that allowed ol' Patton to make his breakout from Normandy across France. It wouldn't have happened if those boys hadn't taken and held it and a lot of others just like it."

I waited for him to explain what he was talking about.

"Now, look at this," he said, picking up another book from the stack on the other side of his bed.

This one was a cardboard-backed diary with handwritten notes in it. The diary included a color photograph.

"What do you see there?" he asked.

The picture had been shot from the air. It looked like rice fields in the delta. The debris of two burned-out helicopters marked the foreground, which was divided by an earthen dike.

"It looks like a paddy dike," I said.

"Very good," he said. "I took it."

"The picture?" I asked.

"No. The dike—all that mud. I was ordered to take it with my platoon against a dug-in NVA unit, and we did . . . at the loss of sixteen men. You know what MACV command did one day after we took it?"

I shook my head.

"After announcing the victory, they ordered me to pull out of there. We gave that mud right back to the NVA."

I was staring at him.

"In other words, it meant nothing," he said. "Not worth one life, much less sixteen."

I got out of bed and handed the two books back to him. He carefully placed them on the stack on the far side of his bed.

"That happens every day over there," he said.

I wondered how he could seem so calm about it.

"When I get out of here, I'm going to be a history teacher," he said next, as if Vietnam had happened a hundred years ago. "American history."

He lay back on the pillows again and closed his eyes. "And I'm going to make damn sure my students don't end up in a place like Vietnam unless there is a goddam good reason for it."

"You don't think we should be over there?" I asked.

"What do you think?" he came right back.

I lay there thinking about it before finally falling asleep again. The next morning I went up to the solarium on the fourth floor. I sat there gazing through the huge picture windows that overlooked Narragansett Bay and watched the wind push the black waves toward shore.

TWENTY-NINE

Two days later, a ward nurse informed me that a Lieutenant Wayne wanted me to report to him at the master-at-arms' office. I knew that the MAA had something to do with hospital security, but I wasn't sure what. When I got there, I was kept waiting in the outer office for almost an hour. No one went in or came out of the inner office. A cardboard nameplate was Scotch-taped on the door. It read JOHN WAYNE, LIEUTENANT JG.

I mused about the possibility that old Duke had finally decided to actually serve. When I was at last summoned inside, Lieutenant Wayne turned out to be a chubby-faced little guy in navy dress blues. He was sitting behind a desk cluttered with papers. Glancing up, he motioned for me to take the chair opposite him.

"I have been given the honor of temporarily commanding the master-at-arms unit of this hospital," he said gravely. "I understand that your doctor has deemed you capable of assuming light duties. Is that correct?"

I nodded.

"The correct response is 'aye, aye, sir,'" he said.

"Aye, aye, sir," I said.

"We have been having disciplinary problems with a number of the enlisted men recently returned from Vietnam," he told me. "If we don't exercise discipline over them now, they can easily become part of a bigger problem. And we wouldn't want that, would we, Ensign?"

"No, sir. Aye, aye, sir," I repeated.

"I have ordered that a commissioned officer be designated as the master-at arms in each ward," he said. "You will be one of them. As soon as an enlisted man is deemed healthy, you will make sure he is assigned to general duties here in the hospital."

"What are general duties?" I asked.

"Sir."

"Sir," I repeated.

"Waxing and buffing the floors, washing windows, policing the smoking lounges, cleaning and sweeping—there are many important jobs to do around here. I am giving you full responsibility," he said.

As I got up to leave, Lieutenant Wayne glanced with distaste at my wrinkled khaki shirt and pants. It was obvious he thought I was a thin reed when it came to winning the Vietnam War.

. . .

I received a written order from him that same afternoon appointing me the MAA of one of the dirty surgery wards. That's what they called the wards with men who had serious combat wounds, guys who had been shot by snipers, had sprung VC-wired booby traps, or stepped on poisoned punji stakes.

At Newport Naval Hospital, they were all marines. Many had just come back from a battle at a hill in Vietnam called Con Thien. I made my first visit to the ward early the following morning in time for reveille at 0600.

In the still darkened ward, I was met with a chorus of snoring that reminded me of the Christmas carol about cattle lowing near the manger. Sleep patterns in the hospital were altered by a lot of things—facial wounds, blocked nasal passages, easy access to alcohol.

Reveille in the hospital didn't involve a trumpet. An electronic amplifier connected to the PA system in the nurses' station was turned up to full volume, and at 0600 a recorded pop song blasted every corner of the ward. The one at that time was always "Soul Finger" by the Bar-Kays.

"Work with it, baby, work with it Hoo, ha."

The ward came alive to the driving beat of the music. Men began turning over in their beds. As the song ended, I could hear a symphony of throat hocking, moaning, farting, and loud cursing.

"Gimme back my fuckin' comic book," somebody shouted.

"I didn't take it," came back another voice.

"I seen you."

A nurse quickly got between them. After the ambulatory men were on their way to the lavatory, things usually settled down to their daily routine of medications, meals, doctors' rounds, visitors, and sleep.

I spent an hour with the petty officer who was to be my deputy master-at-arms. He was a lifer in the navy and told me that Lieutenant Wayne was a horse's ass. Wayne's cousin was the attorney general of Rhode Island, and the hospital administrator had given him the MAA post while he was recovering from a hemorrhoid operation.

I spent most of the days that followed sipping Wild Turkey in the TV lounge of my assigned ward. I would go back to my room for a nap before dinner. Between the liquor and sleeping pills, I managed to avoid thinking about how to respond to Janet Gentry. The days and nights started to run together. One evening I arrived back at our room and Thompson's surgeon was there.

"I think we've given it enough time, Captain," he said with a pained expression after again examining Thompson's withered leg. "I think we should take it."

"Go ahead," said Andy Ray. "I'm ready."

After the surgeon left, he seemed visibly relieved, staring at the leg as if it had become an alien being. Two days later it was removed.

My own soufflé wasn't showing any signs of rising. I'd go over to the ophthalmology wing. Dr. McCormick would strap the miner's lamp on his head and gaze into the eye with his scope. The interior was still too murky to determine if my retina was detached, but he didn't seem discouraged.

One afternoon I was dozing in the TV lounge when three young marines from my dirty surgery ward came in and sat down at one of the card tables. None of them was older than twenty, and they were in their pajamas and bathrobes. One was missing his left arm.

They had just bought new vinyl-padded photo albums at the PX and were inserting their Instamatic color prints into the folders. I assumed they were pictures of their girls or families.

"Check this one out, man," said the kid missing his arm.

One of the other guys glanced at it for a moment before handing it back.

"I kill a gook, it's like stepping on a roach," he said with a schoolboy grin.

"You wanna see some dead ARVN?" asked the third one.

"That's rare, man. Lemme see."

Passing over the print, the third boy said, "Charlie had us sighted in and began to walk in this barrage. These three gooks was sitting up on a track passin' their hash pipe back 'n' forth. And *PHA-BOOM* . . . direct hit."

The other two began chuckling.

"Fuckin' faggots," said the boy with one arm. "Ya remember that bullshit we got at Parris Island? How the South Vietnamese were fighting hard for their freedom? That they wasn't gutless cowards?"

"I can tell you this," added one of the other kids. "If we had Charlie on our side instead of the fuckin' ARVN, the war'd be over in a week."

"Fuckin'-A right," agreed one of the others.

"Look at these," said the one-armed boy handing around another stack of prints.

"This gook has two left ears."

"Yeah, we dragged those bodies in after a night attack. 'Course some fuckwad chopped their ears off. Anyway this brown bar comes over and goes nuts. He tells Sergeant Mackle to sew them back on."

Another young marine wandered into the lounge.

"Cool it. It's the Zombie," said the one-armed boy.

He was a slender kid with unruly hair and looked like Ricky Nelson. He walked slowly and aimlessly around the lounge until coming to a stop at one of the windows. I already knew why they called him the Zombie. In Vietnam, his truck had been blown up by a land mine and the two men with him were killed. Physically, he had recovered. Mentally, he appeared to be in a perpetual daze. Most of the day he plodded around the ward carrying a red diary, the snap-shut kind that a teenage girl might keep, although I never saw him write anything in it.

When he wasn't on the move, he would stand next to the one window in the smoking lounge that faced the bay. His staring eyes were glassy and his lips constantly twitched. He would stay there like a dog on point without moving for an hour or more. I tried to talk to him once, but he turned away as if I had slapped him.

When I got back to my room, two naval officers were waiting for me in the corridor. They were in their blues with starched white shirts, and my first thought was that they were lawyers there to question me about Garland's death.

"Are you Ensign Richard Ledbetter?" demanded the first one. He had three stripes on his sleeves, signifying a full commander.

"Yes, sir," I said.

"Where have you been?" asked the second one. He wore the two stripes of a lieutenant.

"I was having lunch, sir," I said, hoping they wouldn't smell the Wild Turkey on my breath.

"Do you know what a pressed uniform looks like, Ensign?"

I was wearing my bedraggled khaki shirt and stained khaki pants.

"You've kept the admiral waiting for almost ten minutes," he added before I could make up a response.

Noticing the cast on my wrist, he took my good elbow and hustled me into my room. A photographer was standing just inside the door, and beyond him I could see Andy Ray grinning at me from his bed. Another officer stepped toward me.

"Pleased to meet you, son," he said, extending his hand with a wide grin. "I'm Dan Boochever."

I was momentarily blinded by a burst of popping flashbulbs.

Blinking my good eye, I saw that the admiral was about five and a half feet tall with six rows of ribbons on the chest of his blue uniform. Another flashbulb popped as he continued to pump my hand, all the while grinning like we had both won the Super Bowl. The other two officers came over and shook my hand too. I still had no idea what they were doing there.

"I'd like to have a private moment with Ensign Ledbetter," said Admiral Boochever. Before leading me out of the room and into the corridor, he turned to Andy Ray and said, "You're a credit to your race, Captain. I hope you have a swift recovery."

Andy Ray looked up at him and nodded.

When we were alone in the corridor, the admiral said, "Son, this is a real pleasure. I knew your father out in the Pacific during the big one. Trav was my squadron leader—the guts of a goddam Apache. He could do things with a Dauntless they never even designed into that plane."

"Yes, sir," I said, still confused.

"Trav got a raw deal, all right."

"A raw deal?"

"He never told you?" he said. "In Korea he punched the lights out of his commanding officer for refusing to send a rescue mission behind enemy lines to save a downed pilot."

"He never told me," I said.

"The missing pilot was your father's wing man."

I nodded.

"Damn shame," he went on. "Cost him his career. Of course, I probably would have done the same thing."

"Yes, sir," I said, as the two staff officers came out of the room with the photographer.

"Admiral?" the commander began, stopping short when Boochever flashed him a dirty look.

"Anyway, Trav is probably a three handicap by now, the lucky bastard," he said. "Besides, he would hate this man's navy. I could write a book about getting cornholed over the last fifteen years."

"Admiral, you're due at the War College," the three-striper said, almost cringing.

"Right—well, let's get started," he said.

Over his shoulder, I saw a group of the ward nurses gathering at the far end of the corridor along with a few curious patients.

"If you could stand right here, Admiral," said the commander, placing him on the second step of the staircase that led to the ward on the second floor. "Ensign Ledbetter, you stand right here."

He moved me into position at the foot of the steps, which made Boochever appear to be taller than me although I had nearly a foot on him. The lieutenant handed him a black leather folder, and Admiral Boochever removed a sheet of paper. After putting on a pair of gold-rimmed glasses, he cleared his throat and began to read.

"The president of the United States takes great pride in presenting the Navy Cross to Ensign Richard Amory Ledbetter, United States Naval Reserve, for service as set forth herein," he said.

My stomach began to churn.

"For conspicuous gallantry at the risk of his life above and beyond the call of duty while serving in River Squadron Nine, attached to the Mobile Riverine Force in the Republic of Vietnam," he continued as the flashbulbs popped.

"In the course of a hostile attack by enemy sappers who had infiltrated his base, Ensign Ledbetter detected their presence and drove them off, using his personal sidearm, thus saving his squadron from possible destruction. In spite of serious wounds, he then entered his sinking vessel in an attempt to rescue a brother officer. His courage and selfless action upheld the highest traditions of the United States Navy."

Admiral Boochever raised his eyes from the paper and looked at me almost reverently.

"I only wish your father could be here to witness this," he said, pumping my hand again to the sound of more popping bulbs. The nurses down the hall began to applaud. I felt like I was going to throw up.

"The navy doesn't like to trumpet these things with undue fanfare," he said next, "but your local newspapers on Long Island will be receiving this news in the next few days. I'm sure they will give it proper attention. This war needs its heroes too."

The three-striper handed him a small presentation case. Admiral Boochever removed the Navy Cross from its bed of velvet and pinned it above my heart on my khaki shirt.

"Congratulations, Ensign Ledbetter," he said.

All the self-contempt I was feeling must have registered on my face. If I had possessed any real courage, I would have handed him back the medal and told him the truth. Instead, I didn't say anything.

"You look a bit under the weather, son" he said, turning to leave. "You should try to get more rest."

THIRTY

"So I'm bunking with a doggone hero," said Andy Ray as I removed the medal from my shirt and put it back in its case.

"I'm no hero," I said, tossing the box into the drawer of my bedside table.

"Well, I could hear what he said from in here. Sounded like you earned it."

"He wasn't there," I said.

When I sat down on the edge of the bed, he was still watching me intently.

"What about you?" I asked. "You do an Audie Murphy?"

"Naw," he said with a grin. "All I wanted to do over there was finish my thirteen months and then come on home. The only other way you made it home was in a medevac or a brown bag. Anyway, I try not to think about those things now. I just try to remember the good stuff."

"What do you mean—the good stuff?"

He closed his eyes.

"Well—like this one time—I had a big fella from Nebraska in one of my squads. His name was Toby, and Toby's quick-release harness on his rucksack would just pop open for no good reason. He'd be humping along, and it would fall right off his back. So he took some trip wire and wired it shut so it wouldn't pop open on the trail."

His scarred face curled into another wide grin. For a moment, I could see how he must have looked before his injury.

"So one morning we're crossing this creek. It wasn't more than chest deep, but on the other side it was a sheer bank and it got muddier as people pulled themselves up to get out. When I got across, I turned just in time to see Toby slip and fall back into the creek—his rucksack first. The only things sticking up were his legs."

Thompson started laughing.

"Toby was just kicking away and we were laughing like crazy until we noticed that his legs were going slower and slower. And it dawned on me he was drowning because his harness was wired shut and he couldn't get rid of his rucksack."

I couldn't help smiling with him.

"Well, we got him out and he was okay," he said. "I enjoy remembering things like that—that's the only part about war that was any good. The closeness you felt for the men that were stuck there with you. You ate with those men, slept with them, fought alongside them for months—in a lot of ways you got closer to them than your own family."

His voice trailed off, back again in his memories.

I tried to remember a good memory of Garland and one came to me almost immediately. We had been sitting in the officers' club at Coronado when he began doing a wicked imitation of LBJ in the Oval Office demanding a blow job from Robert McNamara.

Another one hit me too. It was the second morning after we had arrived at OCS. We were taking showers when I heard Gene Pitney singing "Twenty-Four Hours from Tulsa." At least, it sounded just like him, but it was coming from the next shower stall. Garland had the same dramatic tenor voice.

I found I was crying. Andy Ray stared at me for a moment and then pretended to go back to his book. I walked out into the hallway and down to the entrance to the courtyard.

. . .

It was raining as I walked outside. Gazing up into the black sky, I knew what I would write to Janet Gentry. It wasn't going to be about how he had died. It would be about how he had lived—the impact he had on the rest of us. The reasons we enjoyed him so much. All the good memories we had shared.

I hoped the day would come when Janet finally stopped grieving and found another man to love. She was too young for that not to happen. And when it did, Garland would be a sweet memory.

I hoped it wouldn't happen too soon.

THIRTY-ONE

The following day I got my news from Dr. McCormick. After probing my eye with the scope for a couple of minutes, he turned off the switch on the miner's lamp and removed it from his head.

"Your retinal wall is detached," he said calmly.

The soufflé was never going to rise. He said he wanted to move quickly before there was any more deterioration. I agreed. That night, he removed my right eye and packed the empty socket with a medicated suppository.

"You'll heal quickly now," he told me. "There won't be any complications."

The only complication was that I was no longer whole. At some point in the near future, I would have a glass eye. The good eye would be looking directly at people. The other would be looking in another direction. I thought about whether I would have preferred to lose an arm or a leg. Those could be hidden in different ways. I shuddered at the thought that people would look away from me. The walleyed man.

I awoke the next morning to find our morning shift nurses standing around my bed. One of them was holding a small chocolate cake with white icing. A single candle was burning in the center of it.

"Happy birthday," they sang as Andy Ray joined in.

It was my twenty-second.

The following Saturday, I went into Newport to have lunch by myself at the Hotel Viking. Afterward, I sat in the hotel bar and wrote a letter to Janet Gentry. I spent the rest of the afternoon walking around town while feeling an odd sense of unease and anticipation that something important was about to happen, but I didn't know what. When I got back to our room that evening, Andy Ray was gone.

"Captain Thompson received his transfer orders to a veterans' hospital near his home in Alabama," said one of the nurses. "He waited for you as long as he could, but his train left at five o'clock."

They had already stripped his bed. Most of his books had been sent back to the library. A few remained on his nightstand, and I found an unfolded letter beneath one of them. It was from his mother.

"My dear son," it began. "Last week, I received the enclosed letter from an officer who served with you in Vietnam. It made my heart swell, and when I showed it to Pastor Wilbon he read it to the whole congregation last Sunday morning. You have made us all proud. I count the days until you are home with us."

The other note was behind the first.

"Dear Mrs. Thompson," it read. "Please forgive the delay in my sending this but I have only recently been released from the hospital myself. I thought you might be interested in the circumstances under which your son was wounded while serving as a platoon leader in my company after we were attacked by a full regiment of North Vietnamese regular troops.

"Andy Ray's platoon bore the brunt of their initial assault and he led it with great skill. When one of his corpsmen was shot, Andy Ray crossed an area of intense fighting to administer first aid. Hit in the leg by enemy machine gun fire, he reached the man and began to treat his wounds. A hand grenade landed nearby and he shielded the man with his body, taking additional wounds to his face. He brought the man back and saved his life. I wanted you to know it was an honor to serve with him."

I remembered asking him what had happened to his leg and he had said, "It got infected."

If I had earned the Navy Cross for killing Garland, what should Andy Ray have received for saving a man's life? They hadn't given him anything. Jarring images invaded my mind, starting with the faces of the young marines in the dirty surgery ward and Harmon Posey on fire after our boat blew up. I remembered Kate's face as she talked at Easter about how all of us were being wounded by this war.

I felt something shift inside me. It was like looking down over the edge of a bottomless abyss and realizing I was about to fall. It started with the stark recognition that I would always have a dead eye. That I would always be looked at as an object of pity.

It was followed by an acute and stabbing pain inside my head. It came from a place I didn't know even existed. At first I thought it might be a migraine headache, but I had never had headaches aside from hangovers, and this was no hangover. It blotted out all coherent thought. I tried to summon up a good memory that would give me escape but was dragged back down every time.

I tried to walk it off by wandering around the acres of lawn inside the walled hospital compound in the darkness. The night was cold and windy near the bay, and the darkness seemed to hold its own special terror.

Drawn back to the light, I sat on a bench near the entrance to the hospital canteen, holding my head in my hands and silently begging to be released from an overwhelming sense of imminent disaster.

A shore patrolman stopped to ask me if I was all right. I knew he was trying to be helpful, but it only made me angry and I moved off. Minute after minute, hour by hour, the anxiety and fear refused to release its grip. I have experienced physical pain in my life. This was different. It was like a hurricane inside my brain.

It ended shortly before dawn with my vomiting up everything inside me onto the lawn. Afterward, I made my way back to the hospital and walked the length of the enlisted ward before arriving at my room. Hearing the men snoring in their beds was actually reassuring in some way and I fell into a restless sleep.

I knew something had died in me.

. . .

I felt utterly drained as I sat in the TV lounge of my dirty surgery ward late the next morning. I tried to remember the things I had been thinking about before my mind exploded after I read the letter from Andy Ray's mother.

Part of it was a fundamental loss of faith, a faith that had been at the core of my being since I was a boy. A faith in the golden gods of war, as Tommy had called them at Obie's Diner. A faith in the leaders who had given us Vietnam A blind faith.

Vietnam was built on a lie. If it wasn't at the beginning, it was now.

I realized that my own yearning to fight was nothing more than a romantic desire to share what my father had experienced in World War II. But as Tommy had tried to tell me, Vietnam was not World War II.

For the first time I saw this war for what it was. An abomination. I had seen some of the human cost of it and how it had wrecked the lives of many of the boys who were fighting it. I thought of the Pale Horse murder squads and the innocent Vietnamese who were being killed out of retribution or vengeance. I thought of the millions of people, Americans and Vietnamese, who were paying the price for the arrogance and stupidity of the leaders in Washington who had driven our country into this quagmire.

I began writing a letter to Tommy. I told him about Garland and how he had died. I wrote to him about the boys in the dirty surgery wards—kids who had never been away from home before who found themselves sent off to fight a war they didn't understand and never would. Iowa farm boys and Alabama rednecks, white high school dropouts from Long Island, and South Los Angeles black kids who got high school diplomas from schools without teachers, the ones who couldn't afford a college deferment or weren't able to figure out all the clever ways to avoid the draft. All the ordinary young men who, when called to serve, did so without complaint. They lined up and went.

I wrote him about the Zombie. And I wrote to him about Andy Ray.

Who was prepared to take responsibility for it all? Who would ultimately care about their sacrifice? By the time I was finished with it, the letter was twelve pages long. I figured it served Tom right, considering some of the missiles he used to launch at me over the years. I took it over to the hospital post office in the morning and airmailed it to the last address my mother had given me for him in Washington.

That afternoon I received a letter from the secretary of the navy's office telling me that as a result of losing my eye, I would be placed on the disabled retired list and separated from active duty once all the paperwork was completed.

THIRTY-TWO

For the next two days I didn't bother going over to my ward to check in with the petty officer. The following morning I was still lying in bed nursing a half pint of Wild Turkey when Lieutenant Wayne stormed into my room.

"You get out of that bed and stand at attention, mister," he demanded. "There'd better be a good explanation for your dereliction of duty, or I will put you on report."

"Fuck you, Duke," I said, taking a swallow. When he spotted the label, a look of shock registered on his face.

"Alcohol is illegal in the wards of this hospital," he declared.

"Fuck you," I repeated pleasantly.

"That's it. I'm bringing you up on charges," he said, going out the door.

. . .

The hospital staff didn't know what to do with me. They were reluctant to enforce disciplinary measures against a decorated war hero with honorable wounds. One of the staff doctors arranged for me to be visited by a resident psychiatrist. When he stopped by my room to get acquainted, I refused to talk to him. A Methodist chaplain got the same response.

The days passed in a hazy blur. One day a corpsman removed the plaster cast from my wrist. By then, the shrapnel wound was also fully healed. Only a scar remained. I also had a new roommate. He was a forty-year-old civilian accountant at the base procurement depot who was suffering from an allergy to milk. After spending one night with me, he asked to be moved to another room but was told there were no other available beds and that the hospital was full of wounded marines back from Vietnam. He threatened to file a formal complaint with the naval inspector general.

It was around six in the evening, and I had just returned to my room after shaving and taking a shower. That was the one concession I made to official decorum, and it was done solely to assure a positive reception at the PX when I went over to buy liquid rations. The weather had turned colder, and I put a hospital bathrobe on over my khakis before heading out of the room. From the radio in the nurses' station, I could hear Engelbert Humperdinck singing "Please Release Me," a song which I had come to truly detest.

"May I help you?" I heard one of the nurses say to someone at the visitors' desk.

"Is Richard Ledbetter a patient in this ward?" came back a familiar voice.

A male orderly was standing ten feet farther down the corridor, staring intently back toward the desk. My eye followed his and there she was, slowly coming down the hallway, checking the numbers on each door.

She was wearing a white silk blouse over a knee-length navy wool skirt. Over her arm, she was carrying a camel overcoat and a small overnight bag. I felt a surge of pure happiness that almost dissolved the energy I needed to stand. As she came up to me, she dropped her things on the floor and opened her arms to embrace me.

"I hope you don't mind my just showing up here," said Kate anxiously, as if unsure how I would react.

"You've got to be kidding," I said. "I can't believe it."

We held each other for several seconds, my warm cheek against her cold one. I took in the clean scent of her. The orderly was looking at us with a goofy smile on his face. When we separated, she smiled up at me.

"I wasn't sure if I had to pass some kind of dress code before they would allow me on the base. I changed into these clothes at the bus station."

The orderly hadn't moved from the spot where he had first seen her.

"You passed with flying colors, ma'am," he said.

"Is there a place we can talk?" she asked.

"Sure," I said, leading her back into my room.

The accountant wasn't there to disturb us. He never returned to the room until he was sure I was asleep. Stepping inside, she turned again to face me. Her hair was a bit longer than it had been at the Worcester jail, not quite shoulder length. Unlike the pallor I had last seen, there was a fresh glow to her complexion.

"Oh my God," she said suddenly.

"What is it?" I demanded.

"You've lost your tan," she said, failing to keep a straight face.

"Well, at least one of us looks pretty fabulous," I said.

"Tom was very moved by your letter," she said, her eyes searching my good one. "He would have come himself, but the demonstration at the Pentagon is Saturday. People are coming from all over the country. Anyway, I said I would come instead. I wanted to come."

"Did you read the letter too?" I asked.

"Yes," she said softly. "I did."

"I'm glad," I replied.

"I was . . . moved by it too, Rick," she said.

There was something in her eyes I had never seen before. I think it was trust.

"How did you get here?" I asked.

"By bus," she said.

"All the way from Washington?"

She nodded.

"When did you leave D.C.?"

"Around four thirty this morning."

"You must be pretty tired."

"I'm fine," she said, stepping back to look me over.

"How much weight have you lost?" she said.

"I don't know," I lied. "I'll get it back."

She nodded again, still smiling.

"You know—with that black eye patch, you almost look like a young Errol Flynn."

"He never wore a patch."

"Long John Silver, then," she said with a laugh.

There was a sudden burst of static from the public address system, and a voice said, "Visitors' hours end in five minutes."

As the words were repeated, my heart sank at the thought of her going.

"When can you leave the hospital?" she asked.

"I'll be separated from the navy very soon, I hope."

"I meant—tonight."

"Tonight?"

"I have to go back tomorrow," she said. "Could we at least have dinner together?"

I felt another rush of pure exhilaration.

"Yeah, sure," I said.

"Can you help me find a room in Newport?"

I nodded.

"The Hotel Viking," I said. "We can have dinner there too."

At that moment I would have carried her to the hotel barefoot over broken glass.

"Let's go," I said, starting to head out of the room.

"Mmm," she came back. "You're wearing your bathrobe."

"Oh, yeah," I said.

I briefly considered borrowing the accountant's overcoat, but he was the size of a jockey. I remembered that one of the things Andy Ray had left behind was a navy crew-neck sweater. I went and got it from the closet, slipping it on over the wrinkled summer tans.

"This will be fine," I said. "There are always taxis waiting near the gate."

. . .

When we came out of the hospital entrance, there weren't any taxis. A cold wind was blowing off Narragansett Bay, and Kate pulled the camel overcoat closer around her shoulders.

"Goddam it," I muttered, shivering as we walked toward the main gate, my head down against the wind.

"You were right," she said.

When I looked up, a lone taxi was heading toward us. There is a God, I temporarily decided. It rolled to a stop and we got in. As rain began to spatter the windows, we headed into Newport. Kate stared out at the dripping trees lining the road.

"Under an oak, in stormy weather, I joined this rogue and whore together," she said.

I realized it had to be something classic but had no idea who wrote it.

"Shakespeare?" I asked.

"Jonathan Swift," she said, turning to look at me.

"How does the rest of it go?"

"And none but he who rules the thunder can put this rogue and whore asunder," she said.

I was still pondering the meaning of the words when we pulled up to the front entrance of the Viking, and a doorman rushed out with an umbrella to escort us inside. While Kate registered, I arranged for a porter to take her small travel bag up to her room.

"I was lucky," she said as we walked to the dining room. "There was only one room left."

An elderly white-haired waiter in a black tuxedo met us at the entrance. Taking a look at my sweater and khakis, he almost visibly recoiled. If I had been alone, I doubt he would have seated me, but when his eyes moved to take in Kate, his attitude visibly changed.

"Dinner for two?" he asked, and I nodded.

The white linen tablecloths set off the dark, mahogany-paneled walls. There were two candles in silver holders at each table. As the waiter lit ours, I watched two navy couples dancing to a five-piece jazz combo in the small open area across the room.

The waiter was sizing me up again, clearly trying to figure out what this fabulous girl was doing with such a loser. He handed us our dinner menus and waited for us to order drinks. She suggested we split a bottle of champagne to celebrate my escape from the hospital. I agreed.

The waiter brought back a chilled bottle and opened it with great ceremony, pouring us each a full glass.

"To safer times," she said, holding her stem glass toward me.

"For you, Kate," I said, before taking the first sip.

She decided on broiled sea scallops in white wine with a Caesar salad. I had no real appetite but pretended to be enthusiastic about the prime rib.

A moment later, she reached out and took my right hand in hers.

"You have been a real puzzle to me," she said.

The look on her face said it all. She saw me as an arrogant and conceited jerk.

"And then at Easter break I learned you were a bit more sensitive than you let on. That sketch you did of your mother is very fine . . . also the way you told me what it was like to grow up in your family, warts and all."

I remembered our sitting together in the outhouse in the rain.

"Another thing that seemed crazy to me—for someone who obviously rejects authority, ridicules discipline and personal responsibility, you volunteered to serve in a military that embraces those same values."

"I just wanted to be a war hero," I said. "Like Travis—like JFK. I grew up with . . . romantic delusions."

"Wanting to be a hero is no romantic delusion," she said.

"A hero doesn't murder his best friend."

"You didn't murder him," she said, her fingers squeezing mine. "Your friend almost certainly would have died."

"In my childhood fantasies, I never actually won a medal for killing anybody," I said. "It was always through saving someone." Like JFK on *PT-109,* I thought.

"I know you don't want to hear it, but I think you are a hero, Rick. I've never really thanked you for what you did for Tom at the jail," she said. "I can't tell you what it meant to me when you rescued him from that nightmare."

"His faith has taken him down a tough road."

"Tom believes he must set an example. That he must *be* an example. Do you know that line from Camus? 'Let certain individuals resolve that they will oppose power with the force of example.' Tom is extending that part of his Christian faith every day."

"I could not have endured those beatings without fighting back."

"Don't confuse meekness with weakness. When someone is weak, they are led by fear. Tom is kind and gentle, but he is also fearless. He believes that he must be a kind of lightning rod to absorb the anger in others."

"Do you think that by submitting to torture he was somehow healing the torturer? That sadistic little bastard?"

"What happened in that jail was simply Tom living his faith. His actions were right out of Matthew. Do you remember the Sermon on the

Mount? 'I say to you do not resist one who is evil. If anyone strikes you on the right cheek, turn to him the other also . . . I say to you love your enemies and pray for those who persecute you so that you may be the sons of your Father who is in heaven.' "

"Matthew five thirty-nine," I said.

"That's very good," she said. "You know your Bible."

"Tom used the same words in the jail, and I looked it up when I got back to Newport."

"The truth teller," she said, grinning.

"You're Jewish," I said. "Where does your faith come from?"

"I don't share Tom's faith."

"What do you believe?"

"The Torah leaves a lot of room for interpretation," she said. "Personally I don't believe in an afterlife. I believe this is all there is . . . this life. You can find heaven and hell right here. We can celebrate heaven in the form of Albert Schweitzer and Mahatma Gandhi and we can see hell every day in what is taking place in Vietnam."

"That's pretty bleak," I said.

"It isn't meant to be. I just think this life is the only chance we will ever have to make a difference and we should live it the best we can."

She smiled and squeezed my hand again.

I found myself wondering where Tom's faith had come from. Nobility and faith were not exactly Ledbetter bywords. Of course, there was the example of Grandpa Sprague, who had mentored him from the time he was a boy. I thought about what had happened at St. John's Pond, and wondered if that played a role.

"Would you have done what he did?" I asked.

"No," she said. "I wouldn't have had the courage."

Although I was a new convert in my opposition to the war, I still questioned Tom's ideas for helping to end it. They seemed self-defeating to me, no matter how noble his purpose or how right he was. What kind of work could he accomplish if he ended up serving ten years in a federal prison?

I was about to raise this point when she said, "It is all-consuming."

"What is?" I responded.

"His faith . . . his work . . . nothing else seems to matter to him anymore." She took another sip of champagne and added softly, "Not even me."

I didn't know what to say.

The waiter brought our dinner. The prime rib looked delicious but I wasn't hungry. I chewed a piece while Kate made short work of her scallops and moved on to the Caesar salad.

"You're never going to regain your weight that way," she said as I shoved a forkful around my plate.

I was already depressed that she would soon be leaving again.

"Don't look so grim there, buddy," she said cheerfully.

The jazz combo began playing "Love Walked In" and I asked her to dance.

"Yes. I would love to," she said.

Then she was in my arms. With the crown of her hair tucked against my throat, and her left hand on my shoulder, we slowly moved across the dance floor. All too quickly the song was over, and I was reluctantly stepping away from her.

But they moved right into "Skylark," and she came back to me again. This time she rested her left elbow over my shoulder, letting her knuckles occasionally graze my cheek.

When the song ended, the combo took a break and we returned to the table.

After finishing the last of the champagne, she started telling me about some of the extraordinary people she had met in Washington, principled people who, like Tom, had no personal agenda aside from stopping the war.

Her eyes coming alive, she talked about how glad she was to have left school, and how important it was for her to have taken her own stand. When the jazz combo came back to start their next set, I ordered another bottle of wine. We danced again. The next hour went by in a kind of daze.

"Well, I'd better go up now," she said finally. "I need to meet the bus at six tomorrow morning."

She could see the immediate reaction on my face.

"You hardly ate anything," she said as we were going up in the elevator.

"Yeah . . . I've gotten spoiled on the culinary delights at the hospital," I said.

She chuckled. Then we were down the corridor and at the door of her room. She looked up at me, her eyes searching my face as if she was trying to memorize it.

"You've gone through hell, haven't you?" she said.

"Nothing even close to a lot of other guys," I said truthfully. "Some of them have been wrecked for the rest of their lives."

"I know," she said. "But it still must be very hard to have had all those illusions of yours shattered."

The elevator door opened back down the corridor. An older navy couple emerged and walked hand in hand to their room. I thought about going back alone to the hospital and my room with the accountant.

I turned to leave.

"Would you like to come in?" she asked.

I nodded.

She unlocked the door, and I followed her inside. It was a small room, single bed, three-drawer stand, one side chair. The single bed left a foot-wide path to the bathroom. Her travel case lay on a wooden rack next to the door.

"Lassie would have trouble stretching out in this bed," I said, as she walked over to check out the bathroom.

Rain was slashing the single window, and the hard spattering jarred loose a haunted memory. I could see the roiling surface of the lagoon during the squall, followed by a vivid image of Garland's face as he lay in the wrecked cabin. I forced it away.

Then Kate was back.

"You look like you've seen a ghost," she said, grinning.

"I did," I said.

"A fire would be good right now, wouldn't it?" she said, glancing at the little brick fireplace. The only things I could see to burn in the room were the Newport telephone book and a Gideon Bible that lay on top of the stand

"No fire," I said, dropping into the side chair, pretending to be nonchalant.

"When we were at dinner," she began haltingly, "I didn't mean to be critical of Tom. It's just that he doesn't seem to need me any longer . . . in the same way that . . . oh, I don't know."

Her eyes found my good one again.

"I don't mean to burden you with this," she said. "You have enough to worry about."

"I'm glad you confided in me," I said, standing up to leave.

"Thanks," she said softly.

"It's still hard to believe you actually came," I said, starting for the door. "I can't tell you how much it means to me."

"Rick?"

I faced her.

"It's a pretty rotten night out there. You . . . you can stay here if you like."

I instantly understood the ground rules. We would both sleep in the bed. Just not together. I didn't care. I only wanted to be with her. Her words were like the commutation of a death sentence.

"I'd like that," I said.

"If you don't mind, I'm going to take a bath," she said. "It will save me time in the morning."

Retrieving her travel bag from the rack, she went into the bathroom and closed the door. A moment later, I heard water gushing into the tub. As the rain continued to slash at the window, I contemplated the idea of surprising her with a roaring phone book fire. Kneeling by the grate, I saw that the flue was blocked with cement.

Leaving the bedside lamp on, I took off my sweater and shoes, pulled back the feather quilt, and crawled under the covers. Through the closed door, I could hear her splashing in the tub while she quietly hummed a song. Then I heard the water gurgling as it went down the drain. Another few minutes passed like an eternity as I stared at the closed door. It reminded me of the same uncomplicated ache I used to feel as I waited in bed as a kid on Christmas morning.

The door opened again, and she came back into the room. A moment later, she was coming toward me. She had put on an oversized flannel shirt and a pair of loose-fitting gym shorts. Sitting down on the edge of the bed, she turned out the light. The mattress sagged toward the center as she slipped under the covers.

"I hope you're not a bed hog," she said, chuckling, as I tried to scrunch up against the wall.

In the darkness, her face was only a pale outline. She lay on her back with her arms across her chest.

"Good night, Kate," I said.

She slowly turned to face me on the pillow. I could feel the sweet ebb and flow of her breath on my face, delicate and invisible. In the faint reflection of the streetlights, I saw that her eyes were open. They gazed at me, luminous and huge. For some reason, she began trembling.

I didn't move.

"Rick?" she whispered.

"Yes."

"Would you . . . just hold me?"

I curled my hand around her shoulder. Taking her gently into my arms, I slowly stroked her back until the trembling seemed to subside a bit. Then her face was in front of me again. I kissed her softly and quickly pulled away.

"I don't know what I'm doing here," I said.

In the silence I only heard the rain.

"I don't either," she said.

"Kate, I want you to know that when I had really bad days over there, I would think of you and . . ."

Her hand came up to stop my mouth. Gently removing the patch over my eye, she kissed the sewn socket. I felt her warm tears on my cheek. They mixed with my own.

She kissed me on the lips, shyly at first, and then with a determination that convinced me she had somehow come to care for me and maybe even desire me.

I had a sudden glimpse of how she would look at me in the morning if we made love.

"We can't," I said.

I gently stroked her face in the darkness and felt new moisture on her cheek. As much as I wanted to make love to her, I knew this wasn't the time. There would be a right time, I hoped, but only when it wouldn't feel like a betrayal.

She turned away from me and I slid behind her, putting my arm around her waist and holding her close. Outside, the sound of the wind grew louder. I held her until we were both asleep.

THIRTY-THREE

It was still dark when I woke again. I could no longer hear the rain. Opening my good eye, I saw that Kate was sitting on top of the bedcovers, fully dressed. Her bag was packed next to the door.

"I have to leave," she said.

"What time is it?" I asked.

"A little after five," she said.

"You can't," I said.

"I have to, Rick," she said.

I sat up in bed.

"I need to check out," she said. "I was hoping you might walk me over to the bus station."

"What if we went down there together?" I said.

"To Washington?" she said with obvious surprise.

"Then I could join you and Tommy in the demonstration," I added.

She gazed at me intently.

"Are you sure you know what you're doing? You're an active duty naval officer."

"Not for long," I said. "And I want to do it. But forget about the bus. I'll rent a car."

"Don't you have to report back to the hospital?"

It would have been a mistake to go back and request a weekend pass. After my recent conduct, they wouldn't give me one. But they also wouldn't want the publicity of punishing a Navy Cross recipient who went absent from the hospital for a couple of days.

"It's fine," I said.

"Do you need anything from your room?" she asked, glancing at the hand-me-down khakis draped across the chair.

"I have everything I need right here," I said.

She leaned down and kissed me again. Slowly pulling away, she smiled and said, "Your hair on one side is standing straight up like a porcupine."

"Yeah, I did that especially for you," I said, getting up to wash.

. . .

After renting the car, I stopped at a deli in Plum Point to pick up coffee and donuts. It was bright and sunny, and as we drove through the Rhode Island countryside, the autumn leaves were blazing red and gold. When we hit the interstate, I headed west toward Connecticut.

"I think you really like me," I said at one point.

"Really?" she replied.

"Yeah, I think you might even love me a little," I said.

"Is that what you think?" she said.

A mile or so farther on she said, "Rick, I don't have any regrets about what happened last night. It was . . . special. But please don't ask me where all this is leading because I don't know. I need time to . . ."

"I understand," I interrupted.

"Whatever happens, I won't forget it," she said.

. . .

We were across the New York State border when a radio news report helped me to realize the magnitude of what was taking place in Washington. The announcer was saying, "More than two hundred thousand people are expected to be here tomorrow in what organizers are calling a march against the Pentagon to peacefully protest the war in Vietnam. At the same time, radical protest groups have threatened to attack the South Vietnamese embassy, and President Johnson has placed the Eighty-second Airborne Division in a state of active alert near the Capitol."

"I think I should call Tom," Kate said.

"Sure."

I pulled off the interstate and stopped for gas. While Kate went inside to call their Washington office, I refilled the rental car's tank. When she came back to the car, her face was ashen.

"He isn't there," she said. "Federal marshals came to the office this morning to arrest him, but he never showed up. My friend at the office said she thought he might be at a church near Dupont Circle. I wrote down the address."

Within minutes of getting back on the road, she began giving herself a hard time. Glancing over at her, I saw a tear slide over the lower lid of her eye, picking up speed as it cascaded down her cheek.

"I should never have left him," she said.

"You had no way of knowing they were coming."

"I wasn't there when he needed me," she said.

"Look . . . this was all inevitable," I said. "Tom must have known they would be coming for him. I'm sure he's prepared for it. That's the whole point. Please don't blame yourself."

"I should never have let him talk me into coming to see you," she said.

"He talked you into it?"

Had he really sent her? At the hotel, she had said she wanted to come.

We made it from Newport to the Maryland border in less than seven hours. Along the way, we passed six slow-moving truck caravans of National Guard and Army Reserve troops heading south. When we crossed over the Susquehanna River and arrived on the outskirts of Havre de Grace, the volume of military vehicles grew even larger.

We passed a sign reading "Washington—74." Kate offered to drive, and I pulled over to change places. A few minutes later we ran into the biggest traffic jam I'd ever encountered. For the next two hours we crept along in stop-and-go traffic, averaging a couple of miles an hour. Police cruisers with flashing gumball lights sat along the edge of the interstate every few hundred yards. Officers were randomly stopping cars to check the drivers' identification.

"They're doing everything they can to impede people from getting to Washington," she said as we waited for the line to move forward. Ahead of us, frustrated drivers were cutting across the grass median strip and heading back in the opposite direction.

Kate's nerves were rubbed raw, and she asked me to take over the driving again. Every ten or fifteen minutes, she would ask if this or that road we were passing might get us there faster. Four hours into Maryland, we finally reached the Washington Beltway, and I headed west toward Silver Spring.

Getting off at the Georgia Avenue exit, we began the next stage of the crawl into the city, passing Walter Reed Army Hospital at around ten thirty. The facility was all lit up, and patients were standing at the windows, watching the crowds going past on the sidewalks.

Kate seemed to know the city and told me to turn west onto Military Road and then south on Sixteenth Street to New Hampshire Avenue. That would bring us directly to Dupont Circle, she said. The church where Tom had possibly found sanctuary was only a few blocks away from it.

. . .

The sidewalks of the avenue were crowded with people all walking in the same direction. Most of them looked like college students. One was carrying a white cardboard sign fastened to a strip of wood that read HAVERFORD STUDENTS AGAINST THE WAR. We encountered another police barricade at the intersection with Corcoran Street. From there, all traffic was being diverted away from Dupont Circle. I found a parking space on a side street and we went ahead on foot.

I was still wearing Andy Ray's sweater over my khaki shirt, but the night air began to cut through me. Maybe it was my weakened resistance. Closer to Dupont Circle, people were pouring into the street like a surging river from the smaller side streets. Many were in high spirits, like they were on their way to a rock concert.

A wail of police sirens began coming from every direction, but Kate was oblivious to it, walking with her long, purposeful strides as she moved through the crush. We emerged from a canyon of tall buildings along New Hampshire Avenue and came to an open park. A sign on one of the light stanchions read "Dupont Circle."

The circular park was ringed by big old trees. The outer rim was bordered by buildings which overlooked a four-lane roadway that ran all the way around the park. Floodlights mounted on several of the buildings lit the entire scene. Behind police barricades, the park was packed with thousands of people standing almost shoulder to shoulder.

Someone was bellowing into an amplified bullhorn from inside the circle. It was impossible to understand his words, but the crush of demonstrators was responding to him with great angry roars. Many looked like they had come prepared for a street brawl and were carrying World War II–vintage gas masks. In the glare of the floodlights, I saw a huge banner waving high above the crowd.

TODAY'S PIG IS TOMORROW'S BACON.

The tension was rising with each dose of rage coming out of the bullhorn. Someone began screaming, "HELL NO, WE WON'T GO," and the tightly packed mass picked up the chant as a guy blundered into me from behind, carrying two paving bricks.

"We're going for the Vietnamese embassy!" he yelled back to the people following him.

"Which way is the church from here?" I asked Kate.

"Over in that direction," she said, pointing to the far side of the circle.

Over her shoulder, I saw the headlights of a car coming around the curve of the roadway ringing the park. It was a police car and moving fast, its dome light flashing and siren blaring. The people at the edge of the roadway began to scatter as the car fishtailed toward them.

Someone from inside the circle hurled an oil drum into its path. The cruiser ran over it with a loud crunch, leaving a trail of sparks under the chassis as it was dragged along. The driver slammed on his brakes, and the police cruiser ground to a halt fifty feet from where we were standing.

In less than ten seconds, the front and rear windshields of the car disintegrated in a hail of bricks. I could see the two officers inside, their faces wild with alarm. The one on the passenger side raised what looked like a small grenade launcher from his lap and fired it through the smashed windshield. A canister exploded on the pavement near Kate and me, and we were enveloped in a cloud of tear gas. In the smoky haze, people began running like stricken animals back down the broad avenue behind us.

"My eyes!" Kate cried out, her hands covering her face.

Tears were gushing out of my good eye. It was like trying to see through a veil of water. I made the mistake of taking a breath and broke into a fit of racking coughs. Kate held my hand as we retreated down the block of commercial buildings along the avenue. I heard a loud crash as demonstrators smashed the plate glass windows of one of them before tossing a flaming Molotov cocktail through the jagged opening. Two blocks from Dupont Circle, we found temporary refuge in the murky darkness of a side street lined with brownstone houses.

"Those policemen," Kate said, gasping. "I thought they were going to die."

Overhead, I could hear the growing roar of helicopters approaching. Searchlights illuminated the darkness, turning night into day. With my good eye shut, I could have been back in Vietnam.

THIRTY-FOUR

We made our way through dark streets lined with brownstones. People slogged past us in both directions, some still looking to join the rioters, others trying to flee the cordon of police and military vehicles that now blocked most of the intersections.

We reached the church a little after midnight. The stained-glass sanctuary windows of the redbrick building were dark from the street, but Kate led me around a hedge-lined path to the basement entrance. The heavy oak door was locked when I tried to open it. After I knocked several times, the door swung open to reveal a young college-age kid with wavy red hair and a freckled face.

"I know," he began, looking at me. "You need a place to crash. Unfortunately the sacristy is full and the fire department . . ."

His eyes moved to Kate, and he stopped in mid-sentence.

"You made it back."

"Hi, Jared," she said, forcing a smile.

Locking the door, he led us down the hallway into a basement meeting hall with white-painted brick walls. It had been turned into a combination flophouse and demonstration headquarters. A couple of hundred people were sacked out in sleeping bags on the linoleum floor. Fifty more sat working at cafeteria tables placed end to end down the center of the room. Jared told us one bunch was checking lists of groups that had already arrived. Another was hand-lettering identification badges, and a third was copying road traffic routes onto a foot-high stack of mimeographed city maps.

"Things are going well," said Jared. "There's no way to tell exactly how many people are here already, but based on the busload tallies reported by the churches and synagogues that have checked in so far, we'll be well over two hundred thousand by tomorrow morning."

"A lot of the people we just saw didn't come on any church buses," I said. "They belong in prison."

"They're not part of our demonstration," said Jared glumly. "They're trying to piggyback on what we're doing for their own ends."

"Where is he?" asked Kate, looking vainly around the room.

"Upstairs in the pastor's study," said Jared. "I'll show you the way."

We followed him across the room and down a dark corridor to a narrow wooden staircase. "Turn right at the top," he said, before heading back to the meeting hall.

At the top of the stairs, we found ourselves at the rear of the church sanctuary. As we walked down the side aisle, my eye rose to a magnificent pulpit that protruded out from the choir loft. Behind the loft was a narrow hallway that led to the sacristy. In the glow of a street lamp outside the window, I could see clerical robes hanging from hooks on the wall. A narrow strip of light came from under a door on the far side of the room.

Kate had just raised her hand to knock when the door swung open. A tall, wraithlike figure stood in the open doorway, outlined in the light from a desk lamp inside the room.

"Tommy?" I asked, still unsure it was him.

Kate didn't have to ask. A moment later, she was in his arms.

"Beau," he said uncertainly as she stepped away and he came toward me.

"Digby," I replied.

As we hugged, I could feel his shoulder blades through his gaunt upper back. In the light of the room, his eyes were red with wrinkled pouches. I thought he looked worse than I did.

"Oh, Tom," said Kate, obviously sharing the same reaction.

"Don't worry about me," he said. "God watches even the smallest sparrow."

Cupping his face in her hands, she said, "Are the federal marshals coming for you?"

"Yeah . . . they're coming," he said, dropping wearily into the desk chair.

"What do you plan to do now?" I asked.

"I'll be arrested," he said calmly. "The marshals will be here at eight o'clock."

"How do you know?" I asked.

"Because I let them know where to find me," he said with an attempt at a grin.

Kate took it in silence.

"Did you drive down last night?" he asked.

I looked at Kate and she glanced away.

"This morning," I said.

"You both must be worn out," he said.

"No more than you, from the look of things," I replied.

"We've been really busy today."

"Well—as of now you have a new volunteer," I said. "Just tell me what you want me to do."

He nodded and smiled. For a few seconds it lit up his face in the same old way.

"That letter of yours was magnificent, Beau," he said. "You write with a power and eloquence I can only envy."

He looked down at some photographs on his desk, and his eyes seemed to lose focus. For a moment, I caught a glimpse of almost pure despair as he covered his eyes with his hand. Kate saw it too.

"I know something is terribly wrong," she said. "Please tell me."

He picked up a manila folder next to the photographs on the desk.

"This arrived today. We're still trying to decide how to deal with it," he said, opening the folder and removing several typewritten pages.

"It's the account of a Jesuit priest describing an air attack on his village near Hue," he said. "The photographs were taken by a Dutch planter who smuggled them out past the South Vietnamese army."

Tom handed me the first page. Written in English, it detailed a napalm strike by six U.S. Air Force Skyraiders, resulting in the deaths of one hundred and sixty eight villagers, most of them women and children. Twenty-one villagers had survived According to the priest, there were two categories of victims. The first were people incinerated in the initial fireballs. Of those who were only splashed by burning napalm, about one third died very quickly. Of the remaining two thirds, the majority died within a few days from shock and infection.

Looking up from the page, I asked, "Why was the village attacked?"

"It's in the rest of the report," said Tom. "Father Mai learned that the local South Vietnamese army colonel had attempted to extort protection money from the mayor of the village and had been rejected. He then told his U.S. Special Forces adviser that the village was harboring a cadre of Vietcong guerrillas. The attack was ordered by the American MACV commanders in Saigon."

I read another account from a Red Cross official who reached the village a few hours after the bombing. He wrote, "In front of me the figure of a boy was standing with his legs straddled, arms held out from his sides. He had no eyes and the whole of his body, nearly all of it visible through his burning rags, was covered with a hard black crust. He had to stand because he was no longer covered with a skin but with a crust-like crackling which broke each time he tried to take a step."

I heard a police siren coming closer and stopped reading. Kate and I turned in the direction of the sound.

"Don't worry. They're not coming for me yet," said Tommy, handing me the small batch of black-and-white photographs.

In the first two, several clumps lay haphazardly on the ground, vaguely human shapes, but unrecognizable as human beings. The third was a photograph of three people who had survived the attack, at least up to that point.

"Our pilots were ordered to do this in the name of our country," said Tommy, his voice husky with indignation, "and then we are told not to worry about it because the responsibility rests with some nameless colonels and generals. In other words, none of us needs to accept personal responsibility for any of it."

"You've accepted responsibility," I said into his haunted eyes. "Because of you, thousands of people are coming here from all over the country to protest the war."

Kate nodded in agreement. "He's right, Tom. You must see that."

His eyes found the photographs in my hand again.

"It won't end," he came back. "Every day it's another obscenity . . . more innocent deaths. They'll never listen."

There was a light knock on the door.

"Come in," called out Tommy.

It was Jared, the freckle-faced kid.

"I'm sorry to interrupt you, but Rabbi Fenster just got back from meeting with the police. They confirmed that two of the bridges over to Virginia will be closed to vehicles at seven this morning, and we can begin sending our groups across fifteen minutes later. He was wondering if you've finalized our speakers list."

"I've got it right here," said Tommy, picking up another sheet of paper and heading out to the sacristy with Jared. While putting the photographs back down on the desk, I noticed an open paperback. It was titled *The Green Beret Handbook*.

Picking it up, I started thumbing through the pages. It was basic stuff, with chapters on how to purify contaminated water and how to survive in the jungle with nothing more than a knife and a length of rope.

"I'm worried," whispered Kate. "I've never known him to be this pessimistic."

"Don't worry," I said. "We'll help him through it."

She squeezed my hand. Then he was back.

"Let's find you a place to sleep," he said. "Have you eaten?"

"No," I said. "Have you?"

He laughed. It was his first since we had arrived.

"Truly—it's so great to have you with us, Beau," he said, pulling me into another bear hug.

The hug felt genuine. But he was right. I was tired, and there would be time in the morning to figure out what to do next. The first thing I planned to do was call Grandpa Sprague. I had no doubt that he was ready to hire a battery of lawyers to keep Tommy out of prison even without his approval.

We headed downstairs to the basement again. It was almost three thirty by then, but dozens of people were still working at the tables in the meeting hall. As Tommy came into the room, one of them recognized him and began whispering to the other people at the table. Even from a distance, I could see the respect in their eyes. Tommy pointed to a pile of blankets and pillows in the corner. Just looking at them reminded me how tired I was.

"Good night, Digby," I whispered.

"Good night, Beau," said Tommy. "Sleep well."

Grabbing a pillow and blanket, I found the first available place on the floor and lay down. The last thing I saw before fading out was Tommy and Kate standing together by the big stainless-steel coffee urn on the serving counter by the kitchen.

THIRTY-FIVE

I smelled frying onions and realized how hungry I was. Stiff and groggy, I got to my feet and went to the men's room. After washing my face, I went back to the meeting hall and walked over to the kitchen counter. A cheerful old lady wearing bib overalls offered me a bowl of vegetable soup with fat chunks of carrots, potatoes, and celery in it.

I was wolfing it down when the big room went quiet. Three men in dark suits were standing at the far end of the basement near the entrance. One of the men was wearing a white Stetson hat like the ones favored by President Johnson.

"I am Special Agent Gillette of the Federal Bureau of Investigation," he called out in a booming voice. He held up his identification badge to all the people scattered around the hall.

"We have a duly executed federal warrant for the arrest of Thomas Matthew Ledbetter, who is believed to be present in this building. Mr. Ledbetter, will you please take one step forward."

No one moved or said a word.

"You should know that there are serious consequences to avoiding a federal arrest warrant," said the agent. "Mr. Ledbetter will become a fugitive from justice and may face additional felony charges. If one of you is a friend of Mr. Ledbetter, you would be doing him a great favor by urging him to come with us right now."

A kid with jug ears stood up from one of the cafeteria tables and held out his hands to be cuffed. One of the agents walked across the room and took him in hand. As he was shackling him, Agent Gillette pulled a photograph out of his breast pocket, glanced at it, and looked at the kid again.

"That isn't Ledbetter," he said sourly. Turning to the rest of us, he called out, "We're going to search this building. No one is allowed to leave without permission."

I slipped past the kitchen to the flight of stairs that led up to the main floor. I was through the sanctuary and into Tommy's office in thirty seconds. Kate was asleep on the couch, covered by an afghan shawl. She was alone. I touched her shoulder and she instantly came awake.

"What is it?" she asked, noting the alarm on my face.

"The FBI is downstairs. They're here for Tommy."

"Isn't he here?" she asked.

"I don't know. I thought he was with you."

"When I fell asleep, he was still working at his desk. What time is it?"

"A little after eight," I said. "Wasn't he planning to give himself up this morning? That's what he said last night."

"Have you checked with Jared? He would know."

"He's downstairs."

On our way back through the sanctuary we were stopped by one of the FBI agents. He was carrying a photograph of Tommy and held it next to my face before allowing us to go on. Back in the basement hall, Agent Gillette was standing at the door with Jared and checking each of the young men's faces as they went out.

"Look," he said angrily. "He called us himself to say he was ready to surrender. This is bullshit. You tell him as of now he's a fugitive from justice. That will guarantee him another two years in Leavenworth."

The other two agents joined him at the entrance and they left. We went over to Jared.

"Where is he?" Kate asked.

"I . . . don't really know," he said.

Her eyes locked onto his.

"Really, Kate," he said, looking down at the floor.

"Jared, I know you're hiding something. Where did he go?"

"I don't—he made me promise not to tell anyone."

"I'm not the FBI. I'm Kate."

"I know." He groaned. "But he said . . . absolutely no one."

"Do you know where he's going?" I asked.

He nodded.

"Jared. This is serious," Kate said. "Rick and I have a right to know. Where did he go?"

"He . . . was going to the Pentagon."

"Why the big secret?" she demanded.

"I don't know," he said. "Honestly, Kate."

"When did he leave?"

"About forty minutes ago."

"Thank you," she said.

Jared was visibly relieved and let out a lungful of air.

"It doesn't make any sense," she said.

"What was he working on last night before you fell asleep?" I asked Kate. "His speech?"

"He doesn't write speeches. The words just come from within," she said. "I think it might have been a letter."

"Well, I guess all we can do is to follow him over there."

"Right. Give me a minute to get my purse and coat," she said.

I sat down at one of the cafeteria tables and tried to remember everything Tommy had talked about in the office. He had told us he was planning to surrender to the agents. Why had he changed his mind? Maybe he wanted to speak at the demonstration before turning himself in. *So what could he have been writing?* I wondered again. Looking up, I saw Jared watching me furtively from across the room. I walked over to him.

"Did Tommy leave anything with you for me?" I demanded.

He stared back at me with that uncomfortable expression again.

Grabbing his arm, I said, "I'm his brother. You know he's under terrible strain. Tell me."

"All right," he said finally, pulling his arm free. "He left me two letters. One of them is for your family."

"Give them to me."

"I can't."

"Why the hell not?"

"He said to wait."

"Wait?"

"Until ten o'clock."

"Give them to me," I demanded again.

"It's not ten o'clock," he said.

"Jared—if you truly care what happens to Tommy, then you'll let me read them."

He stared at my patched eye for a few seconds. Seeming to make up his mind, he walked over to one of the cafeteria tables and pulled out two envelopes buried under a stack of papers. He handed them to me.

The first envelope read "*To be released to the press at ten o'clock.*" It was in Tommy's handwriting.

"Tom wants me to give it to the reporters along with copies of the account we received yesterday about the napalm attack," said Jared, pointing to the pile of mimeographed papers on the table.

The second envelope read "*To my family.*"

I ripped open the envelope for the press and read the lines on the single sheet of white paper.

"What is it?" said Jared.

It was some hideous joke. But I knew it was true. I knew.

"Here is what you have to do," I said, trying to keep my voice steady. "Call the police. Right now, okay? Tell them that Thomas Ledbetter—who is wanted on a federal arrest warrant—is somewhere near the Pentagon."

I jammed both envelopes into my back pocket.

"Give them a good description," I said. "Tell them what he is wearing and call the FBI. Tell them to find that Agent Gillette who was just here and give him the same information."

He nodded.

"Do you understand?"

"I . . . yes. Okay."

"Right now!" I said, struggling to maintain control.

Kate came toward me from across the room.

"Any news?" she said.

"We have to hurry."

Taking her hand, I led her to the door. When we reached the street, I started jogging toward Dupont Circle. Kate followed on my heels. Near the circle, I saw an empty cab cruising the block. Hailing it, we got in. The driver was an elderly black man. A silver crucifix hung from his rearview mirror.

"We need to get to the Pentagon right away," I said.

He laughed out loud.

"You folks'll need wings to get there right now," he said.

Many people may view what I have done today as an act of madness by a man who is mentally unbalanced or deranged. That is not the case.

"What is the fastest way?" I asked, checking my watch.

It was 8:41.

"They got most of the bridges closed," he said. "Even if I take the Georgetown Bridge, the G.W. Parkway is backed up for miles over there. It's that demonstration they're havin'. Your best bet is for me to get you close to the Fourteenth Street Bridge. You can walk across from there."

"That's fine. Please go as fast as you can. It could be a matter of life and death."

"What do you mean?" Kate demanded, now frightened for the first time.

"I mean . . . that Tommy could be thinking about doing harm to himself," I said. "You know how much pressure he's under."

There are things worth living for and worth dying for. One sometimes has to risk everything if the cause warrants this action.

"What's happened?" she cried. "How do you know that?"

I decided not to show her the letter.

"Tommy said something to Jared," I lied.

"You're keeping something back from me," she said.

"I'm not," I said. "But we need to find him as soon as possible."

The old taxi driver did his best, but the next ten minutes had me almost screaming in frustration as we encountered one roadblock after another. Not wanting to alarm Kate further, I pretended to stare out the window until we were on a two-lane access road near the Jefferson Memorial. As we neared the Tidal Basin, traffic came to a complete stop.

"Looks like they havin' another demonstration over this side too," said the driver.

Hundreds of people were standing behind police barricades in a park to our left. It was apparently a counter-demonstration to the March on the Pentagon. A high school marching band in bright orange uniforms stood behind an enormous banner that read ST. IGNATIUS ACADEMY SUPPORTS OUR BOYS IN VIETNAM.

A band was playing "The Stars and Stripes Forever." Farther on, a man was holding a sign that read VICTORY OVER ATHEISTIC COMMUNISM. Another sign said TEAMSTERS LOCAL 703 SUPPORTS LBJ.

"If I was you, I'd get out right here and walk the rest of the way," the old man said. As I paid him he added, "Good luck, my friend—may God help you get there in time."

"Can you run?" I asked Kate. She nodded, and we began to jog together at a good pace toward the approach ramp of the bridge. A flood of people lined both aprons of the roadway ahead of us.

Through this act I wish to speak to my country. In the name of life.

I checked my watch again as we passed the Jefferson Memorial. It was 9:14. A few minutes later, we reached the entrance ramp leading up to the bridge. As far as I could see in the distance, the bridge was jammed with people.

We would run twenty steps and then have to wait for a hole to open in the solid mass ahead of us to slip through. In the sky above us, police helicopters were swooping low toward the Pentagon. Television news helicopters hovered in fixed positions, filming the spectacle.

"Please let us through," I kept calling out to the people ahead of us. "Please let us through."

Everyone in the crowd seemed very polite, and would quickly step away to clear a space as we came past. Unlike at the previous night's demonstration in Dupont Circle, it appeared as though college students made up only a small portion of this crowd. For the most part, the protesters struck me as ordinary middle-class people of all ages.

Very few carried signs or placards, and they looked to be there as individuals, not as part of any organized group. Veterans in World War II campaign hats were walking next to women dressed as if they were on their way to church, followed by young mothers wheeling baby carriages. About halfway across the bridge, we overtook a man carrying a large transistor radio. I could hear the radio reporter's voice as we ran past.

"There appear to be two different groups here at the Pentagon . . . those who have come to demonstrate peacefully and a small group that has come to fight. From where I'm standing, I can see Vietcong flags with a yellow star on a red and blue field being waved above the crowd. Some of the demonstrators are starting to hurl rocks and cans at the soldiers. The soldiers are falling back."

Today we are releasing a documented report of just one of hundreds of napalm attacks made by U.S. warplanes in Vietnam. This attack was carried out in our names. Yours and mine.

The Pentagon building slowly rose up ahead of us in the distance off to the right. I glanced at my watch again. It was 9:36. I wondered how much leeway Tom had left himself.

The first exit from the other end of the bridge led down to the George Washington Parkway. It looked like a good shortcut, but when we arrived at the exit ramp, I saw that the parkway was separated from the Pentagon complex by a deep lagoon. Cabin cruisers were anchored next to the crowded marina loaded with people watching the demonstration. As I rushed on toward the next exit, I looked back for Kate. She was about twenty feet behind me and coming to the end of her strength.

"We're almost there!" I shouted.

She raised her hand in acknowledgment.

As I approached the second exit, a man wearing a blue sash stood on the edge of the ramp. "This is a nonviolent protest!" he called out loudly. "When you reach the Pentagon, please disperse immediately to the left. Buses are there to bring you back to Washington."

Today, Secretary McNamara will have the chance to see what napalm does to a human being. I have made the napalm myself from a formula published without shame in "The Green Beret Handbook."

Up ahead I could see that the Pentagon was ringed by ranks of helmeted troops. At the northern end of the massive building, several hundred demonstrators appeared to be in a skirmish with the soldiers along a section of their defense perimeter. Vietcong flags fluttered above them. Intermittently, a thin cry was carried back on the wind.

The line of peaceful protesters ahead of us was swinging off toward a fleet of buses parked beyond the cloverleaf exit. Desperately, I tried to imagine where Tommy might have decided to make his final stand. I knew he couldn't have gotten inside the defense perimeter around the Pentagon itself. Where would he go? It wouldn't be toward the violent protesters. Where else? I could see two other Pentagon parking lots from the overpass. One was to the north of the attacking demonstrators, and the second extended out from the southern rim of the building. The lots were cordoned off by a small sea of blue-and-black-uniformed police officers.

My watch read 9:44 as I stopped at the edge of the concrete retaining wall to wait for Kate to catch up. I surveyed the surrounding landscape in both directions, fighting back a wave of nausea at the thought of what he was planning to do.

"Where could he be?" she cried out in frustration.

Only one place in the whole panoramic landscape was empty of people. Down to the right of us, an open promenade extended out from the columned front entrance of the Pentagon to the deep lagoon we had passed at the previous exit. Near the edge of the lagoon there was a long concrete walkway, anchored at each end by flagpoles a hundred feet high. An American flag waved from the top of each one. Just beyond the walkway, colorful beds of flowers were bordered by permanent guard shacks.

My eye was suddenly drawn to a lone figure in the center of the concrete walkway. He appeared to be kneeling there, maybe fifty yards from one of the guard booths. His head was bowed as if in prayer. I pointed at the solitary man. Kate's eyes followed my extended finger and locked on to the kneeling figure.

"Tom!" she screamed in immediate recognition, although there was no way he could have heard her over the roar of the helicopters and the crowd.

"Tom!" she screamed again.

I glanced down at the concrete abutment. Below where we were standing, there was a fifteen-foot drop to the grass apron beneath the overpass. Climbing across the abutment, I scrabbled over the edge until I was hanging free. Letting go, I made sure not to lock my knees, rolling out as soon as I felt my feet make contact with the ground.

I have chosen to say This is the gift of my life so that the use of napalm stops here. Today. With me.

I started running toward him. The first fifty yards melted away and I could see him clearly now. A gallon-size plastic jug sat next to him on the cement. I was about halfway there.

"Tommy!" I cried out. "Tommy!"

A police officer emerged from the guard booth next to the flower beds. He saw me running and I pointed toward Tommy. As he looked in that direction, Tommy calmly picked up the gallon jug and began to pour the contents over his legs and body. The fluid flowed out like molasses.

The police officer started toward him. When he saw what Tom was doing, he began to trot. As Tom lifted the jug higher, I saw it drench his hair. Then he carefully set it down beside him. I could still hear Kate screaming far behind me.

Tommy hunched forward, as if leaning into a wind.

May God accept my life in reparation for what we have done.

The police officer was maybe five yards away when Tom saw him coming and held up his left hand like he was silently ordering him to stop. In his right hand, he was holding a nickel-plated Zippo lighter like the ones I had seen in the military exchanges. He turned to look straight ahead at the Pentagon building as I came running up.

"Tommy, don't!" I yelled, but a split second later he became a human fireball, the flames engulfing his body and shooting ten feet into the air.

He stayed in position, kneeling upright for almost five seconds, and then began to sink slowly forward. Reaching him, I dropped down on the ground. There was nothing to suppress the flames that were shooting out of his upper body and head.

Ripping off my sweater and shirt, I was about to try to smother the flames erupting all over his body when someone knocked me sideways and my arms were pinned behind my back. People were now running toward us from every direction.

"Stand back!" the policeman shouted. "He's gone."

I watched as the plume of greasy smoke rose from Tommy's body, climbing higher into the clear blue sky. I can see him now.

THIRTY-SIX

What he did that morning was pretty much forgotten in less than a week. The story of his self-immolation was buried on an inside page of the *New York Times* next to a photograph of Defense Secretary McNamara being hustled out of the Pentagon later that day by a security detail. Although McNamara had been in his office and in direct line of sight from where Tommy had set himself on fire, the old hypocrite was quoted as saying he hadn't seen anything and had no comment on whatever took place.

A columnist for the *Washington Post* wrote, "It is perplexing to understand the motivations of a young man who professes to be nonviolent and then resorts to violence. A true idealist would have devoted himself to the persuasion of the public by words, not by an act of fear."

Another journalist called it "the deluded act of a lunatic who became convinced he was the Prince of Peace." Most major newspapers didn't cover his suicide at all, nor did any of the television networks, which focused only on the massive demonstration and the speeches of the celebrities.

Aside from our family, twenty people came to his funeral. It was as if he had done something so alien to American culture that everyone wanted to forget about it as quickly as possible. Four of his childhood friends were there as well as a young black man Tommy had met as a Freedom Rider in Mississippi. A handful of the activists he had worked with down in Washington also showed up. The rest were apparently too busy with plans for the next demonstration. Kate drove up from Washington with Jared, the freckle-faced kid.

My mother asked Rod Carpenter to deliver the eulogy. By then he had resigned as pastor at our church after a majority of the congregation voted to ask the district superintendent to remove him. Tommy's memorial service was held at St. John's Episcopal Church, right next to the pond where he had fallen through the ice in 1961.

The lawn around the church was blanketed in red and gold leaves. An offshore breeze carried the scent of the sea.

Our family sat together in the first row. Travis was sober and dignified in his Brooks Brothers blazer and gray worsted pants. Grandpa Sprague sat at the end of the pew, weeping silently. He had been inconsolable ever since the news reached him. My sister Hope was in India with Cliff and the Maharishi, and there was no way for her to get back in time. Dave and Laura were there, but they didn't bring the kids. And they didn't acknowledge me. Rod Carpenter chose to base his eulogy on the part of the Sermon on the Mount in which Jesus said, "Blessed are the meek, for they shall inherit the earth."

"The dictionary tells us that a person who is meek is gentle and kind and humble," he said. "Thomas Ledbetter was certainly all of those things. But in today's world, too many people confuse that with a lack of courage."

As he spoke, I remembered Kate telling me the same thing when she came to see me in Newport. I turned around to look at her. She was staring straight ahead at Rod Carpenter, her eyes rimmed in red.

"There was no lack of courage in Thomas Ledbetter. To the contrary, he was fearless when it came to his faith. Tom lived by the precept that even if a man were to possess all the wisdom of the world or acquire all its riches, he could not be as fulfilled as one who called nothing his own except his faith. Tom never lost that faith. His final act was an act of love for his fellow man. Truly, he believed that love will conquer in the end and will endure for all eternity."

From where I was sitting I could look out the window at St. John's Pond and see the place where Tommy and I had gone through the ice. The old boathouse had been torn down since then, but I remembered what Tommy had whispered when we were lying there together under the winter coats.

"I was in heaven, Beau," he had said.

Maybe since he thought he had been there once already, he wasn't afraid to go back.

"It's very hard for those of us who knew him and loved him to say good-bye to Tom Ledbetter," Rod Carpenter continued. "Though our hearts are sad today, that sadness will one day be turned into joy. The sorrows of this world will pass. And in the words of Abraham Lincoln, his memory—instead of an agony—will yet be a sad sweet feeling in our hearts of a purer and holier sort than we have known before."

I looked at my mother. As she sat there in her black dress, I knew she already had Tommy tucked away in a corner of heaven. Maybe it was the power of suggestion in Tommy's last letter to the family. When Rod finished his eulogy, she went up to the altar, carefully unfolded the letter, and began to read it aloud.

"When dawn broke this morning, I could hear birds singing outside the windows of the sacristy where I slept," she read in her smoky voice. "The birds seem to know more freedom and joy than we humans with all our gifts of intellect and our knowledge of the pure reward that awaits us after this brief existence on earth.

"I would have liked to say so many things to you in farewell. It is hard, knowing that I will not see you again. I would have liked to spare you the pain and sorrow you must bear because of what I have done. But what can give us greater comfort than the knowledge that we need never fear death? Even if we could live for a thousand years, what would it be compared to God's greatest gift to us? Now, when you read this I will be gone. Dear Mother, forgive me, and stand fast in His love."

She read the whole thing without losing control and walked back to her seat.

When the service was over, I followed Kate outside and watched as she said good-bye to the handful of Tommy's friends who had come. When she was finally alone, I went over and asked if she would be coming back to the house with us.

"I have to drive Jared back to Washington," she said.

Her eyes sought every direction but my face.

"I love you, Kate," I said.

She shook her head.

"I blame myself," she said, her eyes finally looking straight up into mine. "If I had stayed with him, this never would have happened. If I had been there, I could have changed his mind."

"He didn't make this decision in one night," I said. "He had obviously been thinking about it for some time. The napalm attack was just the final trigger."

"I don't believe that," she said. "I wasn't there when he needed me most."

"I think he meant for us to be together," I said. "When he urged you to visit me in Newport, I think he was putting things in place for the people he loved."

"I still love him," she said. "He is inside me like a second heart. Truly, I wish you the best in your life, Rick, but I have to go."

Jared was standing by the door of the car as I walked over with her, trying to think of something to say to change her mind. She didn't look back at me after starting the car. Putting it in first gear, she drove out along the lane next to the pond.

I watched the car until it disappeared.

THIRTY-SEVEN

The day after the funeral, I drove back up to Newport.

At the hospital, I found out that they hadn't brought me up on charges for being absent without leave. Instead I was told to report to the captain in command. As he paced around his office, he gave me a stern lecture about the importance of maintaining a high standard of personal conduct as an example to the enlisted men. He wished me good luck in civilian life. After being fitted for a future glass eye by a hospital technician, I went over to the dirty surgery ward where I had been in command as MAA. The petty officer who had reported to me was still there. He told me that John Wayne had been removed from his post for striking one of the patients.

He also said the Zombie had killed himself. They had found him hanging from a water pipe in a custodians' closet. I asked the petty officer what the Zombie's name was, but he didn't know. At the nursing station they told me it was Eric Hagen. I asked for his address so that I could write to his family, but the nurse said that was confidential information. I wondered what his life had been like before he went to Vietnam.

A few days later, I received another letter from the secretary of the navy's office stating that I had been placed on the disabled retired list and was officially released from the service.

I drove back home.

. . .

A lot has happened in the five months since Tommy died.

Grandpa Sprague outlived him by only a few weeks. After the funeral, he just seemed to waste away. One afternoon, my mother had asked me to go with her to see him at his home in Oyster Bay. By then she was visiting him every day and told me he was near the end.

His estate was on Cove Road near Youngs Memorial Cemetery, where Teddy Roosevelt is buried. It's bigger than our place in Cold Spring Harbor, and the property is surrounded by a ten-foot-high brick wall. He hadn't given all his money away.

One of the maids escorted us up to his mahogany-paneled bedroom on the second floor. It had amazing views across the bay, but the curtains on his windows were drawn against the light and my mother had to turn on a table lamp at his desk to relieve the darkness.

Grandpa Sprague was lying asleep in the four-poster bed. Blankets covered his body right up to the chin. His eyes were closed and his breathing was very loud. His false teeth were submerged in a glass of water on the table beside the headboard. There were several pill bottles alongside it. The smell of Vicks VapoRub was almost overpowering.

"Papa?" she said gently, taking his hand.

His eyes opened and took us in.

"Papa, Richard is here to say good-bye," she said.

He looked up at me with desolate eyes. If I didn't know it was him, I wouldn't have believed he was Thomas Sprague. He had been frail a month ago, but you could still see the life force in him. Now he was all shriveled up and his face was chalky white. He whispered something incomprehensible. Not understanding him without his false teeth, I looked at my mother for an interpretation.

"He's asking what you are going to do with your life," she said.

I thought about it for a few seconds.

"I don't know, Grandpa," I said.

He kept staring up at me until what little energy he had left seemed to drain out of him. With a slight movement of her eyes, my mother motioned for me to leave.

"Good-bye, Richard," Grandpa Sprague whispered clearly enough for me to understand him.

I turned around for a last look.

"Good-bye, Grandpa," I said.

He died the following morning. They held a big service for him at Christ Church, the Episcopal parish in Oyster Bay that's been there since about 1700. More than five hundred mourners showed up, including Vice President Humphrey, Governor Nelson Rockefeller, and Senator Robert Kennedy.

. . .

A few days later, I got a letter from Pete Demetropolis. He had read a story in the *Ithaca Journal* that I had been awarded the Navy Cross and was back in the States. He wrote that he needed someone to manage his roller rink near the Cornell campus. Pete had called it Skate-A-Go-Go.

It was a cash business, he said, and there was no one else he could trust to do it. The rink was doing gangbuster business, but he wanted to focus his own efforts on buying up student rental properties. He promised to make it worth my while.

I didn't need his money. At twenty-two, I could start drawing on the trust Grandpa Sprague had set up for me anytime I chose. But I had a lot of good memories of Cornell. It would give me something to do until I sorted things out. I told him I would come up and take a look. When I arrived in Ithaca, I drove straight to the rink. The building had once been a seed supply warehouse, and Pete had paid to have a circular hardwood floor laid down inside it. Somehow he had also gotten a license to serve wine and beer. Aside from the bar, there was a concession stand for sandwiches and snacks. Another room contained a few hundred pairs of rental skates.

It was around five thirty when I got there and the place was packed with students, most of them mingling at the bar. A dozen skaters were cruising around the oval track to the amplified blast of Robert Knight's "Everlasting Love." Suspended from the ceiling in the center of the oval track, a girl wearing a bikini was dancing inside a large cage.

I found Pete behind the bar stacking cases of beer. His hair was shoulder length and he was wearing bell-bottom trousers. His shirt looked like it had been dyed with Easter egg colors.

"Buddy, it's so great to see you," he said, pumping my hand and smiling wide enough for me to see the full set of braces that had gotten him out of the draft. "Jeez, I've missed you."

Two coeds went by, pausing to stare at me.

"I love that eye patch—the man of mystery—the wounded warrior. You're always on the cutting edge. The girls will love it. I've already spread the word."

I helped him finish stacking the beer as "Everlasting Love" gave way to the Who singing "I Can See for Miles."

"I've converted the storeroom upstairs into an apartment," he said. "You're welcome to live here rent free."

"Pete," I began, but that was as far as I got.

"Listen," he said. "We'll have plenty of time to catch up. In the meantime, let me explain what's happening here. We're not selling roller-skating. We're selling fun and a great place to meet up. I've got every evening covered. There are still plenty of old farts who love to skate to the organ music. They come on Sundays. Then we have country night for all the gap-toothed rednecks out in the sticks. And of course oldies night for the crowd that loves fifties rock and roll."

The rumbling roar of the skaters grew louder as more students joined the fray on the oval track. I wondered what the noise level would be like in the apartment upstairs.

"But my bread and butter is all the horny coeds who are hoping to meet Mr. Right or Mr. Wrong. You are the essence of Mr. Wrong. As my manager you're going to be a pig in shit, buddy. Take the cream for yourself and just be nice to the rest."

He was grinning at me like I had just tapped into the mother lode. Between the music and the rumbling skates, the noise was now so loud I had to shout to be heard. I took his arm and led him outside through the back door.

"I don't have time to . . ." he began and I said, "Just shut up and listen for a minute."

Fine—fine," he said.

"If you want me to manage the place I'll do it until I decide on something else," I said. "But forget those fringe benefits or you can find yourself someone else."

He looked up at me, clearly confused.

"What is this, *The Twilight Zone*?" he came back. "You look like Rick Ledbetter. You talk like him, but you're not the Rick Ledbetter I knew.

"That guy is a distant memory," I said.

"Whatever you say. You ready to go to work?"

Needless to say, it wasn't hard. There were people to work the bar and run the concession stand, clean the bathrooms, and handle the skate rentals. I just kept track of the money for him and watched the parade go by. Pete left me in charge while he pursued his other projects.

Girls started hitting on me right away, and at first it was awkward to tell them I had no interest in them no matter how good-looking they were. The need to score in the sack was gone. The rumor got around that I was neutered from my Vietnam wounds like Jake Barnes in *The Sun Also Rises*.

The truth is I'm waiting for Kate. At night I go to sleep thinking of her, replaying our short time together over and over in my mind. Even though we didn't make love, the image of her lying next to me in that dog bed at the Hotel Viking is still vivid in my mind. Like when I was in Vietnam, I find myself wondering where she is and what she is doing.

. . .

One change in my life came about one morning after breakfast in the Ivy Room at the Straight. I walked over to Uris Library and climbed up into the stacks to my old study room. It was in a back corner of the sixth floor behind the library's repository of federal government publications. Normally an undergraduate didn't rate one. I had gotten it by writing off a poker debt from a library staff member who owed me a few hundred dollars. I had used it senior year to store my books and as a rendezvous spot with willing coeds.

The musty smell inside the room hit me as soon as I unlocked the door. When I turned on the light, it was obvious no one had used it since I was last there. The dry husks of a dozen flies lay on the interior sill of the small window. A half-empty pint of Jack Daniel's was lying where I had left it in the top drawer. The shelves above the maple desk still held the books for all the courses I had blown off.

I randomly pulled one of them out. The title indicated that it was something about American empire. The author was Cornell professor Walter LaFrance. I remembered failing Professor LaFrance's history course. I had never taken the time to skim the book, much less read it.

I sat down at the desk and opened it to the first page. Two hours later, I was still reading. I was not only enjoying it but jotting down questions as they came to me. I realized that in four years of an Ivy League education, I had never asked a tough question about anything related to our political system.

The following days fell into a familiar pattern. I woke up in my apartment above the rink, had breakfast, and then made the two-mile walk through Collegetown over to the library to read one of the books on my shelves. I would have lunch in the Ivy Room, play in a daily pickup basketball game at Teagle Hall, head back to the rink, and work until it was time for bed again.

Nobody commented on the patch I was still wearing until the glass eye was finished. With the right socket sewed shut, the only awareness I had of the injury was a lack of depth perception when I tried to play tennis. Otherwise, there was no lingering impact on my ability to play sports or anything else.

When I had finished reading all the books in my study room, I began writing letters to many of the authors with some of my thoughts and questions. I was pleasantly surprised to receive a long letter back from Professor LaFrance. After complimenting me on a few of my observations, he invited me to audit a graduate seminar he would be teaching in the spring semester on the failed diplomatic initiatives that had led to the Vietnam War. I accepted the invitation.

. . .

Another change took place when I was walking along the Fall Creek Gorge Trail one afternoon and happened to see a "For Sale" sign on a house that was set right on the bluff at the edge of the gorge. If you stepped out of one of the windows along that side, the next stop was one hundred and fifty feet down. The property also had a small brick outbuilding with casement windows at the tip of the bluff with dramatic views of Cayuga Lake. Using a small portion of Grandpa Sprague's trust money, I bought it.

In January, I said good-bye to Skate-A-Go-Go. I told Pete I was planning to try something else, but that wasn't the truth. I just didn't want to be around him or his mouthful of braces anymore. Pete is like the vast majority of guys I know. They aren't for or against the war. They just don't want to fight and maybe die in it, and they are too busy moving on with their lives and careers to waste time opposing it. They're content to stand on the sidelines and watch.

The gorge house has become kind of a sanctuary for me. I rarely want to leave it. I set up the little brick outbuilding as a kind of study with an old post office desk and a comfortable leather couch. With the constant rush of black water racing down the gorge below me, it's a good place to ponder things.

That was when I started writing this story. I've spent most of every day working on it since, beginning well before dawn each morning. I like to feel the light of the world coming up around me as I write.

It's given me a chance to reflect on all that we've lost, to remember the things I was too ignorant to understand back when I should have, and most of all to justify myself to Kate. As I wrote at the beginning, if only she could know what I know now, she would understand. She might even forgive me and forgive herself enough to love me.

I haven't stopped dreaming about her. I haven't stopped thinking that I see her sometimes, walking up ahead of me across the arts quad with those long, purposeful strides, her chestnut hair bouncing off her shoulders.

A few weeks ago, when I had finished my writing stint for the evening and was enjoying a few cold beers, I happened to remember one of the things Tommy told me when he was in that jail in Worcester. He was recalling the time when we were kids and had camped together on Whiteface Mountain in the Adirondacks, the morning we hiked up to the summit to watch the sun come up. I remembered that on the way back down the mountain, we promised each other we would climb all forty-six of the Adirondack High Peaks together some day.

I decided to make good on the promise. I started with the highest of the forty-five left, Mount Marcy, then did Algonquin Peak, followed by Haystack and Skylight over the course of several weekends. The Adirondacks aren't the Himalayas, but once you get above the tree lines, they're a worthy challenge.

Last Sunday night I returned from the Adirondacks to find the phone ringing. It was my mother calling from her apartment in Manhattan on Sutton Place.

"Your father is dead," she said in a flat monotone.

It was impossible at first to believe the news. He had always seemed so indestructible. I asked her how it happened, and she told me he had disappeared while swimming off Montauk Point.

She said he had broken up with Michelle and was staying with another woman in a guest cottage at Gurney's Inn right on the beach. The woman told police he went swimming every morning regardless of the weather, and usually returned within an hour. When three hours passed without any sign of him, she notified the police. The Coast Guard and navy immediately mounted an air and sea rescue operation, but they didn't find him.

A man staying at another guest cottage on the beach told the police he had been walking his dog and had seen Travis come striding down to the shoreline. It was a cold morning with raw winds and high surf.

He said Travis was naked.

According to the man's statement, Travis paused for a few moments at the edge of the surf line before tossing away something he had been holding. As he was wading out into the breaking waves, Travis saw the man standing there with his dog.

"I'm meeting someone in Penzance for lunch," he had called out before diving in and starting to swim out through the surf.

When he was gone, the man went over to where Travis had been standing. As a wave receded, he saw something shiny sticking out of the sand and picked it up. It was Travis's Medal of Honor.

In thinking about what finally brought him down, I figured booze had to be a factor. Although he stayed in decent shape, he was probably knocking off close to a fifth of liquor every day, from the vodka tonics at lunch to his "sleep-blasting" whiskey and sodas after dinner. His attitude was always "I can take it or leave it," but in those last couple of years I never saw him leave it.

If it was suicide, he didn't leave a note.

He lived by his own set of rules. I remember him once telling me that he had never stolen anything in his life. I don't doubt it, unless it was another man's wife. I never saw him cheat at games or sports. As competitive as he was, he was a true sportsman. For all his failures as a husband and father, he considered it a sin to ever let a friend down.

In all the time I knew him, I never heard him use the word love. As I look back on it, he was working pretty hard to avoid saying it. Hell, most of us use it talking about a favorite movie or a great piece of prime rib. I'm not sure if he ever realized what it meant. Maybe coming from six generations of warriors, he never heard it himself when he was growing up dirt-poor in Texas.

What are the odds of losing three generations of your family in six months? I wonder. Pretty long I would think, but maybe all three were inevitable. Grandpa Sprague's death came from old age, heartbreak, and disillusionment, Tommy's through the inevitability of the path where his faith took him, and finally Travis, who had either defied the odds once too often or decided to cash it in.

I'm meeting someone in Penzance for lunch.

Penzance is on the southwest coast of England.

I guess we'll never know for sure one way or the other, but I think he was ready to go. My mother said there would be no memorial service for him. Travis had made it clear in his will that he didn't want one.

The *New York Times* obituary made him sound like one of the stalwart members of the Gold Coast elite, a debonair socialite who had overcome his humble origins in Texas to become part of privileged society on the North Shore of Long Island.

I remember him telling me once that if there was ever another war like the one we fought against Japan and Germany, he would go again. Thinking about Vietnam, I doubt too many of the guys I served with would say the same thing.

I don't see any sign that God plans to end the war.

As I write this, we have more than five hundred thousand American troops there, and the American death toll stands at thirty-seven thousand. For the Vietnamese it's already in the millions. The recent Tet offensive by the North Vietnamese army makes it clear they aren't ready to quit anytime soon.

. . .

Speaking of God, I sometimes wonder if he planted Tommy in our family like a seed that's blown into the crevice of a rock and somehow manages to grow in spite of the hostile surroundings. I know I'm not like him. I've never met anyone else like him either. I think he was one of a kind.

He was only twenty when he died. If he had chosen to run into a burning house to save someone else's life, he would have been called a hero. Instead, he set fire to himself in the belief that he could save thousands of lives in the middle of a war that is still tearing our country apart. In a way, he gave his life fighting war itself.

I asked my mother to allow me to have his ashes, and after I told her my plan for them, she agreed. I still have forty-one high peaks to climb, and I will spread a portion of them on all the summits. On each hike, I always camp just below the peak so I can reach it in time to watch the dawn light spread across the vastness of the Adirondacks.

I always pause to look up at the sky and repeat the same words.

"Hey, Digby," I call out. "I love you."

ACKNOWLEDGMENTS

A small number of Americans chose to immolate themselves in protest of the Vietnam War, including Roger LaPorte, a twenty-two-year-old former Catholic seminarian, Norman Morrison, a thirty-one-year-old Quaker, and Alice Herz, an eighty-two-year-old pacifist. Their sacrifice is little remembered or understood. My hope is that this novel might provide insight into their possible motivations.

There are still lessons to be learned from that war's impact on every one of us who lived through it. The lessons continue to apply today for the generations of Americans born since the war ended who have no direct memories of the Vietnam years and the divisions that it created.

I began writing this book during the two months I spent as a patient at Newport Naval Hospital in 1967–68. At the time, the hospital's wards were filled with wounded marines back from Vietnam. Prior to my own injury, I was a supporter of the war. Seeing the terrible impact of it firsthand on those young men, both physically and psychically, changed my life.

For their contributions to this novel over the many years I have worked on it, I would like to thank the late brilliant film director and my cherished friend, Fred Zinnemann, Melody Miller, Bob Keeler, and Julia Stone. I am also grateful to my literary agent, David Halpern, who has always believed in the book.

Finally, I owe a deep debt of gratitude to my editor at Cornell University Press, Michael J. McGandy. Sadly, such superb line editors are fast disappearing. His wise observations and recommendations greatly strengthened the story and its characters.

I am likewise grateful to the team at Cornell University Press, Dean Smith, Ange Romeo-Hall, Scott Levine, Martyn Beeny, Jonathan Hall, and Amanda Heller, who decided that this book should become the first original novel ever published by their imprint, and who all helped to bring it to life.

For anyone wishing to reach the author, please contact rjmrazek1942@gmail.com.